SAVING GRACE

SKY PICTURES PRESENTS IN ASSOCIATION WITH PORTMAN ENTERTAINMENT
AND WAVE PICTURES A HOMERUN PRODUCTION

BRENDA BLETHYN CRAIG FERGUSON 'SAVING GRACE' MARTIN CLUNES TCHEKY KARYO

COSTUME DESIGNER ANNIE SYMONS HAIR & MAKE UP DESIGNER ROSEANN SAMUEL

ORIGINAL SCORE COMPOSED BY MARK RUSSELL CASTING DIRECTOR GAIL STEVENS EDITOR ALAN STRACHAN

PRODUCTION DESIGNER EVE STEWART DIRECTOR OF PHOTOGRAPHY JOHN DE BORMAN,

B.S.C. CO-PRODUCED BY CRAIG FERGUSON & TORSTEN LESCHLY LINE PRODUCER STEVE CLARK-HALL

EXECUTIVE PRODUCERS CAT VILLIERS & XAVIER MARCHAND STORY BY MARK CROWDY

SCREENPLAY BY CRAIG FERGUSON & MARK CROWDY PRODUCED BY MARK CROWDY DIRECTED BY NIGEL COLE

SKY
PICTURES™
A division of British SKY Broadcasting

DOLBY DIGITAL
IN SELECTED THEATRES

WAVE pictures

20th CENTURY FOX

© 2000 TWENTIETH CENTURY FOX

SAVING GRACE

Tom McGregor

HarperCollins*Entertainment*
An Imprint of HarperCollins*Publishers*

HarperCollins*Entertainment*
An Imprint of HarperCollins*Publishers*
77–85 Fulham Palace Road,
Hammersmith, London W6 8JB

www.fireandwater.com

A Paperback Original 2000
1 3 5 7 9 8 6 4 2

A catalogue record for this book
is available from the British Library

ISBN 0 00 710711 0

Set in Sabon

Printed and bound in Great Britain by
Clays Ltd, St Ives plc

PROLOGUE

'*Morris dancers?*'

'Yes.'

'How undignified.'

'Oh don't say that. They get terribly miffed, you know. Apparently it's rather serious ... something to do with fertility and the rights of agrarian societies.' Martin Bamford grimaced and leaned over the bar. 'Actually, I agree with you. All those bells and the hanky-waving are ...'

'No, I mean, how undignified for *him*.'

'For John?' This time it was Martin who looked surprised. 'Well, not really. He wouldn't have known. He was dead by the time he hit the ground. Of course, if he'd landed *on* one of the dancers, that might have broken the fall ...'

'... and killed one of the dancers.'

'Well, yes. Yes, I suppose that could have happened.' Supremely unconcerned, and possibly rather bucked-up by the idea of deceased morris dancers, Martin shrugged and downed the rest of his whisky in one large gulp.

'Another?' prompted Charlie from behind the bar.

'Nah. Wouldn't do to be drunk at the funeral.' Martin wagged an admonitory finger at the barman. 'Now *that*, my man, really would be undignified. Can't have the good doctor stumbling about in the churchyard.'

No, thought Charlie. At least, not again. He looked at his

companion. But Martin's expression betrayed no recall; no sheepish recognition of his antics at the previous funeral in St Liac. But then Charlie remembered that Martin had been so comprehensively sozzled, so titanically wrecked when he had all but stumbled into the grave, that the episode had been blanked by his pickled brain and had passed – like an alarming number of his patients – into oblivion.

'Right,' said Martin, standing up and patting his pockets. 'You not coming?'

'Er ... no. I'll come up to the house later. Best stay here and mind the fort for the moment. You ... er ... well, you never know who might drop in.'

'Oh *bad taste*, Charlie.'

'Eh?' The barman looked at his departing customer. 'What d'you mean?'

Martin raised his right arm. 'Zoom,' he said, gesturing downwards. 'Dropping from the sky.'

'Oh, *please*,' said Charlie. 'I just meant ...'

But Martin Bamford was no longer around to hear what he meant. Whistling to himself, he had left the pub and was making his way up the steep narrow street towards the edge of town.

Alone in The Anchor, Charlie smiled to himself, sat down and reached under the counter. His favourite pastime – talking to customers – was now denied to him, but his other great pleasure in life was almost as rewarding. With a satisfied sigh, he opened the book and settled down for a good read. Always abreast of the latest trends in literature, Charlie also hoped to find contemporary relevance in his reading matter. He'd never heard of the author Jim Crace before, but the title looked promising. True, it was hardly likely to be about a Cornish squire who had fallen from a plane, but the subject-matter was similar.

Five minutes later, Charlie was lost to the world, immersed in the haunting pages of *Being Dead*.

John Trevethan's death had shocked the citizens of St Liac. The fact of it had been surprise enough, the manner of it had been astounding. People were attuned to the concept of planes occasionally falling out of the sky: not by people falling out of planes. But that was exactly how John Trevethan had met his maker – and made the posthumous acquaintance of a startled troupe of morris dancers. Out of respect for his widow (and prior to Martin Bamford's learning of it) the morris-dancing aspect had been down-played. Now, on the day of his funeral, there was no mystery left about the manner of John Trevethan's death.

There was, however, a huge question mark about the reason for it. John Trevethan had been a healthy, wealthy fifty-five year old with a beautiful house, battalions of friends and a long-standing and, as far as anyone was aware, happy marriage to Grace. Wonderful, charming, down-to-earth Grace. For Grace, although chatelaine of Liac House, held no truck with graces. Grace was hugely popular; she had time for everyone; she was the bedrock of the community – and good though she was with people, she was a saint when it came to plants. Grace's garden was a Cornish legend. Grace could make anything grow.

But Grace herself, on the day of her husband's funeral, was wilting. An hour before the service and dressed in her widow's weeds (her only acquaintance with the dreaded word was in her attire – certainly not in her garden), she was in her greenhouse, engrossed in the familiar ritual of watering her orchids. Or rather, physically engrossed:

mentally she was miles away.

Her thoughts were revolving round the word still upper-most in her mind: *why?* Why had John died? Had it been, as everyone was at pains to assure her, a tragic mistake? Had he just opened the wrong door of the plane – or had he deliber-ately opened the one he felt was right for him? And if so – again why? Why would John commit suicide?

It was only now, five days after his death, that Grace allowed herself to ponder those questions. In the immediate aftermath of his sudden demise she had been reeling with shock, disbelief and grief: emotions that had largely been contained by the very English phenomenon of Good Behaviour. People had descended on Grace, dispensed sympathy in a well-behaved way and Grace had responded in the expected manner by being brave, stoic – perhaps a little tearful at times – but essentially and fundamentally graceful. Grace, everyone agreed, had been 'a brick'. She had accepted sympathy as she had accepted everything else in her twenty-five years of marriage to John Trevethan: calmly, politely and without that unwelcome intruder into a well-ordered life: 'fuss'.

But now Grace found herself assaulted by a rather different and equally unwelcome visitor: introspection. A relative stranger to the concept, she was surprised by its force and, even more alarming, by the number of questions it posed. Would she have known, for instance, if John had problems? Would she have known if he were unhappy? The answers rang quite clearly in her ears. No; she wouldn't have known because John wouldn't have told her and she wouldn't have dreamed of asking.

Even worse were the persistent little question marks that hovered over the state of her marriage. Grace had never thought to question her marriage: she had always been too busy being half of it. But now that it was over and she was busy trying not face the issue that she was someone else, she found herself looking back.

Her marriage, she realised with a jolt, had progressed rather swiftly from bliss to contentment and then to … to what? Grace had a nasty suspicion that, for the last decade, it had settled down to become a habit. A nice habit, to be sure – but still a habit.

Grace sniffed and fought back a tear. Then she picked up her humidifier and sprayed an orchid. Habits, she knew, were extremely difficult to break. She had spent the last few years trying to stop smoking, but always kept a packet of cigarettes in a kitchen drawer 'just in case'. She had never tried to break the John habit. There had been no need. It had been a good habit: nothing about it had been harmful. Than Grace checked herself as another issue she hadn't faced reared its unpleasant head. There *had* been something harmful; something very hurtful. But like the cigarettes she pretended didn't exist, she had locked it away in a drawer in her mind. And this time she had thrown away the key.

Grace squirted another orchid with rather more force than she intended. Questions. She didn't like this barrage of questions: she couldn't answer most of them. Then, as if on cue, came a question that she could answer. The words wafted with the breeze and through the greenhouse door, nudging her out of her reverie. 'Mrs Trevethan? Are you ready?'

Yes, thought Grace. Mrs Trevethan is ready. Resolute and determined, she examined another orchid with an expert eye, snapped off the head and pinned it to her lapel. Then she turned, picked up her black hat and placed it firmly on her head. 'Yes,' she called. 'Coming!'

Composed now, she walked into the beautiful garden that, to many people, had symbolised a perfect life. Then she reached the driveway and stepped into the car that would take her to her husband's funeral.

———————————————

Matthew Stuart would have done anything for the Trevethans. Especially for Grace. Always cheerful and accepting, she had never questioned Matthew about his aspirations. Nor, verbally, had John. But Matthew had always sensed a curiosity, bordering on disapproval, emanating from John. Behind the friendly, charming countenance, there seemed to be criticism. While the mouth said 'hello', the eyes asked questions – and foremost amongst them was 'what's a strapping young man like you doing wasting your life odd-jobbing in a place like this?'

Matthew looked up from the grave. Perhaps John Trevethan, born in Liac House and bred to inherit it, had taken his surroundings for granted. Perhaps he had failed to appreciate the staggering beauty of the Cornish coastline, the extraordinarily close yet reassuringly diverse community he lived in, and, most of all, the real meaning of the phrase 'quality of life.' Born and raised in inner-city Glasgow, Matthew learned about life at an early age. But he was a relative newcomer to quality.

Matthew looked down again, not at the grave, but at the restrictive cuffs of his one and only white shirt. Feeling slightly guilty that he should be celebrating life whilst surrounded by death, he concentrated on his fingernails. A mistake. They were caked with mud. Matthew's heart missed a beat. He would have done anything for the

Trevethans, but the very last thing he had anticipated doing was digging John's grave.

Matthew wasn't aware that he had flinched, but his companion was. Sensing his disquiet, Nicky took his hand, offending fingernails and all, in her own and gave it a reassuring squeeze. Mathew smiled. Nicky. Where life met quality.

But death was the reason they were here today. Gerald Percy's measured tones were reminder enough of that. 'Grant us, Lord,' he was saying, 'the wisdom and the grace to use right the time that is left to us here on earth. Lead us to repent of our sins the evil we have done and good we have not done.' The Reverend Percy paused and looked over to Grace. So did Matthew. Her eyes were closed; her expression unfathomable. Was she contemplating John's sins and the good he had not done? Surely not. John's only sin, as far as Matthew was aware, was to spend far too much time away on business.

Which showed how little Matthew, in common with nearly everyone else at John Trevethan's interment, knew about the lately-deceased. One of the few people who knew was the Reverend Percy himself. The reason why he had stopped, mid-oration, was his concern about Grace: he wondered if she had noticed the stranger in their midst. Her closed eyes indicated that she hadn't. Breathing a sigh of relief, Gerald continued his eulogy. But Grace had noticed. Her eyes were closed because they refused to acknowledge the woman standing at some distance from the grave. Grace didn't want to notice her. Grace was going to be graceful to the bitter end.

And she was. When, eventually, John's coffin was lowered into the ground, she stepped forward, unpinned the orchid from her lapel and threw it into the grave. As soft as Grace's tears, it landed without a sound. Then Grace turned away and led the funeral cortège back to Liac House, where Good Behaviour would see them all though the rest of the sorrowful day.

That, at least, was the intention. Martin Bamford had already behaved impeccably. Fond as he had been of John – and as devoted as he was to Grace – manners could not sustain him for much longer. He felt in need of something else. So did some other inhabitants of St Liac. So, unwittingly, did somebody else. Someone who, in the process, would catapult the little Cornish fishing village of St Liac into the world's headlines.

ONE

'More tea?'

'Please.' Gerald Percy proffered his cup and pretended not to notice that Grace's hand was shaking. And Grace, for her part, pretended not to notice Gerald's look of concern. She didn't need sympathy now. Other people needed tea – or wine – and as long as she could busy herself fulfilling their needs she would be all right. Smiling rather too brightly, she left Gerald and passed through the archway into the drawing room.

Formality was not, and had never been high on the agenda in St Liac. There had never been any doffing of caps to Grace and John. Guests, whether they be local fishermen or neighbouring landowners, were welcomed, and behaved, in exactly the same relaxed manner. And Liac House itself reflected that manner. It was grand in scale, but its appearance was more lived in than luxurious. The drawing room epitomised that: while there were numerous valuable pieces of furniture, a good portion of them were slightly battered or stained from the contents of wine glasses or mugs. And although there were several good Persian carpets, half of the traffic that had walked on them over the years had been wearing muddy wellington boots.

But not today. Today everyone had made an effort to look smart: an endeavour which, in conjunction with why they were there in the first place, made most people feel rather self-conscious. As a result, their conversation was of the strained and achingly polite variety that is usually, if not exclusively, heard at funerals. People who had known each other – and Liac House – all their lives found themselves making remarks like 'lovely house' and 'have you been keeping well?' Then, embarrassed, they would fall silent and suppress the urge to giggle, because nobody wanted to be the first to laugh at a wake.

'House looks lovely,' said Charlie to Grace when she entered the room.

'Thank you,' said Grace. 'Tea or wine?'

'Wine, please.'

Grace deposited the teapot on a side table and picked up the bottle of Chablis. She had agonised – not for very long – over what wine to serve: the quaffing stuff or John's best? The decision had made itself. John would have wanted nothing but the best. She poured a glass for Charlie and smiled tentatively up at him before picking up the teapot and continuing on her way. The role of hostess was second nature to her: the fact that until five days ago it had been a supporting role was something she cared not to think about.

'Thank you, Grace' said Vivienne Hopkins from the Women's Institute as Grace replenished her tea. She wanted to say something else but the only thing that sprang to mind was 'lovely service' and that belonged to the lexicon of wedding-speak. She wasn't too sure if there was a funereal equivalent so instead she smiled at Grace, accepted a sandwich she didn't want and waited for Grace to go away before she dared speak again. Grace went away with her teapot, her plate of sandwiches and a smile so brittle that it could have cracked at any minute. But it didn't. It survived an endless onslaught of 'thank you Grace' and continued round the room. Grace, herself invisible, went with it.

Michael Penrath thanked Grace for her offer of more tea, waited until she had left his side and then turned back to his companion. 'Will she stay here, do you think?' Alfred Mabely looked at the other man. Then he remembered that the Penraths lived over Bodmin way and hadn't really known the Trevethans that well; like the Trevethans, they lived in the 'big house' in their area, and so they had come to John's funeral to show solidarity rather than sorrow. Had they known Grace better, mused Alfred, they would have known that she wasn't interested in the concept of old, established families sticking together. And they would certainly have known that Grace would never contemplate leaving Liac House.

'Oh aye,' said Alfred. 'Grace'll never leave here. Not in a million years. This house is her life. Or rather, the garden is. You don't get many gardens like this in Cornwall.' He paused, turned to the window and contemplated the garden for a moment. Then, warming to his theme, he turned back to Michael Penrath. 'Take Heligan, for instance. That's what some might call a garden, but give me this any day. Heligan's too formal, y'see. Contrived. There's nothing contrived about Grace's garden.'

Michael turned and looked out of the window. He had to concede that the local policeman had a point: whoever designed the garden had somehow managed to make it look completely organic; as if it had grown out of itself, by itself. It was lush without being luscious; cultivated without being contrived. But to rank it above one of the greatest gardens in the British Isles was a gross exaggeration. 'Well,' he said, 'it's certainly very beautiful.' He looked across the wide expanse of lawn to the lake beyond and then turned back to Alfred. 'Grace'll need help with it now that John's gone.'

'Oh, John never had anything to do with it. That was always Grace. And, of course, Matthew.'

'Matthew?'

'Yes.' Alfred Mabely scanned the room for the man in question but failed to locate him. 'Scottish chap. Good-looking, craggy sort of fellow. He's Grace's gardener. Dotes on her, too.' Then, frowning, he paused. 'Nothing funny going on there, though. No, no.' Self-styled guardian of morality as well as local law enforcer, Alfred took a very dim view of all things 'funny'. He smiled at Michael. 'Matthew goes out with the skipper of the *Sharicmar*. Very settled, they are.'

'Er ... right.' Michael assumed, correctly, that the *Sharicmar* was a fishing boat and, incorrectly, that the skipper was a man and that the craggy gardener was therefore gay. Not entirely approving of the concept of gay fishermen and gardeners, and not sure of what to say next, he looked round the room for inspiration. It didn't take long to find.

Standing at the other end of the room, and evidently under the impression that the large orchid on the table in front of her was shielding her from view, a middle-aged woman in a black felt hat was surreptitiously emptying the entire contents of a bowl of peanuts into her handbag. Michael watched, intrigued, as she snapped the bag shut and turned back to her companions; a taller woman in a similar hat and a smartly-suited, younger man. 'Who on earth,' he said, turning back to the policeman, 'is that woman?'

'Which woman?'

Michael nodded in the direction of the trio. 'The short one in the hat.'

'Ah. That's Margaret Sutton. She runs the post office. With Diana Skinner – the one on the other side of

Dr Bamford. Local institutions, they are.' Alfred smiled benignly. 'Don't know where we'd be without them.'

'But she just …' Then Michael remembered who he was with, and trailed into silence. Sergeant Mabely looked like the sort of man who would take crime – any crime – extremely seriously, and Michael didn't want to be the catalyst for a local institution being arrested at the wake of a local landlord. Instead, he took his leave of Alfred and went in search of his wife. He found Grace before he found Hermione. She was hovering beside another large orchid, holding a teapot like a shield to her breast. She stood quite still, but her eyes were bright: dancing round the room as if looking for someone in particular.

'Lost someone?'

'Oh! Oh, Michael. No … no. Just, you know … well …' Grace lowered her eyes. 'More tea?'

'No, thank you Grace. In fact, I think we'd better be going. It'll be dark in about an hour and my eyes aren't what they used to be. Driving, you know.'

'Yes,' said Grace, who hadn't heard a word.

'Thank you, Grace. It's been … well … look,' he added, donning the reassuring mantle of the older and wiser protector and adviser, 'if there's anything you need … anything at all we can do for you, just phone. You know where we are …'

'Yes. Moore Manor. How are the gunneras?'

'I beg your pardon?'

'Gunneras. A sort of Brazilian rhubarb. You grow it.'

'Do we?'

'Yes. We … I can't because we're too near the sea and the salt gets to the leaves and …' and then Grace noticed the expression on Michael's face and realised he hadn't the faintest idea what she was talking about. 'Well,' she finished with a half-hearted smile, 'I must come and see your garden one day.'

Relieved to be back on familiar territory, Michael bent forward and touched Grace's arm. 'Do that, Grace. Hermione would be delighted. *We'd* be delighted. Any time, Grace.'

'Thank you.' Grace beamed at Michael, grateful more for his impending departure than for his offer of hospitality. She liked what she knew of Michael and Hermione. She knew they meant well. She also knew that she was wilting again.

So, across the room, was Martin Bamford. He desperately needed a break from Diana Skinner and Margaret Sutton. While they were both the epitome of kindness, and whilst St Liac would be poorer – especially as regards gossip – without them, neither woman was the sharpest knife in the drawer. And Martin, although he cultivated the image of lad at large, was highly intelligent, deeply concerned about his patients – Grace included – and thrived on witty conversation. He was beginning to tire of the ladies. He needed a breath of fresh air. More specifically, he needed a smoke.

'Well,' he said, interrupting Diana's thesis on peanuts, 'I really think it's time …'

'What kind of injuries,' asked Margaret, 'would someone have if they fell from that height? Thirty thousand feet, wasn't it? Must have been pretty bad.'

'Yes. Very bad. Very bad injuries,' said Martin. 'Although, of course, he was dead by the time …'

'… Why did he do it?'

'Sorry, Margaret?'

'Why did he fall out of the plane?'

'I've never been on a plane,' offered Diana. 'And now I know why.'

'Um … why?'

'The doors.'

'Doors?'

'Yes.' For one who had never been on a plane, Diana assumed great authority on the subject. 'You see, he probably thought he was going to the toilet and picked the wrong door by mistake.'

'Um … yes, probably.' Slightly desperate now, Martin looked from one woman to the other. Both were lost in thought. And both, he surmised correctly, were about to elaborate on the subject of planes and their doors. 'Look,' he said. 'Would you mind awfully? I've got to go to the …'

'… toilet,' said Diana.

'Yes. I'll … um, be back in a mo.'

But he didn't mean to be. And he wasn't. Leaving Diana and Margaret to their musings on planes, doors and, probably, toilets, he rushed out into the hall and bounded up the stairs. And he wasn't heading for the lavatory. Five minutes previously, he had seen Matthew march upstairs. And Matthew, he suspected, was in possession of the particular brand of fresh air he needed. He found his friend emerging shutting a door behind him and, judging by the fact that he was still buttoning his flies, it had obviously been the right door. 'Matthew,' he whispered through the banister. 'You got any?'

Matthew blinked. 'What?'

'Any stuff?'

Matthew looked horrified. This was, after all, a funeral. 'No,' he whispered back. 'There's none about.'

Martin responded with a look. A highly charged look.

What the hell, thought Matthew. A little light relief wouldn't go amiss. He winked at Martin. 'Oh all right, come on.'

Martin Bamford breathed a sigh of relief.

19

'But not in the house,' cautioned Matthew.

'No!' This time it was Martin who looked horrified. He was, after all, a doctor. Blatant consumption of illicit drugs which were – as far as he was concerned – of the healing variety was one thing. Surreptitious toking was quite another. 'Garden, then?'

'The old laundry,' said Matthew.

Liac House, being three hundred years old and, at its inception, a self-sustaining community, had numerous outbuildings originally designated as laundries, cold-stores, dairies and tack rooms. Nearly all of them had been made redundant after the First World War; and some of them had been allowed to decline to the point of desolation. But under Grace's régime, the buildings that were still intact had become part of the garden rather than the house. The crumbling edifice that was the old laundry, for example, was now completely covered in ivy and, with its archway leading into a now grass-covered courtyard, was more leafy bower than building.

It was also rather secluded.

'Grace bearing up okay?' asked Martin when they reached it. 'She looks a little strained.'

'She's got every right to,' replied Matthew, carefully extracting a joint from his breast pocket. 'It's not every day you play hostess at your husband's funeral. Must be grim.' Matthew lit up and inhaled deeply. Closing his eyes for a moment, he relaxed, leaned further against the wall and then exhaled with a long, satisfied sigh. He watched the smoke curl lazily up into the bright blue sky and then took another drag.

Waiting impatiently, Martin found his mind wandering to the subject of drugs in general. 'I offered her sleeping pills, you know. Said she didn't need them.'

'Not Grace's style, is it?' said Matthew. 'Anyway, she has other methods of winding down.'

'Oh?' Martin was intrigued.

'Yeah. Gardening. It's incredibly cathartic.' Matthew grinned. 'You should try it sometime.'

'Me?' Martin looked appalled. 'No … not my thing. Don't know where I'd find the time anyway. Too busy … um … doctoring.'

Matthew smile broadened as he proffered the joint to the other man. He tried, and failed, to conjure up an image of Martin pottering around his garden. Despite the fact that he lived in what holiday brochures described as a 'rural idyll', Martin Bamford was impossibly urban. The smart suits, the sleek Jaguar, the stark modern furniture of his house – they all screamed London rather than Cornwall. Indeed the people of St Liac had treated Martin with no small degree of suspicion when, five years previously, he had successfully applied for the post of the town's GP. He wouldn't have been the first Londoner to fall in love with the place and then attempt to spoil it by imposing his views, his customs and his loud city friends on the community.

But Martin had done none of that. Instead he had muttered vaguely about 'falling in love with the surf', and then puzzled everyone by failing to go anywhere near the beach. It took two months for everyone to realise that, in reality, he had fallen in love with a bronzed surfette who later decamped to Bondi leaving Martin as deflated as the dinghy he had never used. Dark rumours about his own imminent departure back to London reared their heads but were never founded. Martin Bamford stayed on and became a respected, if slightly eccentric, mainstay of the community. Suspicion turned to admiration tempered, occasionally, with sympathy. For while it was true that a disproportionate number of his patients died whilst in his care, it was also true that the parish of St Liac harboured a disproportionate number of elderly people. Young people who were raised in St Liac tended to leave for the bright lights and big cities. Yet, over the last few years, the population had remained stable. It was even beginning to grow as people like Martin arrived, fell in love (with whatever) and stayed. Matthew himself was one of them. And like Martin he had fallen in love with a person: someone who was still very much part of his life.

'Where's Nicky?' asked Martin, as if on cue. Nicky, he knew, couldn't understand dope. He suspected she rather disapproved of it.

'Nicky? Oh … dunno. She was trying to help Grace a minute ago, but Grace was having none of it. Silly, really. She's got too much on her plate.'

'Mmm. Sandwiches.'

'What?' Matthew reached out for the joint.

'Sandwiches. Last time I saw her she had too many sandwiches on her plate.'

'Oh very funny. No, she's got too much on her mind. She's asked me twice to check the humidifier in the greenhouse – and I've told her twice that I did it yesterday.'

'D'you think she'll stay?'

'Stay where?'

'Here.' Martin gestured vaguely around him. 'At Liac.'

'Course she'll stay.' Matthew was surprised by the question. 'She loves it here. Christ, she's been here for twenty-five years. She wouldn't just up and off. This is her life.'

'And yours now, eh?'

Matthew hadn't really addressed the question before, but he supposed Martin was right. He couldn't imagine himself ever leaving. 'Yeah, I guess. Anyway, there's no way Grace could manage the garden on her own.'

'Do you think John left her well provided for?'

'Oh yes. No question of that. He was pretty loaded.'

Martin looked suddenly thoughtful. 'D'you know, I don't think I ever really knew what he did? I know he was always jetting off somewhere, but what did he actually *do*?' He stared down at the joint and then raised it to his lips for another drag. Contrary to rumours, the dope wasn't a source of enlightenment.

Nor, more to the point, was Matthew. 'Well ... he did ... well, business. He was a businessman.' But even as he spoke, Matthew realised the feebleness of his diagnosis. 'Um ... well,' he finished, 'I suppose I never really knew either. Still, he had masses of investments.'

'Did he?'

'Yeah. Grace was always laughing at the amount of mail they got. From trusts and things. Said John had a pie in every finger.'

'Finger in every pie.'

'What?'

'You've got it the wrong way round. Wrong end of the stick.'

'Eh?'

'So did Diana.'

'Martin, I haven't a clue what you're talking about.'

Seemingly unaware of his non-sequitur, and slightly stoned now, Martin recalled his conversation with the post-mistress. 'Diana seems to think it was some sort of accident. She reckons that he was just going to the lavatory and opened the wrong door.'

Matthew pondered that one for a moment. 'He probably did go,' he said at length. 'On the way down.'

'What's on the way down? The crime rate, if it's anything

to do with me!' The hearty words were followed by an even heartier laugh and, belatedly and to their horror, Martin and Matthew found themselves staring at Sergeant Alfred Mabely.

Matthew, the first to recover, glared at Martin and, pointedly, at the joint in his hand. Martin froze for a second and then hid the offending item behind his back.

'All right, Alfred?' smiled Matthew.

'Yes, yes.' Alfred was standing, as was his wont, with his hands clasped behind his back and his head craned forward in a slightly questioning manner. But he was, thankfully, smiling. 'Ah, Dr Bamford,' he said, noticing Martin. 'Hello there.'

'Hello.' Suddenly aware of the need to expel a lungful of smoke, Martin wheezed and edged backwards towards the wall. Behind him, the joint sizzled slightly as it made contact with the ivy.

But the policeman continued to beam up at him. 'Now … I wonder if you could do me a favour?'

'Er … yes. Um.' Martin coughed loudly and put his left hand to his mouth in a valiant attempt to disguise the smoke.

Alfred put his own left hand to his ear and winced. 'It's my ear. It needs to be looked at again. It's still giving me gyp.'

Martin spluttered and patted his chest. Words, however, failed him.

'What if I pop into the surgery tomorrow, eh? Would you be able to see me then?'

Still unable to speak, the hapless doctor looked wide-eyed at the policeman and then, rather harder than he had intended, slapped him on the back.

If Alfred was surprised by the gesture, he didn't show it. He merely nodded. 'Right then, I'll be off then. I've said my goodbyes to Grace and there's work to be done.' With a zealous glint in his eye, he looked back at Matthew. 'There's reports of salmon poachers out on the estuary.'

Both men remained deathly still until Alfred was well out of sight. And, they hoped, earshot. Because when Martin eventually opened his mouth, it was in the throes of a paroxysm of hacking that forced him to bend double and clutch his hands to his chest.

'Are you all right?' asked Matthew.

'I'm dying,' moaned Martin. 'God, you have no idea! You have absolutely no idea ....' Unable to finish the sentence, he bent forwards again and coughed his lungs out.

'You're not a very good ambassador for the medical qualities of dope,' remarked Matthew. 'What have you done with it anyway?'

Matthew gestured to the grass behind him. The joint had been extinguished by the damp leaves of ivy and lay forlornly at the foot of the wall. Matthew picked it up and re-lit it. 'I can't believe,' he said as he savoured the sweet smoke, 'that Alfred didn't suspect anything.'

'I can.' Martin groaned and drew himself to his full height. Then he saw the spliff. 'Feeling better now. Give us a drag, there's a good chap.' He reached out for it. 'It's pretty easy to fool old Alfred, you know. Pulling the wool over plod,' he finished with authority, 'is child's play.'

'Well you'll not get a chance to play that particular game again for a long while,' said Matthew. 'That's the last of the stuff.' He looked up into the sky. 'Enjoy while you can; it's going to be a long, cold winter.'

He was probably right, but the flowering camellias, azaleas and magnolias indicated that they were in the middle of a long, warm spring. And Matthew had no idea that, well before winter set in, he would be playing the game in an altogether different league. 'C'mon,' he said as he watched

Martin burn his fingers on the red-hot roach. 'We'd better find Nicky and say goodbye to Grace.'

Grace was in the kitchen, clearing up the remains of her life. At least that was what it felt like. In reality, she was hovering uncertainly beside the bin, half-heartedly scraping food from plates. Behind her, sitting at the debris-strewn table with a can of lager in front of him, Harvey Sloggit was lending her moral support. At least that was his intention. In reality, he was getting on her nerves.

'My mum,' he said as Grace stacked the plates beside the sink, 'wanted to get one of those dishwashers.' He paused, waiting for a reaction from Grace. None was forthcoming. Harvey shrugged and pressed valiantly on. 'My dad said she's already got one.' Another pause. Again no reaction. 'Him,' finished Harvey. He knew it wasn't very funny, but the old Grace would have at least replied. At the very least she would have grinned. The new Grace simply turned back to the table for more plates. 'He means well,' she told herself. 'Like the others. Like Matthew and like Nicky.' That, she knew, was true. Of all the mourners in St Liac, it was the younger generation, not her peers, who were rallying round her most. And Harvey, Nicky's mate on the *Sharicmar*, was rallying in spades. But Grace didn't want rallying. She wanted to be left alone.

Harvey looked up at her with his dark, brooding eyes. 'Look, Grace, if there's anything I can do. You know, round the house or ....'

'... No!' snapped Grace. Then she saw the startled expression on Harvey's face and smiled. 'No, really,' she said softly. 'Everyone's been very kind, but ... but I'm fine. Really.' Looking away from Harvey, she picked up the large, glass cake-stand that had, she dimly remembered, been a

26

wedding present. She was about to go back to the sink when Harvey suddenly sprang to his feet and tried to wrest it from her. 'Here, look. I'll do that for you,' he insisted.

'Harvey!' Surprised by the sudden movement, Grace momentarily lost her grip on the cake-stand. So, startled by the look in Grace's eye, did Harvey. The cake-stand went crashing to the floor. Grace looked at Harvey. Harvey looked at Grace. Then they both looked at the shattered fragments at their feet.

There was nothing accusatory in Grace's expression as she looked back at Harvey. But there was an unmistakable warning to leave her alone. 'I'm fine. Really. I'm fine, Harvey.'

Harvey knew when he was beaten. He smiled sheepishly, muttered something about not being back late, and reached for the jacket on the back of the chair. It was then that Matthew, Martin and Nicky made their appearance. The awkward atmosphere in the kitchen told them their own decision to leave hadn't come a moment too soon; so did the look in Harvey's eyes. And while Grace put her smile back on to escort them through the house, while everyone made the right noises and said 'thank you Grace' with feeling, there was still something hollow and hurried about their departure.

As they scrunched their way along the gravel drive, Nicky looked back at Grace. She was standing in the doorway, dwarfed by the façade of her huge house and by the large palms that flanked the front entrance. Nicky waved: Grace raised a hand and smiled. But Nicky was too far away to see the look in her eyes. Nor could she guess what was going on in her mind.

Grace didn't really know either. Her brain was assaulted by a barrage of conflicting emotions. Grief, despair and exhaustion battled with each other – as well as with anger and surprise. Anger because of the woman's presence in the graveyard: surprise that someone else had known about her. And that someone had been Gerald Percy. 'She's not here,' he had whispered as he saw Grace fruitlessly scanning her drawing room earlier in the afternoon. 'I know, but don't worry. No-one else does.' Then he had squeezed her arm in what he hoped was a reassuring gesture. 'She left straight after the service. Try to forget, Grace. And try to forgive. You've seen the last of her.'

But as John Trevethan's widow closed the door behind the last of his mourners, she recalled Gerald's words. And with them came a sneaking suspicion that he had been mistaken. Grace had a horrible feeling that she hadn't seen the last of John Trevethan's mistress.

TWO

Grace had been in her early twenties when she first came to Liac. She had immediately been captivated by the small fishing village, by the harbour that was the hub of all activity and by the narrow streets that wound their way upwards and away from the coast. She had been entranced by the lobster pots and crails drying on the waterfront; by the fishermen who lived their lives according to the tides; by the weather that changed from howling gales and storms to bright sunshine in, it seemed, an instant. She had revelled in walking across the cliffs and then down to rocky, beautiful – and deserted – beaches to gather great bucketfuls of mussels.

So complete had been her love for the place that even dyed-in-the-wool cynics gave up trying to brand her a patronising Londoner and welcomed her into their midst. Most people had long suspected that John Trevethan, working in London, would marry someone he met there. Their only reservation after the engagement was announced was that Grace would become bored and bolt back to the bright lights to indulge in cocktails and sin or, worse, invite her fast friends to do likewise at Liac House.

But they had reckoned without Grace's burgeoning passion for gardening. In Chelsea, she had worked in a highly-respected garden centre for no other reason than she liked being around things that grew rather than people who withered in offices. But in Cornwall, the seeds of her desire to nurture were firmly sewn – and soon they began to reap astonishing rewards. Cornwall's micro-climate, she discovered, was a gift for plants. Even for sub-tropical plants. Grace soon found that she had a flowering Camellia at Christmas (albeit with a little help from her greenhouse), huge pink *Magnolia campbellii* as early as March and that, long before the summer trickle of tourists which later turned into an invasion, she had violets, wood anemones, comfrey and campion flowering in various parts of her garden.

Then Grace began to experiment for herself and became slightly dispirited. A garden, she realised, was never finished. In her first few years, she began to feel like the mythical Sisyphus, condemned for eternity to push a boulder to the top of a mountain only to find, just as he neared to summit, that the boulder would roll down again. Grace learned the true meaning of uphill work, but it never deterred her. One day she would reach the summit.

She did. She discovered orchids and orchids, it seemed, discovered her. She would do anything for them and they, in turn, appeared to reward her by flourishing throughout the year. Even recalcitrant varieties, choosy about their pollinators, adapted to Grace's methods. If they were used to feeding on moths they would, if Grace desired, adapt to crawling insects. Grace became famous for her hybrids.

And then, five years into her marriage, the rumours began to spread. Grace, the gossips declared, was infertile. (They never countenanced the possibility that it was John. He was, after all, local.) And Grace was using orchids as a cure for her infertility. They were, after all, exceedingly sensual plants, sharing the appearance of certain parts of the human anatomy. They were – as the late and not-much-missed

Helen Norbury had put about – derived from the Latin word for testicle. They were possessed of powerful aphrodisiac qualities. 'Especially the roots,' she had declaimed. 'They're hot and moist and, under the dominance of Venus (she meant Grace), they provoke lust.'

Most people thought Helen was spouting nonsense, but even Grace's ardent fans started to feel sorry for her. They accepted the notion that she was desperate to conceive and was sublimating her desires into her plants.

Grace wasn't stupid. She knew more about orchids than anyone else (including that fact that *orchis* was indeed the Latin for testicle), and was well aware of their reputation. Yet, even years after she had accepted the fact that she and John would never have children, she continued with her orchids. Not because they were a substitute for children, but because orchids were what she did best.

The orchids were Grace's saviours in the dark days after John's funeral. She nurtured, she potted, she experimented and, most of all, she thought. Not about orchids themselves but, whilst tending them, about her life. The conclusion she reached surprised her. She had vaguely assumed that once one was widowed, life changed dramatically. Now she realised that wasn't the case. Far from it. Her life, in fact, was going to continue much as it had before, the only major difference being that John's absence was now permanent rather than intermittent. She had been accustomed to business trips that had lasted days or even weeks: now she would have to get used to the fact that his last trip had been one-way.

That John was no longer with her in spirit was rather more difficult to deal with. When the pain hit her it hit hard – and it hurt. Her method of coming to terms with it was to hit back, to recall the woman at the funeral and the part of John's life that had been a lie. It was quite an effective method: Grace found herself becoming angry as she remembered the letters that John (surely he must have suspected she knew?) had left for her to post to a woman called Honey Chambers. A woman who he never mentioned in a business context. A woman who he never mentioned at all.

And then Grace found that she had to quell her anger, which she did by telling herself that as she no longer had a husband then *he* no longer had a mistress and that was that. It was all in the past and there was nothing she could do about it. And she dismissed from her mind that unhappy, fleeting sensation that had visited her on the day of John's funeral. That, too, belonged to the past.

So, really, it was strange logic as much as orchids that saw Grace through her darkest moments. And, of course, Matthew. Grace didn't know what she would do without him. He was always smiling, often laughing and forever willing. That he wasn't especially skilled wasn't important to Grace. Any aspect of gardening that required skill and, dare she say it, delicacy, was undertaken by herself. Matthew did the digging, the dead-heading, the pruning of the more robust plants and the mowing. And that last job, as spring gradually gave way to summer, was becoming ever more time-consuming. Even with the tractor-style mower John had bought her for her last birthday, it was still a huge task, but one that Matthew took on with vigour. And as far as Grace was concerned, the new mower had another advantage: the powerful engine comprehensively quashed the sound of Matthew's singing. Singing was something Matthew undertook with equal vigour – and a corresponding lack of skill. But he was fun to have around and

Grace, a few weeks after John's funeral, was beginning to appreciate fun again.

So it was with a spring in her step, on a Monday morning exactly a month after John's death, that she left Liac House for her customary, if hardly exciting, round of chores in the village. Grace loathed shopping, her appointment with the bank manager was sure to be a bore – but she didn't care. It was warm, the sky was crystal clear and Matthew, bless him, was singing.

'Morning!' she called as she saw him at the lake. Or rather, *in* the lake. Matthew had decided to dredge it.

'But it's not a *proper* lake,' Grace had protested when he had mooted the idea. 'I mean, there's no traffic on it. It's too shallow to swim in. It's artificial – only for looking at. It doesn't really,' she had finished, 'need dredging.'

Matthew had fixed her with a laconic glare – offset by the twinkle in his piercing blue eyes – and told her that there was nothing he didn't know about water where he came from.

'But you're from *Glasgow*.'

'So?'

'There's plenty of artificial lakes. You never know what you'll find cluttering them up. Which is why,' he added with finality, 'they need dredging.'

'Good God!' shouted Grace as she walked towards him. 'How on earth did that get there?'

Matthew shrugged. 'Dunno. Probably the grisly drowning of a housemaid in the eighteenth century.'

'They didn't have bicycles in the eighteenth century, Matthew.'

'Didn't they? Oh.' Matthew looked down at the mangled, thoroughly rusted machine. 'Nineteenth century then. Might be worth a bob or two if it was cleaned up.' He looked appraisingly at Grace.

But Grace's expression told him she wasn't interested in making a bob or two. So, thought Matthew, she doesn't know. Yet.

But she would. Very soon.

The rumours had started, as St Liac rumours did, in the post office. More specifically, they had started when Diana Skinner had noticed the amount of mail that Archie the postman was required to lug up the hill to Liac House.

'Grace is getting a lot of mail,' she had said to Margaret.

'Well she would, wouldn't she?' Margaret, generally considered the more sensible of the two postmistresses, hadn't expressed surprise. 'Letters of condolence and all that.'

'In brown envelopes?'

'Well … those'll be from John's business people. Sorting out his affairs. Things for Grace to sign.'

'Molly Pentyre didn't get nearly so many when old Jack died.'

'Oh *Diana*,' admonished Margaret. 'You've been counting again.'

'No. Just … just concerned about Grace.' That was undoubtedly true. Diana saw it as her mission in life to look after not just Grace, but the entire population of St Liac. She also saw herself as the village's patron saint of lost causes and lost things. In this she was helped by her demeanour: she looked, and acted, like a questing vole. But she was thwarted by her almost complete absent-mindedness. Diana forgot things. And her ability to find things was nothing to do with extra-sensory powers but because the things she found were things she had taken, and forgotten about. Usually they were things of little importance (like the peanuts she had found in her handbag on the day after John Trevethan's funeral). But

Diana never took anything valuable, so her little habit was tolerated. It was even regarded with some amusement.

But Margaret wasn't amused by Diana's intelligence regarding Grace's mail. She knew all about brown envelopes. Nothing good ever came of brown envelopes.

Just to make sure that she was right, she voiced her fears to Joyce at the bakery who corroborated that brown envelopes were nasty. Who, she asked, would be getting piles of brown envelopes at such a sad time, what with the place still in mourning for John Trevethan? But Margaret couldn't possibly say and changed the subject to Grace who was bearing up so well under all the strain she must be under, wasn't she? And so the story of the brown envelopes gained momentum and, indeed, credibility when Melvyn Stott from the bank drank too much at The Anchor one night and told Charlie that Grace had passed her mail to him and that he didn't, really, know what to do. The next day the head office of the bank started to bounce Grace's cheques and the stories became facts: Grace was broke.

Perversely, while everyone had believed the rumours, no-one was prepared to accept the facts. It was quickly decided that John's untimely death had wrong-footed his lawyers and accountants and that his estate was suffering from administrative rather than financial problems. It wasn't about a lack of money, just about a lack of access to it. There was, in fact, heaps of money. John's affairs were so complex because he had been so wealthy and, once everything was sorted out, Grace would be thrillingly rich.

This appealing rumour became far more popular than the stories of brown envelopes and fuelled speculation about what Grace would do once she came into her vast inheritance. In the meantime, and until everything was sorted out, everyone agreed that it would be best not to tell Grace about the little matter of the bouncing cheques. After all, they were for small amounts and what was the point of living in a close community if you didn't rally round in times of crisis? There were some who didn't believe a word of this rumour – and Matthew Stuart was one of them – but they still kept quiet. No-one wanted to upset Grace, and Matthew, for one, didn't want to address the possibility of losing his job.

Because the rumours concerned Grace, she remained in blissful ignorance of them. It was true that she had sent the brown envelopes off to Melvyn Stott, ruefully admitting to a total lack of financial acumen and, indeed, understanding. And Melvyn had promised that he would deal with everything. Two weeks after he had received the first batch of Grace's mail he had phoned to request what promised to be one of the most miserable and upsetting appointments of his life.

But Grace didn't know that. As she left Matthew to his dredging and walked down the lane into town, she was at one with the world; smiling, happy, greeting people she passed with a friendly 'hello' and not noticing that they failed to look her in the eye and rushed passed rather more quickly than was the norm.

Her first port of call was the post office, an establishment which doubled as a general purpose store and (unbeknown to Margaret and Diana) a tourist attraction. First-time visitors to St Liac would invariably stop in their tracks and gawp at the window display of the store. The place hadn't changed to any considerable degree since the 1950s. Nor, for that matter, had Margaret and Diana. Their last great concession to modernity had been a resigned acceptance of decimal coins and that, they felt, had been traumatic enough.

So their shop became enveloped in a time warp that bothered neither its owners nor their customers. The shop sold everything any sane person could ever require – and if some other wares were insanely out of tune with modern life, nobody in St Liac cared. Locals had long been used to the golliwog in the window, the pointy-bosomed mannequin in pink bra and knickers on the counter, the lobster claws dangling from the ceiling and the fact that cornflakes shared shelf space with carbolic soap and plimsolls with toothpaste. They were also used to the fact that, from time immemorial, Diana and Margaret had stood together behind the counter – the former in her purple apron and the latter in her woolly hat – ready to serve all customers at all times. And the fact that the counter was beside the window left them well-placed to observe the comings and goings of St Liac.

So Diana and Margaret were prepared for Grace even before she pushed open the door and walked into the shop. They had primed the two other customers to act as if nothing was wrong and to greet Grace in the usual manner. Grace was therefore met with a strained atmosphere, a deathly silence and, from behind the counter, two rictus grins. She didn't, however, appear to notice.

'Hello, ladies,' she said with a bright smile.

Diana couldn't trust herself to speak.

Margaret managed a 'Morning, Grace,' and relapsed into silence.

The two other women in the shop developed a pressing need to search for items as far away from Grace as was possible.

Grace looked at her shopping list and frowned. 'Nothing really from here today, but I thought I'd come in and settle my account and, oh yes, I'd like some paracetamol.'

This was worse than they had expected.

Diana merely gawped, but Margaret rallied to the fore. 'Um ... no ... you can't settle. We've ... er ... we've lost our accounts.'

'Oh.' Grace looked puzzled. That was highly unusual. Even in an establishment where Diana worked. 'Oh. Well ...'

'... it's very mysterious,' whispered Diana.

'Yes. Yes, I suppose it is.'

'So why don't you just pay us next month?' suggested Margaret.

Diana nodded. 'When we've found our accounts.'

'Oh. All right. If you're sure. So I'll just have the paracetamol then.'

Diana and Margaret exchanged a look. 'We'll put it on the account, then, shall we?'

But Grace had already opened her purse. 'No, no,' she said to Margaret. 'It's only pennies.'

Margaret reluctantly reached under the counter and produced the required bottle. 'That'll be five pence.'

'What?'

'Five pence.'

'It can't be!' Grace peered down at the price-tag. 'It says one pound twenty-five.'

'Special offer,' snapped Margaret.

'Oh.' Looking a little uncertain, Grace delved into her purse and produced a coin. 'Well, if you're sure.' She popped the bottle into her shopping bag and turned to leave. A small voice in the back of her head told her there was something not quite right about the atmosphere in the shop, but she couldn't put her finger on it. It was only after she'd said her goodbyes that she realised what it was: Margaret and Diana had practically been monosyllabic. Grace had been in and out of the shop in a minute. Normally it took ten to say hello.

Diana breathed a sigh of relief when the door closed

behind Grace. 'Well,' she said with pride. 'We saved her a pound.'

'Yes. Every little bit helps.' Then Margaret looked out the window and raised a hand to her mouth. 'Oh my God!'

'What?'

'Look. She's heading for the lady from the lifeboat fund.'

Diana looked. Sure enough, Grace was making a beeline for the lady with the lifeboat-shaped money box. They knew what that meant: Grace was inordinately generous to local charities. She would part with more than the pound she had saved – and could ill-afford – in the post office.

But Diana and Margaret needn't have worried. Mrs Reid, the lady from the lifeboat fund, who didn't even come from St Liac but from nearby Constantine Bay, was well-acquainted with the Grace situation. She had met her once, and remembered the tentative smile, the honey-coloured hair and the bearing that matched her name. She also knew a thing or two about worthy causes and if ever there was one it was Mrs Trevethan in her current predicament. So as Grace approached, Mrs Reid hid the charity box behind her back and smiled in the embarrassed way you do when you're trying to prevent someone giving money to charity.

Grace faltered slightly but then rummaged in her bag for her purse. Mrs Reid backed away.

'I'd … er … just like …'

'… No!' In a panic now, Mrs Reid clutched the lifeboat to her breast, retreated even further and then, aware that her behaviour was at the very least a little uncharitable, smiled sweetly at Grace. 'Lovely day,' she said.

Grace was completely dumbfounded. 'Won't you …?'

'Bye then!' shrieked Mrs Reid. Then she turned on her heel and ran away.

Watching from the post-office window, Margaret nodded

her approval. 'That was well done,' she said to Diana. 'But I can't help feeling if this isn't sorted out soon then Grace may begin to suspect something.'

'No, no,' countered Diana. 'Not if we continue to be subtle about it.'

Being subtle was something Melvyn Stott was rather good at. He had to be. As manager of the St Liac branch of the Southern Bank, he was accustomed to imparting bad news rather than good: this wasn't anything to do with St Liac in particular, more with bank managers in general. For like the rest of the species, Melvyn had been trained to ignore customers who were in credit ('no use to us' was the dismissive line at the management courses) and to direct his subtleties towards people who owed the bank money. ('There's nothing better than a debtor' was the management mantra on that one). Debt meant interest. And unauthorised debts meant interest calculated at dizzying percentages.

That was all very well if you were a faceless individual sitting in an anonymous office, dealing with pieces of paper rather than broken pieces of people. But as manager of a regional branch, Melvyn was far from faceless: he was on first-name terms with all but a fraction of his clients; he was on dinner-party terms with about half of them and, worse, he cared about them. He cared deeply about Grace. But for the life of him – and even if he deployed every trick in the subtlety book – he couldn't see how he could break the news of Grace's predicament without upsetting her. Or perhaps predicament was an understatement: catastrophe was nearer the mark.

So when Grace was announced at 11am precisely, Melvyn

himself was in a predicament. And it was Grace who helped him out.

'There's something wrong, isn't there?' she asked as soon as he had ushered her to the chair opposite his own.

'Er ... what do you mean?'

'Well I'm not stupid,' said Grace with a half laugh. 'Just now ... they wouldn't let me pay in the post office and then that woman from the lifeboat fund wouldn't let me give her any money.'

'Really?' Melvyn was outraged. Then, remembering, he bit back his instinctive response. Now was not the time to tell Grace that donations to charity were tax deductible. He looked down at the neat, if hefty, pile of papers on his desk. 'Well, yes, Grace. Now that you mention it, John's affairs were ... a little tangled.'

'Yes. He had fingers in lots of pies, didn't he?'

If only he'd had a finger in a lot of tills as well, thought Melvyn. He coughed. 'Yes. Only ... look, Grace, is there anything you haven't told me?'

Grace blinked. 'About what?'

'About John's affairs. Are you sure this is all the relevant correspondence? All the right papers?'

'Ye-es. I gave you the entire contents of his desk and, well ... you've got all the letters that I was sent since ... after ...'

'Fine. Good. Um ... well, not good, as it turns out. Look,' he all but implored. 'There must be other things. Life insurance policies. Endowments. Investments?'

Grace shook her head. 'I don't think so.' Then she leaned over the desk. 'Melvyn, there's something very wrong, isn't there? Are you trying to tell me that John wasn't well off? That he hasn't left me much?'

'Oh he *was* well off. No doubt about that. Only ... only he wasn't when he died.'

'Oh.'

'In fact he wasn't *at all* well off.'

Grace looked as if she had been hit. 'I don't understand, Melvyn. There must be some mistake. I mean it wasn't even that long ago that John's father died, and I *know* he left a lot. I mean, the house alone is worth …'

'… The thing is, Grace, John used the house as an asset to raise capital.'

'There's nothing wrong with that, is there? That sort of thing's quite common, isn't it?' Grace quelled a wave of panic. 'I still inherit the house, don't I?'

'Oh yes. But … but you also inherit the mortgage.' Too late, Melvyn realised that was hardly being subtle.

The mortgage. That wasn't right: it *couldn't* be right. Grace managed to persuade herself it wasn't right. She smiled across at Melvyn. 'That's fine, then. The house is three hundred years old. The mortgage must be paid off by now.'

Oh dear, thought Melvyn. He gestured again at the pile of documents. 'Er … you don't understand.' He sighed. 'He used the house as collateral for loans to finance business deals …'

'He did a lot of deals. Yes.'

'… None of which actually … took off.'

The smile was still hovering on Grace's lips, but Grace herself wasn't aware of it. She was beginning to feel as if she had lost her grip on reality; as if she had wandered into someone else's nightmare. And now she wanted out. 'What about,' she suggested, 'the money he left me?' The question came out in a near-whisper.

So did the answer.

Grace blinked rapidly.

'The thing is, Grace, not to panic,' said Melvyn.

'No.'

42

'We'll sit down and draw up a strategy, eh?'

'Strategy?'

'Yes. A schedule, if you like. A list of priorities.' Melvyn meant payments. It was going to be a very long list. Heart sinking, he reached for his pen. 'Now ... Liac House. I don't suppose you ... want to sell?'

'No.'

'Fine. Good.' But it wasn't at all good. Melvyn chewed the end of his pen and looked down at the sheet of paper in front of him. 'So the first priority is the mortgage payments.'

'How much are they?'

'Er ... two thousand pounds. A month.'

Grace went rigid with fear. 'But Melvyn ... I don't have two thousand pounds. A month. I don't even have two thousand pounds.'

Melvyn knew that. He also knew that the mortgage payments were the tip of the iceberg. And he knew that, however long he managed to stall the payments, Head Office would eventually step in and scoop up the miserable remains of Grace's life.

'What,' whispered the shell-shocked woman, 'am I going to do?'

Melvyn hadn't a clue; couldn't really help her. For in his heart of hearts, he knew there was no way of saving Grace.

THREE

'What will she do?'

'Sell up, I suppose.'

Nicky was horrified. 'But she *can't!* Liac is her life. There must be something she can do, Matthew.'

Matthew shrugged. He was trying not to think about Grace's situation – partly because it directly reflected his own. But that, of course, was precisely why Nicky wanted to talk about it. And Martin and Harvey, leaning against the pool table beside them, could think of little else to talk about either. Grace's finances, or total lack of them, were public knowledge now, principally because Grace, on her return from the bank, had confided in Matthew. She had also sacked him.

Matthew's reaction had been to feel heart sorry for her. When her cheque of the previous week had bounced he, like others in the same predicament, had kept quiet about it. He had tried to believe in the myth of the administrative mix-up and had assumed business as usual. But when Grace had returned from town, her agonised expression told him that nothing would be as usual again. Her words were confirmation of that: she said she was sorry but had no option. She paid him, in cash, until the end of the week. Then she went into the house because, Matthew suspected, she couldn't look him in the eye anymore. She knew that

Matthew couldn't afford to stay in St Liac if he didn't have a job. And jobs in St Liac were extremely thin on the ground.

Nicky knew this more than most. She had lived there all her life and had witnessed the exodus of many of her schoolfriends when they had realised that the words 'work' and 'Liac' were largely incompatible. Nicky, however, had been one of the lucky ones. Her father had been a fisherman and she had inherited his love of the sea and, on his death five years ago, his boat. She had also inherited Harvey which was fine because the boat needed, and could support, a crew of two. But the money it made couldn't support three people.

Nicky sighed and cupped her hands around her glass. Beside her, sprawled on the sofa with a whisky in one hand and a cigarette in the other, Matthew looked as if he hadn't a care in the world. But this was typical. It was actually what had attracted her to him in the first place. That and the rugged good looks, the furrowed brow and the sparkling blue eyes. It was only after she had got to know him that she realised his carefree attitude belied a careworn childhood in an unprepossessing housing estate in Glasgow, and that he had become a drifter, taking any job in any place, because he somehow felt he didn't fit in Glasgow or indeed anywhere else. Much later, Matthew had told her that he always felt like a fish out of water but that in coming to Liac he had somehow come home.

Which was deeply ironic, because Matthew didn't really like the sea and felt sick on boats. Another reason why, even if she had the means, Nicky couldn't employ him. But she didn't want to employ him. She just wanted to be with him. And, by far the more pragmatic of the two, she knew that they couldn't continue living together if he didn't have a job. Financial considerations apart, she was well aware that, however much of a maverick Matthew claimed to be, no thirty-seven-year-old Glaswegian would take to being supported by a girlfriend who was nearly ten years his junior and a fisherman to boot.

Sighing, Nicky decided to address the subject directly. 'Matt, d'you think it might be a good idea to start looking for another job right now? I mean, even if Grace doesn't sell, she's never going to have enough money to employ you again, right?'

'She'd be mad to employ him again even if she won the lottery.' This nugget of wisdom, offered from beside the pool table, came from Martin Bamford.

'Thanks, Martin.'

'Well it's true. Gardening's about nurturing, not killing.'

'People who live in glass houses, Martin …'

'Well, honestly, if you can't even grow a bit of weed, then what's the point? You really are a plonker, Matthew.'

'Weed?' said Harvey, perching on the edge of the sofa and lighting a roll-up. 'What *is* the point of growing weeds?'

'Not weeds, Harve. *Weed*,' corrected Matthew.

'Oh, yeah. I remember. What happened to it?'

Martin looked pointedly at Matthew.

Besides conveying the news of Grace's tragedy, Matthew had imparted more bad tidings to Martin. News that, he supposed, he was now obliged to share with Harvey.

'It's … er, dying.'

'What? The stuff you bought in Bodmin?'

'The stuff *I* bought,' corrected a peeved Martin. 'I paid for it and Matthew was going to grow it. *Was* being the operative word.'

Harvey looked mournfully into his pint. Admittedly this was hardly a disaster on the same scale as Grace's, but it was ominous. And Harvey, in common with his dark Celtic looks, held dark Celtic beliefs. He believed in omens. 'Maybe you shouldn't have tried to grow from seed,' he said.

'I didn't have much choice. It was all I could get. And it was *great* stuff. A hybrid of *indica* and *sativa*.'

'What?' asked Nicky. Contrary to what Martin thought, Nicky didn't disapprove of dope. She just didn't smoke it. Or know much about it.

'*Indica*,' explained Harvey, 'is Afghan stuff. Gives you a really heavy high. And *sativa* is Mexican – gives more of a heady high. So if you cross them you get …'

'… a heavy and a heady high …'

'Yeah.' Harvey grinned at Nicky. 'You get really, *really* wrecked.'

'Oh.' Nicky turned to Matthew. 'Have you tried plant food?'

'Tried everything. I reckon they're dying on purpose. I even talk to them.'

'What do you say?'

'Would you mind not dying?'

Martin snorted and downed the rest of his pint in one. 'You really are a crap gardener, Matthew.'

'Well, what do I know about gardening? I'm from Glasgow. Anyway, you don't have a great track record when it comes to keeping things alive.'

'Oh stop it, will you?' sighed Nicky. Then she grinned up at Martin. 'He can't help it. He's from London.'

'Huh.' Martin pretended to look offended. 'Another round?' he suggested.

'We've had five already.'

'So?'

Matthew held out his glass. 'So the next one will be the sixth.'

'I've already got the sixth,' said Harvey.

'Eh?'

47

'The sixth sense.'

Martin snorted again and ambled off to the bar.

'It's true, you know,' Harvey explained to Matthew. 'I have the gift. I've seen things, haven't I Nicky?'

'Er.' As far as Nicky was concerned, Harvey *did* have an extraordinary gift – of a hugely fertile imagination.

'And this is ominous,' continued Harvey. 'It's like the signs.'

'What signs?'

'Armageddon.' Harvey looked into the mid-distance. 'A man falls from the sky. You lose your job. And all the plants are dying. It's like the devil's at work.'

Harvey wasn't the only person that night with the devil in mind. Nor was he the only resident of St Liac possessed of a fertile imagination. Picking his way through the pitch-black woods at the back of Liac House, Gerald Percy was delighting in thoughts of ghouls, spectres, witchcraft and the bad lord Lucifer. The owl hooting somewhere overhead helped, as did the bats flicking through the trees. A howling wolf, Gerald felt, would really have done the trick. But wolves, howling or not, were not part of the Cornish landscape. Supposedly. Gerald reckoned otherwise. The Beast of Bodmin, Cornwall's answer to the Loch Ness Monster, was out there somewhere. And Gerald was convinced the beast was a wolf. A giant wolf. With huge fangs.

For obvious reasons, Reverend Gerald Percy kept his passion (he called it a hobby) for horror to himself. For while it was all good and well – necessary, even – for someone of his calling to believe in the devil, it wasn't entirely seemly to imagine him with such flair and pizzazz and invest him with glamour. And the fact that it made Gerald's own master look a little drab in comparison was something he preferred not to think about.

But Gerald did think about God. A lot. He had believed in him from an early age, had worked in the ministry since he was twenty-five and was still, forty years later, as happy to serve his Lord as he had ever been. The only doubts he had ever experienced related to the way he served him. In the depths of his soul, Gerald regretted not having embraced the Catholic faith. Being a Protestant was fine, but Catholicism knocked the hell out of it when it came to talk of the devil, tortured souls, brimstone and sheer scary drama. It also meant more colourful clothes. But then one couldn't have everything.

Grace Trevethan, mused Gerald, knew all about that. Grace was the reason why he was haunting the woods at night. For the vicarage garden backed onto the woods which, in turn, led to the grounds of Liac House. Gerald was here to give Grace comfort, solace and his heartfelt sympathy. He had already decided that he wouldn't harp on about God because Grace didn't hold strong beliefs and may anyway be wishing that her husband had gone to the devil, what with the colossal debts, the mortgage and the mistress. And Gerald didn't really want to go down the devil route with a parishioner. Nor, more to the point, did he really want to discuss the mistress.

Grace, however, didn't look as if she wanted to discuss anything. When Gerald arrived at her front door, she took several minutes to answer his ring and, when at last she opened the door, seemed distinctly unenthusiastic about inviting him in. And that was very un-Grace.

'Hello,' he said in response to her greeting of 'Oh.' Then he peered closely at her and realised she had been crying. That, too, was very un-Grace. But it wasn't entirely surprising. Gerald held up the plastic bag he was carrying. 'I've brought you some fish fingers and some of my potato wine.'

'Oh.' Grace looked blankly at the offering. 'Thank you.'

'I've come to see if you're all right.'

Still showing no signs of inviting him in, Grace smiled and said she was fine.

Gerald decided a more light-hearted approach would be better. ' Um … Grace, there are a few traditions that have made Britain great. One of them is that when the vicar comes to call, he must be invited in to sit awkwardly with you and offer platitudes in your time of sorrow.' To his relief, Grace giggled.

'Sherry,' he finished, 'is optional.'

'Of course you must come in, Gerald,' said Grace, beckoning him into the hall and closing the door behind him. 'I'm sorry. I was just … well to be honest, I'm feeling a little distracted at the moment. I'm sorting through the paperwork and … well …' Grace ran a hand through her already tousled hair and smiled bleakly at him. 'It's … not good.'

'No.' Gerald reached out and patted her on the shoulder. 'I heard.'

'I'm in the kitchen. You don't mind, do you? ' Grace turned towards the passage that led towards the back of the house. 'I suppose I should treat company more formally, like they do in films, but to be honest the drawing room's a bit bleak and the garden room's horrid at night and we never used the morning room anyway …'

'Grace!' Gerald laughed and stopped her mid-flow. 'You

don't have to be formal with me. Anyway, I'm not like the sort of vicar you find in films.' But then Gerald wasn't the sort of vicar you found anywhere. He followed her down the passage to the back of the house, thinking as he went, that Liac House would be a hopeless location for the films that suited his particular taste. It was far too beautiful and too welcoming to be haunted. Haunted houses, in his celluloid experiences, were not festooned with foliage on the outside and warm and inviting inside. They had forbidding turrets and stark, sheer walls that plunged down to the cliffs being pounded by angry, frothing waves. Gigantic waves that thundered ceaselessly against those cliffs and threatened to drown anyone foolish enough to be sailing past, and even if they didn't drown, there would be a vampire out there somewhere which Gerald knew because Dracula had come to England – Whitby, he remembered – in a boat and that was ominous because …

'Sorry about the mess,' said Grace, startling him out of his reverie as they entered the kitchen. 'As I said, I've been trying to sort things out. Melvyn Stott gave me back all the letters and things and I'm trying … well …' she turned to Gerald. 'I'm not making much sense of them.'

'No.' Inappropriate and rather embarrassing vampire-type thoughts vanished from Gerald's mind as he looked at the papers, bills and letters strewn across the table. 'No. I'm … er, not very good at paperwork either.'

'Wine?' offered Grace.

'That would be lovely.' Gerald held up his plastic bag again. 'And you'd better put the fish fingers in the freezer.'

'Oh, right.' Grace took the bag, popped the fish in the freezer and the potato wine in the fridge. Wondering why someone who lived in a fishing village felt the need to buy things masquerading as frozen bits of cod, she then opened the cupboard where she kept the real wine. Even in her current state of abstraction, there was no way she was going to drink Gerald's dreadful concoction.

Behind her, Gerald looked relieved. Potato wine was all very well as a gift, but there was no need to drink it. It was perfectly foul.

Grace opened a bottle of red, poured two glasses and took them to the table.

'Can I be of any help?' asked Gerald as they sat down.

'I don't know. I don't think so.' Grace picked up a bundle of papers and stared at them as if they were strange, foreign bodies. 'None of it really makes any sense. Well, to me anyway. How are you on financial things?'

Gerald shook his head. 'Not good, I'm afraid. Did … er , did John really leave things in a mess?'

Grace laughed; a sound bereft of humour. 'Oh worse than that. He left a complete catastrophe. Or rather,' she added flatly, 'he left nothing but debts.'

Gerald's heart sank. He looked at the sea of papers in front of him. The he frowned. 'What about a stock portfolio. Do you have one of those?'

'I don't know. What is it?'

'I don't know either.' Gerald shuffled uncomfortably in his seat. 'I just thought you might have one.'

'No.' Grace took a sip of wine and then picked up a bank statement. 'But we do have a Swiss bank account.'

'Well that's marvellous, isn't it? They're always full of money, aren't they?'

'This one isn't. There's nothing in it.' A sad smile hovered on Grace's lips. 'But at least we've got one.'

'Yes.'

Grace flicked through more papers and, for the umpteenth time since Melvyn Stott had returned them to her, ran a distracted hand through her hair. 'I just don't understand it Gerald. There are accounts here for companies I've never heard of. And letters of credit. And then the bills ...'

'Isn't there something ... something tucked away somewhere?'

'No. That's what I was hoping I might find. But no. There's nothing.' Grace leaned back in her chair and stared, unseeing, at the ferns cascading over the units opposite her. 'What in God's name,' she whispered, 'am I going to do?'

Gerald didn't know. He suspected God wouldn't know either. Under less appalling circumstances, Gerald would have advised Grace to take a devil-may-care attitude to her financial troubles, but that, he felt, would be highly inappropriate. Not to say irresponsible.

Then, breaking a silence that seemed to last for ever, Grace turned to him and asked him the question he dreaded. 'How did you know about her?'

'Er ... who?'

Grace took a sip of wine and looked over the rim of her glass into Gerald's eyes. 'Honey Chambers.'

Gerald fingered his dog-collar and then ran his hand through his receding hair. 'Ah. I thought you might ask that.'

'I was going to ask before,' sniffed Grace. 'But I thought that if I could bury John I could bury the past as well and just forget. And forgive. That's what you said, isn't it Gerald? That I should forgive.'

'Yes.'

Forgetting her question, Grace took a gulp of wine. 'I read the first letters,' she said.

'Letters?'

'Yes. He wrote letters to her.' Grace sniffed again. 'He was so silly,' she said with a half-smile, 'he always left his letters for me to post and I suppose he thought that I wouldn't notice there was no company name and that they were always hand-written and … I don't know. There was just *something* about those envelopes. I'd always thought that female intuition was … what's that word Martin uses all the time?'

'Crap.'

'Yes. I always thought intuition was crap but there was something about those letters … so I opened one.'

Gerald reached for Grace's arm.

'It gave me quite a shock.'

'I can imagine.' Gerald gave a reassuring squeeze.

'No … not in the way you think. Most of it was about me.' Grace's eyes were moist as she looked at Gerald again, seemingly unsure about whether to laugh or cry. 'About how much he loved me. It was very strange, you know. He said that he loved me and would never leave me and that she must never ask that. He … he said that we were very happy together …' Grace paused. 'We *were* very happy together, you know.' The remark was slightly defensive: a question in disguise and in need of an answer.

'Yes,' said Gerald. 'I know you were.'

'In a way I suppose it was my fault.'

'What was?'

'The … the Honey thing. John travelled so much in the last few years and I had the garden and the greenhouse … and the orchids were going so well and I couldn't feel I could leave for long so John would go off and … well, I stayed here.' Then Grace laughed again. 'So he sought companionship elsewhere. Such a cliché, isn't it? More wine?' she added rather too brightly as she suddenly sprang to her feet.

'Please.'

'It *was* companionship more than anything else,' continued Grace as she came back with the bottle. 'Or at least that's what I thought until …' she gestured at the piles of papers, 'until all this happened.'

'I'm … not quite sure what you mean, Grace.'

Grace looked guiltily at the vicar. 'I opened another letter and … and it was all about the friendship they had. Oh, I suppose they must have … well, you know, but it seemed more of a *friendship* than anything else, so I managed to convince myself that as I had my orchids and my garden then it wasn't so bad if John had his … his Honey.' Grace frowned. 'Such a silly name, isn't it?'

'Er …'

'But now *this*,' continued Grace as she poured more wine. Her hand, Gerald noticed was shaking. 'I really don't know how he could have done this to me. And I don't know *why*. John was very generous, you know.'

'Yes, I know. He was always the first to donate to church appeals.'

'And he was very good to me. He never imposed any limits on how much I spent. Not that I ever spent very much anyway.' Grace fingered her cardigan and looked down at her sensible skirt and the shoes that were, if she remembered correctly, at least five years old. Maybe, she thought, that was another reason for Honey. Maybe she, Grace, was a dowdy frump and Honey was a brittle, glamorous creature with endless legs and a vast wardrobe. Paid for by John. She tried, and failed, to recall her; to recapture the image of the woman in the graveyard.

'So,' she said to Gerald, 'the only conclusion I can draw is that Honey was a high-maintenance trollop who robbed John blind.'

Startled by the viciousness of Grace's words, Gerald nearly knocked over his glass of wine. 'I … well, Grace, I really don't ….'

'And as you're the only person who knew she existed, I want you to tell me.' Leaning closer to Gerald, Grace looked imploringly into his eyes. 'What did you know about her, Gerald? How did you know?'

Gerald sighed deeply and leaned back. 'John came to me about a year ago. That was surprising enough. He wasn't, as you know, a particularly religious man. And when he said he had something to confess, I ... well ...' Gerald closed his eyes, trying to remember what he had said. But he could only remember what he had thought, and that wasn't much use to Grace. He had thought that if only he had been a Catholic, he could have bundled John into confessional and dealt promptly – and conclusively – with the whole situation. But that, of course, hadn't happened.

'You what?' prompted Grace.

'I ... I asked him to tell me more. He said that he had been seeing someone occasionally ...'

'Occasionally?'

Gerald nodded. 'Yes, that's definitely what he said. And that he knew it was wrong but that ...' Gerald looked away from Grace, '... that he enjoyed the companionship when he was away. That it was someone he could ... enjoy dinner with.'

Grace bowed her head. Enjoy dinner with. Hadn't he enjoyed dinner with her? Hadn't they sat around this very table, laughing together and drinking wine? Had that all been a sham? No, she thought. It had been a reality. As had been the fact that she hadn't gone on business trips with John, leaving him to dine on his own. Or not.

Gerald reached out to her again. 'For what it's worth, Grace, I think it was exactly as you suspected. More of a friendship than anything else.'

'Yes,' said Grace in a small voice. But her next words were

raw and bitter. 'I'm amazed at how easily I let myself believe that. But it can't really have been the case, can it?'

'I don't see why …'

'… because John got into debt because of this Honey person. He wanted to impress her. She was a money-grubbing little minx and … and …' Grace bit her lip. 'And what I'm really trying to say, Gerald, is that I think he had a family with her and that's where all the money went.'

'Ah.'

'I want you to tell me,' continued Grace after a moment's silence, 'that that wasn't the case. Gerald?'

'I can't, Grace. I'm sorry but I can't. Not for a fact.' He leaned closer to her. 'But I firmly believe that if that *had* been true then John would have told me. Why only tell me half the story? You of all people know that John never did things by halves.'

'Yes,' sniffed Grace. 'That's true.' She jabbed at the papers in front of her. 'No half measures here.'

'I mean it, Grace. I really think he would have told me.'

Grace sighed. 'What I don't understand is why he told you about her in the first place. We all know he wasn't religious. What did he want from you?'

Gerald shrugged. 'Forgiveness? Absolution?' Then he shook his head. 'No. He knew he wouldn't get that. I think he just wanted someone to corroborate the fact that he was doing wrong.'

'And you did that?'

'Yes. And I told him what he clearly wanted to hear.'

'What was that?'

'That he had to stop.'

'But he didn't, did he?' said Grace in a small voice.

Gerald didn't reply. He didn't want to give voice to the thoughts that were beginning to nag at the back of his mind.

John hadn't stopped seeing Honey. Instead, Gerald suspected that he had applied masculine logic (often a contradiction in terms as far as Gerald was concerned) and come up with a deeply flawed solution to the problem. He would make up for his betrayal of Grace by making huge amounts of money for her; by buying his way out of guilt. And then John's plans had gone so horribly wrong that, faced with a guilt he couldn't deal with, he had chosen the ultimate solution and jumped out of a plane.

If that had indeed been the case, it compounded the tragedy. Because Grace, who had never even been interested in money, now had little else to think about.

Gerald was right about this. When she went to bed an hour after Gerald left, Grace couldn't sleep. She was physically exhausted, but her brain refused to give her any respite. It kept her awake most of the night, buzzing with unanswered questions. The ones that assaulted her emotions concerned Honey. But Grace kept pushing them to the back of her mind because she had made a decision about her immediate future. She would not leave her house. She would not even allow herself to contemplate losing the only thing she had left to love. Somehow she would find the money to keep it. But how?

FOUR

Grace had always been the sort of person to leap out of bed early and seize the day with gusto; not the sort to greet the morn with a heavy heart, even heavier eyelids and a horrible premonition that the day was not going to be a pleasant one.

Her first action of the day was always to throw open the curtains and (she always slept with the window open) sample the air. Today, as with the last few days, it was cool and damp, the sky hazy with the promise of sunshine. In one respect at least, the day looked as if it were going to be glorious. Grace's mood lifted slightly.

It sank again when, still in her dressing-gown, she went downstairs and saw the three large brown envelopes that, courtesy of Archie, were lying on the doormat. Sighing, she bent to pick them up and put them under her arm to take with her to the kitchen. Then she noticed the wastepaper bin out of the corner of her eye. She looked at the envelopes again. She really didn't need to open them to know what they were. Grace threw them in the bin.

Like an automaton, she went through her morning routine of tea, toast and the newspaper before dressing and, as briskly as possible, tackling her household chores. Chores were exactly how Grace viewed them; keeping the house clean and tidy was a necessary evil and something to be undertaken as quickly as possible. They used to be undertaken – very slowly – by the elderly Maeve who had come for two days a week and then, after she became unwell, for one, and then none because she was now dead.

Grace had never replaced her because, by then, John had started to travel more, Grace spent most of her time in the garden or the greenhouse and as a result the house required very little maintenance. A far cry from the days when Grace and John, in London during the week, lived in the gate lodge at weekends and John's parents lived in the big house with a two maids, a cook, a chauffeur and an endless stream of house guests. They had also employed two gardeners who, shortly after John's mother passed away, had retired; their passing had not been mourned by Grace because, frankly, they had been hopeless.

Thinking about them, Grace allowed herself a little smile. At least she had carried on with that particular Liac tradition: Matthew was utterly delightful company, but no-one could accuse him of being green-fingered. Then the smile vanished as she remembered that Matthew would soon be no more. He would be gone at the end of the week. And Grace would mourn him greatly.

He arrived two minutes after Grace had finished sweeping the kitchen floor. She had been intending to wash it, but when Matthew sauntered in wearing a huge grin and muddy wellies she realised, to her relief, there would be no point. 'Hiya,' he said, plonking himself down at the table. This had become part of their ritual: he would sit with her over a cup of tea with the intention of discussing what needed doing in the garden but, in reality, they would chat about anything in general and nothing in particular.

Today was slightly different. Matthew appeared as robust as usual but was suffering the effects of too much alcohol the previous night as well as from the strain of trying to pretend that everything was normal in Grace's world. Which it wasn't.

'I thought,' said Grace, pretending as well, 'that it might be an idea to start the lawns today. The weather looks like it'll hold. What d'you think?'

'Fine by me.'

Then Grace wished she hadn't suggested that because it meant Matthew would be sitting on the lawn mower for the next two days and she would have preferred to have him around her. Even if that meant hearing him sing all day.

'Good night last night?' she asked for no reason in particular.

'Er ... yeah. Why d'you ask? Do I look hungover?'

'No,' said Grace, laughing as she poured the tea. 'Are you?'

'Yeah. A bit. I didn't think we drank that much last night but we must've. Even Nicky felt a wee bit strange this morning and she *never* gets hangovers.'

'How is she?'

'Hungover.'

'No, I mean how is she generally?'

'Fine. You know ... fishing. Christ knows how she can go out on a boat with a hangover.'

'Well, Nicky was practically brought up on a boat.'

'True.' Cradling his hands round his mug, Matthew grimaced at the thought.

'And how's the decorating going?'

'Oh, fine.' Matthew looked sheepish. 'Well ... not fine. Nicky's a bit pissed off with me. Says I'm not pulling my weight.'

'Aren't you?' That would be most unlike Matthew.

'Well ... I hate stripping wallpaper. Boring.'

'Mmm. I suppose you're more of an outdoors person.'

'Yes.'

They exchanged an uneasy glance. Not an outdoors person, the look said, for much longer.

'Right.' Matthew pushed his chair back and stood up. 'Work to do.'

'Yes.' Grace got to her feet as well and pointed at the cutting in a pot on the worksurface beside them. 'One of my new projects.'

Matthew peered at the tiny plant. 'Oh? What is it?'

'My new hybrid. *Phalaenopsis pathopedilum*. It's going to be beautiful.'

Matthew looked intrigued. 'I don't know how you do it, Grace. I mean, how do you know what it'll look like?'

Grace shrugged. 'Oh, you know … just a little bit of practice.'

'Huh! A "little bit"? You're a walking encyclopaedia, you are.' And she was. But, being Grace, she would never admit to it. Grace was ludicrously modest about her abilities.

When Matthew meandered out into the garden, she set to work on her indoor plants. She knew it was the last thing she should be doing, but the alternative – trying, yet again, to make sense of the papers she had studied last night – was too depressing. More depressing than the anguished thoughts that had kept her awake most of the night and that would, she knew, disappear if she buried herself in her orchids. So that's what she did.

Grace couldn't understand people who thought orchids were 'just plants'. To her they were marvels of nature that had been evolving for 120 million years and that would probably be doing so long after mankind had vanished off the face of the earth. She thought they were the most exciting family of plants in existence, endlessly adapting and populating every corner of the globe; and if they didn't grow in Antarctica it was only because – as Vivienne Hopkins was fond of saying – Grace hadn't been there with her green fingers and her compost.

Grace had heard her say that once and had laughed because, really, there was so much she didn't know about orchids. She knew there were more than 35,000 different species in existence; far more than she could ever get to grips with. But she did know – and this was part of the secret of her success – that it was vital to know the provenance of each species she tried to grow.

Wandering into the drawing room with her watering can, she paused beside the showy *Dendrobium* on the piano. The man in the nursery had told her it was Australian. But she knew it was Himalayan, that it required a higher nitrogen feed in spring and that, probably, was why she succeeded in getting it to bloom regularly. Even if she said it herself (and she only said it to herself), Grace was rather proud of this particular plant.

She was in the process of watering it when the doorbell rang. Grace frowned. She wasn't expecting anyone and even if she had been it was customary for visitors she knew to let themselves in after ringing the bell and shout 'hello?' from the hallway. Then if there was no response, they would look for Grace in the garden. Grace waited for the door to open. It didn't. Sighing as she remembered her horrible premonitions about the day, she deposited her watering can on the piano and went into the hall. When she opened the door she was more than a little surprised to find Vivienne Hopkins, Diana Skinner and Margaret Sutton standing on the doorstep.

'Oh!' Wrong-footed – literally – Grace stepped back. 'What ... what a pleasant surprise.' She smiled rather weakly and, noticing what the women were wearing, suspected that it probably wasn't going to be pleasant. They were clutching their handbags in front of them (defensive), wearing hats (serious) and smiles that tried a little too hard.

'Hello, Grace,' said Vivienne. 'I hope we're not disturbing you.' Beside her, Margaret and Diana beamed.

'No. No ... not at all. I was just ... making tea. Won't you come in and have a cup?'

The invitation was accepted with alacrity and Grace's heart sank. The hats and the handbags merited tea with china in the drawing room and not mugs in the kitchen and she couldn't, really, be bothered. She gestured towards the former. 'Please. Go on in. I'll be with you in a minute.'

Diana, however, stepped closer and looked up at her with her questing nose. 'Would you like a hand, Grace?'

'No. Really.' Grace smiled at the little woman and waved again towards the drawing room. 'I'll only be a tick.'

'Right you are, then.' She made to join the other women and then looked back. 'Sure?'

'Sure.' Grace sped down the passage. The last thing she wanted was to have Diana watching her make tea. The woman meant well but she was obsessed by tea and reckoned there was only one way to make it – hers. And that involved endless brewing and fussing and admiring ornaments in the process which in turn meant that something would go missing. And that, in turn, meant that Diana would come back at some stage claiming that she'd found the missing item in the shop and was it Grace's and Grace would say yes and then find herself offering Diana a cup of tea. Grace had been down that route many times before.

In the kitchen, she threw a couple of tea bags into the pot, grabbed cups and saucers and banged them onto a tray and, when the kettle boiled, filled the pot. She was back in the drawing room before Vivienne Hopkins had even sat down. 'So peaceful,' said Vivienne, turning from the window as

Grace entered. At that very moment Matthew gunned the engine of the lawn mower, shattering that peace.

Grace laughed. 'That's Matthew. Don't worry, he'll start at the far end of the lawn. The noise will die down in a minute.' Then she put the tea tray beside the *Laelia purpurata* on the coffee table and asked them to sit down.

'Lovely plant,' said Margaret.

'Oh thank you. It is pretty, isn't it?' Grace poured the tea as she listened to the sound of the lawn mower receding, handed a cup to each of the ladies and, once they'd gone through the business of it being a lovely day as well, she repeated what a pleasant surprise it was to see them.

'Well,' said Vivienne after a covert look at her accomplices, 'we're here about the week after next.'

'I'm sorry?'

'The W.I. do.'

'Oh.' Grace looked apprehensive. 'What about it?'

'Given your recent troubles,' continued Vivienne, picking her words carefully, 'we rather thought you'd want to cancel.'

'Yes,' said Diana and Margaret in unison. 'We didn't think you'd want all the bother,' finished Diana, taking a tentative sip of her tea.

'It's only a tea party,' said Margaret. 'We could have it anywhere.'

Grace looked across at the women, ranged against her on the sofa opposite. She didn't much care one way or the other about the tea party: what she minded was their reason for wanting to cancel it. Her 'troubles'. Was this the shape of things to come, she wondered? Was this what it would be like from now on: everyone rallying round Grace with the best of intentions, serving only to emphasise what a desperate financial plight she was in?

Trying not show her disquiet, Grace sipped her tea and, eyebrows raised, merely said that the tea was always held at Liac House. 'It's tradition,' she finished with a smile. 'I see no reason to break from it.'

Diana and Margaret looked doubtful but Vivienne, who was the President of the W.I., appeared delighted. Grace surmised – correctly – that the other two had bullied her into coming here today.

'As long as you're sure …' she said.

'Absolutely. Anyway,' said Grace, 'I've been growing a new hybrid. *Phalaenopsis pathopedilum*. It should be budding by next week.'

'Perhaps you'd like some help with the tea?' said Diana. Her own half-drunk tea, Grace noticed with amusement, was now back on the tray.

'Oh … I don't think so. It's never been any trouble.'

'But …'

'All right, ladies,' said Vivienne Hopkins, successfully stalling Diana mid-flow. 'Let's get back to business. Do we invite Dr Bamford, given his disgraceful display last year?'

Grace grinned. But before she could reply, a strange, strangled sound floated through the window.

'What's that?' asked a startled Vivienne.

'I don't know.' Grace leaped to her feet and ran to the window. She shaded her eyes against the sun and looked out into the garden. Another roar assaulted her ears. It was Matthew. He was sitting on the lawn mower, yelling at two strange men beside him.

Alarm flickered across Grace's features and, turning to the three women on the sofa, she asked to be excused for a moment. Not giving them a chance to answer, she hurried out of the room. With a sense of foreboding, she rushed across the lawn, reaching Matthew just as he screamed another anguished 'No!' at the two men standing over him.

'What's going on?' panted Grace. Then she realised she knew both men. 'Hello, Terry,' she said to the taller of the two. Then, with a smile, 'Bob. How's your mother's hip?'

Both men looked thoroughly abashed. 'Much better, Mrs Trevethan,' mumbled Bob.

Then Grace noticed their expressions, the large van parked in the driveway behind her, and Matthew's mutinous countenance.

'Matthew?'

'They want to take the lawn mower, Grace.'

'What?'

'It's not us!' protested Bob, whom Grace had dandled on her knee when she had been newly-married. 'We wouldn't do that to you, Mrs Trevethan.'

'It's the company,' said Terry in a small voice. The last time he had seen Grace had been at his last school sports day when she had presented him with a trophy. Now, in the course of his first job, he was obliged to repossess one of Grace's favourite trophies. Developing a pressing desire to study the ground at his feet, he looked away from Grace.

'I ... er, I don't understand.'

'The, um, the hire purchase payments are way overdue,' explained Bob. 'It's in the rules. And, 'cos the last letter went unanswered, we've ... um ... come to take it away.'

'Oh. But ...' Grace had been on the verge of saying 'but it was a birthday present' and then bit her lip. It wasn't, of course. It was just something else John had lied about. She straightened her shoulders and smiled at the two men. 'Well, you'd better take it then.'

Matthew snorted, shrugged, alighted from the machine and, without looking either at Grace or the repossession men, marched across the lawn and disappeared round the back of the house. Diana, Margaret and Vivienne watched him from the drawing room window. Diana's eyes were like saucers as she turned to her companions. 'What a fuss! I wouldn't treat repair men like that.' She shook her head. 'Bad manners. Scottish,' she added with a dark look.

'I don't think they're repair men, Diana. In fact,' said Vivienne, 'I really think we should go. Something tells me Grace isn't going to be in the mood for discussing tea parties any more.'

Margaret pursed her lips as she watched Bob and Terry wheel the lawn mower onto the tailgate of their van. 'Poor Grace,' she whispered and, taking Vivienne's cue, followed her through the drawing room, into the hall and out the front door.

'Grace!' called Vivienne. 'Anything we can do?'

The forlorn figure at the edge of the lawn turned, belatedly remembering her visitors. 'No. No thanks.' She was too far away for the three women to read her expression, but the way she was wringing her hands told them quite enough. 'If you don't mind,' she added, 'can we continue this another day? I've … I've got things to discuss with Matthew.'

'No problem!' cried Vivienne, raising a hand in salute.

'And remember,' called Margaret, 'if there's anything we can do …'

'Thank you!'

'Thanks for the tea!' Diana clutched her handbag close and fell into step behind the other two women. 'How on earth,' she whispered as she caught up with them, 'is she going to cut two acres of lawn without a mower?'

But that was the last thing on Grace's mind as she watched the three ladies disappear down the drive and, after them, Bob and Terry in their van. Shoulders hunched, she trudged back towards the house, fervently wishing that John was still alive.

Not because she missed him, but because she wanted to kill him.

As she reached the stone balustrade separating the lawn from the wide sweep of gravel in front of the house, Matthew reappeared, dragging an ancient, rusty manual lawn mower behind him. Face set, he pulled it onto the lawn and, with a monumental effort, set the protesting blades into motion. He looked as if he was even more upset that Grace.

Touched by his determination, Grace sat on the balustrade and smiled wanly in appreciation of his efforts. 'You don't have to do that, you know.'

Matthew didn't respond. 'Matthew ...?'

'You've paid me until the end of the week. The lawn needs mowing and so ...' but even as he spoke the effort of pushing became too much even for Matthew and he let the machine drop and went to sit with Grace on the wall.

Grace looked away. 'I can't believe he did this. I can't believe he even lied about a lawn mower. He said it was for my birthday.'

Sensing she was close to tears, Matthew draped a brawny arm round her shoulders and pulled her close.

Grace sniffed. 'He lied about everything. *Everything.*'

'Yeah.' Matthew couldn't allow himself to think about John Trevethan. Anger would overwhelm him and that wasn't what Grace needed at the moment.

They sat in silence; two small figures in the middle of an idyllic landscape and an almighty mess.

'Couldn't you get a job?' asked Matthew after a moment.

'What could I do?' There was more rueful amusement than self-pity in Grace's response.

'Well, you could ...' Then Matthew realised she couldn't. 'Right,' he said after another silence. 'What about ... what about a cup of tea or something?'

Grace shook her head. Then, as Matthew jumped to his feet, she reached out and touched his hand. 'Matthew, I'm really sorry about your job.'

Matthew nodded. 'S'all right.' He looked at the lawn and, with a twinkle in his eye, back at Grace. 'You're gonna have to get a goat.'

'I will, won't I? But, Matthew, if there's anything else I can do for you …'

'Actually, I was hoping you might say that.'

'Oh?' Grace looked rather startled. 'Why?'

The twinkle in Matthew's eye turned to a gleam. The plan, when it had jumped unannounced into his head in the middle of the night, had seemed ludicrous at the time. But now he couldn't see why not. Grace wouldn't have to know what they were. He took a deep breath. 'Um … I've got some plants that are really sick. They desperately need help.'

The gardener in Grace looked deeply concerned. 'Oh. I didn't know you had any plants at home?'

'Well, no. They're not exactly at home. Y'see, we don't have a garden …'

'… I know that.'

'… and I couldn't really grow them in the house so I planted them somewhere more secluded.'

'Matthew! You could have planted them here. I'm amazed you didn't ask. I'm upset that you didn't …'

'No!' Matthew looked horrified at the prospect of upsetting Grace. 'I couldn't have planted them here.'

'Why?'

'Er … it's a bit complicated. But will you come and see them with me later?'

'Of course.' Grace was only too delighted. 'We could go now if you want?'

Matthew shook his head. 'No, no. That wouldn't be fair.

I've work to do here, and you're still paying me. We could go ... sort of ... after hours?'

Grace shrugged. It didn't really matter to her when she went to look at Matthew's plants, but she supposed 'after hours' was better. It would give her an excuse not to sit at the kitchen table trying to salvage something from the wreckage. She was still determined that this something was going to be Liac House – but still she didn't know how.

Matthew spent the day working like a man possesssed. He trimmed the ivy on the house; he began work on the enormous hedge behind the old kitchen garden; he swept the gravel on the driveway and, intermittently and without much success, he tackled the lawn with the rusty old manual mower. A goat would have made a far greater impression.

Grace spent most of the rest of the day in the greenhouse tending to her more delicate orchids. Some of them were valuable. And Grace had a nagging suspicion that some of them had been illegally imported. The rare Indonesian *Paphiopedilum supardii*, for instance, had reached her a circuitous and convoluted route about which she deliberately hadn't asked. For while Grace was appalled that unscrupulous smugglers plundered the world's forests and jungles for increasingly rare species, she hadn't been strong enough to refuse what was, by anyone's standards, a gem. She looked at it, as she always did, with a mixture of awe and guilt. She knew she shouldn't have it, but here it was. In the greenhouse of Liac House.

Then the idea began to form in her mind. The more she thought about it, the more ludicrous it seemed. Then, quietly and without realising it, she began to hyperventilate. Because the idea was also exciting – and realistic. Grace knew all about orchids. She knew, if not personally, then of the names of most orchid collectors in the country. And she regularly corresponded with other experts all over the world.

How much, she wondered, was her collection worth? More to the point, how much would it be worth if it included a few more species that were … unusual? Grace knew this meant illegal. Surprising herself, even shocking herself by the direction her thoughts were taking, Grace then began to feel guilty because she was smiling. Smiling at the thought of Grace Trevethan becoming an orchid smuggler.

About ten years ago, she dimly recalled, there had been a sensation (in the orchid world at least) over an orchid smuggler who had been stupid enough to get caught. How much had his collection been worth? Grace was sure it had been tens of thousands of pounds. Then her smile vanished as she realised he had also been fined tens of thousands of pounds and, worse, imprisoned. But perhaps he had just been stupid. Or perhaps he hadn't known the right people. Perhaps …

Then Grace looked at her beloved plants with a critical eye and knew she couldn't do it. Not because (here, again, she surprised herself) the thought of breaking the law was anathema to her, but because she saw herself as a contributor to orchid science and conservation – not to the theft of botanical resources from other countries. Grace Trevethan, criminal, was amusing in an absurd sort of way, but Grace as an engine of destruction was quite another. She dismissed all such thoughts from her mind, buried herself in her work and, such was her concentration, jumped in surprise when, hours later, Matthew poked his head round the greenhouse door.

'Grace …?'

'Matthew! You startled me.' Then she smiled as she realised it was dark outside and that Matthew should have gone home hours ago. 'Oh Matthew, you really shouldn't be here. I know there's a lot to be done before … before the end of the week, but, really …'

Matthew grinned and raised his eyebrows, deepening the pronounced furrows on his forehead. Adding, thought Grace, to his attractiveness. 'But I'd really appreciate it if you could come and look at my plants now.'

'Oh!' Grace wiped her hands on her skirt. 'I'd completely forgotten. Of course. Where did you say they were?'

'Oh … just follow me.' Then he paused. 'D'you think I could borrow a torch?'

'Of course.' Grace reached for one of the torches she kept on the shelf beside the door and handed it to Matthew. Then she closed the greenhouse door behind her and followed him across the lawn and into the woods.

'Matthew,' she began as he plunged into the thicket that marked the border between Liac House and the vicarage. 'Where on earth …?'

'Sshh!' Matthew put a finger to his lips and with his other hand, cupped the end of the torch so that its beam shone thinly onto the ground, illuminating Grace's way.

Grace came up to him and, in a whisper, asked why they were whispering.

'I just don't want to wake up any squirrels or anything.' Then, indicating that she should follow, Matthew broached the thicket and entered the wild end of the vicarage garden.

'Matthew! This is Gerald's …'

'I know. It's just … well, here they are.' Matthew knelt down and shone the torch on one of the saddest collections of cuttings Grace had ever seen. Frowning, she knelt beside him.

'Are these Gerald's plants?'

'No, they're mine.' Matthew frowned at the wilting leaves.

Grace grabbed the torch from him and, now on her hands and knees, crawled closer.

After a moment of careful scrutiny, she turned to Matthew. 'I'm not stupid, Matthew. I know what this is.'

Matthew had rather suspected she might. 'Um … what is it?'

'Hemp.'

Matthew scratched his head. 'Yeah. It's hemp. I was going to go into business. Hemp trousers are really popular just now.'

Grace shot him a look that implied she wasn't born yesterday. Then she shone the torch on the plants again. 'Well, they're not getting enough light, are they?' She looked at the trees above them and the undergrowth encroaching on the tiny plants. 'Even in daylight it's too dark. They're never going to grow down here.'

Matthew looked sheepish. 'Yeah … well, I didn't really want anyone to see them.'

'Of course you didn't, Matthew,' smiled Grace. 'The world of trousers is a really dangerous one, isn't it?'

Matthew looked even more embarrassed. It had been stupid not to confide in Grace in the first place. And it had been even more stupid to plant cannabis in Reverend Percy's garden.

As if on cue, Grace looked behind them. She had always thought the vicarage a rather spooky residence for a man of the cloth. A Gothic Victorian construction, it seemed – like the hemp – to be shrouded in perpetual darkness. But as Grace looked, she saw a flickering light at a downstairs window. She also fancied she heard a faint yet high-pitched scream coming from the direction of the house. But that was probably her imagination.

The rumble of thunder, however, was not. A thunderstorm was brewing. Grace had sensed it for the past few hours and the last thing she wanted to be doing when the rain started lashing down was to be kneeling on a patch of earth in the vicarage garden examining dying plants.

'Look, Matthew, if you really want these poor things to grow they need better soil and better light.'

Matthew sensed rather than saw Grace edging backwards out of the clearing. 'Right,' he said.

Then Grace noted the disappointed slump of his shoulders and, sighing, reached forward again. Hadn't she been contemplating a career as an orchid smuggler, not even baulking at breaking the law? Growing one little cannabis plant was hardly in the same league. Anyway, she wanted to help Matthew. Sighing, she crawled forwards again and pointed to one of the plants. 'Let's take this one back to the greenhouse. See what we can do.'

'You might not want to do that,' said Matthew without much conviction.

Grace raised her eyebrows. 'I'm a gardener,' she said. Then, nodding to herself, 'and these are sick plants.'

A delighted Matthew fumbled in the pocket of his boiler-suit and produced a small trowel.

'What's that?'

Matthew looked surprised. 'A trowel.'

Grinning, Grace shook her head. Then she reached into her own, voluminous pocket and extracted a far more serious implement. '*This*,' she said, eyes glinting, 'is a trowel.' Then she scooped up the little plant in one expert movement and backed out of the clearing. As Matthew followed her, a great flash of lightning lit up the sky. 'Quick,' he urged, 'it's going to start chucking it down any minute.' Then he looked towards the house. 'Oh *shit*!'

'What?'

Matthew put a finger to his lips again. 'It's Gerald. He's at the window.'

Grace looked. Sure enough, the spectre of Gerald Percy was looming at the window, the flickering lights of the television just visible behind him. As another flash of lightning crackled overhead, Grace saw him rubbing his hands in glee. 'It's all right,' she whispered to Matthew. 'His eyes aren't good enough to see us. I think he's just waiting for the rain. It'll do his garden good and ...'

'Come *on*, Grace!' Cupping the torch to contain the beam, Matthew headed back into the woods. Grace followed.

A moment later Gerald Percy turned away from the window. This time he was sure he hadn't been mistaken; knew that it hadn't been his imagination. He was positive he had seen the ghosts flitting through his garden. If he had been a ghost, he knew he wouldn't be able to resist a night like this either. The close night air; the thunderstorm beginning to rage above and, of course, the signs in the ether. Gerald turned back to the television just in time to see Dracula sink his fangs into the milky-white neck of his latest bride. She screamed in terror. Gerald sighed with satisfaction.

Matthew and Grace parted company outside the green-house. 'Are you sure you don't want me to help?' asked the former.

'No, really, Matthew.' Her slightly impish smile told him that she was actually enjoying herself. He was glad. Grace needed a lift; something to take her mind off her worries. But, belatedly, Matthew began to worry about Grace. He was sure she had never broken the law in her life.

'Well ... um, keep it out of sight, okay?'

Grace cast her mind back to her earlier notion of contemplating a career in smuggling and suppressed the desire to giggle. Best not tell Matthew about that, she thought. He would be horrified.

She gave him a playful push in the direction of the drive-way. 'Be off with you. Nicky will be wondering what's happened to you – and don't worry about me. As if anyone's going to imagine a middle-aged widow growing cannabis in her greenhouse!'

FIVE

Nicky *had* wondered what had become of Matthew. When he had finally returned home and confessed that he had spent the evening recruiting Grace to save his plants, she was less than enthusiastic.

'But she's doing it as compensation for having to lay me off. Isn't that nice?' he had said.

And that, Nicky had thought, was just Matthew's problem. He was too nice. And too willing to believe in the niceness of everyone else around him. True, his optimism and enthusiasm were two of his most endearing qualities, but they went hand-in-glove with something that Nicky suspected bordered on naivety.

'Well,' she had said. 'I just think that Grace has got enough problems without getting involved in drugs.'

'Drugs! *Drugs!*' Laughing, Matthew had pushed her onto the bed. Then, trying to look fierce, he had jumped in beside her. 'It's only a wee bit of dope.'

'You know what I'm talking about, Matthew. It's still illegal. And Grace is very vulnerable right now.' She had looked deep into his eyes. 'I hope you're not taking advantage of her.'

Still looking fierce, Matthew had reached out for her and told her that there was someone else he intended to take advantage of. Nicky hadn't demurred about that one, and, within seconds, the dope was forgotten.

But then Nicky had woken up in the middle of the night and fretted, not so much about Grace but about Matthew's Jack-the-lad attitude to life, his refusal to worry about finding a new job and her suspicion that their lives together were about to take on a more serious dimension.

Now, in Martin Bamford's surgery, those suspicions had just been confirmed.

'Yup,' said Martin. 'Pregnant indeed.' His tone was light-hearted, almost flippant, but as he looked across the desk at Nicky, he was watching for her reaction. He knew he had a reputation for treating life – and sometimes death – as a joke. He knew also that it was a highly successful way to establish a rapport with his patients. And Nicky, although a close friend, was also a patient. 'Is that a good thing?' he asked, watching her closely.

Nicky tried to look inscrutable, but she failed to disguise the momentary look of pure joy. She looked down into her lap and then back up again at Martin. 'Yes,' she said, 'it's good.' Then she gave up the pretence. Dark eyes glowing, she smiled across at Martin. 'Actually, it's brilliant.'

Martin nodded. 'Er … any idea who the father is?'

For a split second Nicky looked outraged. Then she tried to look cross. Martin, however, ignored her and examined the medical records on his desk. 'Well, I think I know. I looked at the test slides. Some of the chromosomes had little kilts on.'

'Very funny, Martin.'

Martin looked up again, the picture of concern. 'I do have some bad news, though.'

Alarm flickered across Nicky's face. 'What d'you …?'

Martin leaned forwards. 'There is,' he whispered, 'a slight risk of ginger hair.'

Nicky breathed a sigh of relief. Then she told Martin to piss off.

Martin nodded amiably and replaced the records in his file. 'Anything else you want to discuss, you know where to come.'

'Is that it?'

'At this stage, yes. You're only a few days gone, Nicky. All I can advise you to do is make an appointment for two weeks' time, stay off the fags ...'

'... I don't smoke.'

'Oh, yes. Forgot. Well, go very easy on the booze and stay off the drugs. Er ... talking of which, how are our plants doing?'

Nicky grimaced. 'Matthew's called in an expert.'

Martin looked highly impressed. 'Oh. Sounds good. Those seeds cost an arm and a leg, you know. It would be a tragedy if they didn't grow. I hope ...'

'Look, Martin,' interrupted Nicky, 'don't mention the baby yet, okay? I just want to ... to tell him when the time is right.'

She looks worried, thought Martin. Then he remembered why. Matthew had no job. That, combined with the fact that Nicky simply wouldn't be able to do her own job in an advanced state of pregnancy, was going to pose problems. He sincerely hoped there would soon be a 'right time'.

He shot Nicky a look of utter bafflement. 'Mention what baby?'

Nicky grinned.

Then Martin indicated the jar of sweets he kept on his desk. 'Have a sweetie. They're normally reserved for my favourite patients, but ...'

'... bet that's what you say to all the girls.' Nicky reached for a boiled sherbet. 'And the boys. And the little old ladies.

And …'

'Yes, yes. Well off you go now. Can't have you cluttering up my surgery all day.' But Martin's gruff dismissal was, they both knew, a cover. He was delighted for Nicky. And for Matthew. But as Nicky closed the door behind her, Martin also felt a gnawing concern. He wanted his friends to be happy in every way. And Matthew didn't have very much to be happy about at the moment.

Matthew, however, knew better. At the same time as Nicky walked out of the surgery in the village, he was ambling into Grace's greenhouse. Grace was standing at one of the potting tables in front of last night's cannabis plant. 'Will she live, doctor?' he asked as he approached.

Grace was trying terribly hard not to look pleased with herself. Suspecting she might be failing, she continued staring at the plant. 'I think so,' was all she said.

Matthew peered down at the innocuous-looking plant. Was it just wishful thinking, or did it look healthier than it had done last night? It seemed somehow more robust; more sure of itself.

'Where did the seeds come from?' asked Grace.

'Oh … um … guy in a pub in Bodmin.'

Grace laughed. 'No, I mean, what *kind* are they?'

'Oh, I see what you mean. They're hybrids. *Indica* and *sativa*. Er … Purple Haze with Early Pearl crossed with *Ruderalis.*'

Grace looked momentarily non-plussed. 'Well, anyway, they're designed to grow in a very sunny climate.'

Matthew looked crestfallen. Even in Grace's very sunny greenhouse, he suspected they might not flourish. 'Oh … if you say so.'

Grace was aware of Matthew's disappointment, yet a

smile was hovering at the corners of her mouth. 'Is it the bud, the bit you're after?' she asked, bending down to the plant.

Beside her, and trying not to look like a naughty schoolboy, Matthew cleared his throat. 'Well, um ... yeah.'

'Look.'

'What?'

'Look.' Grace handed Matthew her magnifying glass and he looked at where she was pointing. To his utter astonishment, he saw a tiny bud sprouting.

'Christ!' Matthew nearly dropped the glass. 'You did that in less than twenty-four hours?'

Grace shrugged.

But Matthew was looking at her in a new light. 'You're a witch,' he declared.

Grace laughed again. 'Oh it's not me, really. It's just a question of having enough light. No light, no buds. Simple.'

'But the bud grew *overnight*. When it was dark.'

'Ah, but not in here.' Grace drew back from the plant and pointed at the various pieces of apparatus without which many of her plants would have died. 'I had the humidifier trained on it all night. Not soaking it; it gave a gentle squirt every few minutes. And then on the other side I had this lamp, so ...'

'... so as I said, you're a witch.' A bemused Matthew shook his head in wonder. 'Harvey and Martin will be chuffed to bits.' But so was he. And so, beside him, was Grace. Growing marijuana, or cannabis or hemp, or whatever it was they called it, may well be illegal, but it was still rewarding.

Because Grace was Grace and believed that the gardener's only real enemy was ignorance, she returned indoors later in the morning to consult her extensive array of gardening books, searching for more information on her latest patient.

While Matthew claimed his plant was a hybrid, the most Grace could ascertain was that it was a variety of hemp called *Cannabis sativa*. And to her amusement, she discovered that *sativa* meant useful. The book she was reading, however, didn't find that at all funny. It cautioned her that while it was perfectly legal to possess the roots, stalks and stems of the plant (useful for making paper, clothes, fuel and food), it was a heinous crime to possess the flowers or leaves. Grace didn't have to read further to establish why. She did, however, marvel at the perverse logic of the law relating to the cannabis plant. Then she laughed out loud when she read that it was legal to possess the seeds (and to eat them), but only if they were sterilised. She made a mental note to tell Matthew about that.

Her book went on to describe in depth the various properties of the plant, but fought shy of providing her with details of how to accelerate its growth because it was 'not possible to grow *Cannabis sativa* without being in possession of the illegal drug marijuana'. So much, thought Grace in wry amusement, for Matthew and his trousers. Then she frowned. How *did* they make clothes out of hemp, then? But her book wasn't going to tell her that.

Yet she knew enough about the properties and provenance of the plant to be able to guess how best to cultivate it quickly. It should be well-drained and would probably benefit from sponge rock or pearlite. Soil-wise, Grace reckoned she had been right on a pH balance of 6.5, as a highly acid soil would encourage the plant to be predominantly male. That wouldn't have boded terribly well for the buds. Grace frowned. The buds were going to be her biggest problems. Artificial light was all very well, but the common light bulb – no matter how strong – emitted a high percentage of infra-red and that would encourage the plant to concentrate its growth on the stem. All very well if you wanted to use the plant for making canvas, but Matthew wasn't intending to sail away. Grace giggled to herself. He wanted to be blown away instead.

Grace was now completely immersed in her new subject. Her worries about her financial plight were forgotten: her only concern was to grow as many buds as possible on Matthew's plant.

She closed the book she had been reading, crossed the sun-drenched drawing-room and stopped by the bookshelves. Somewhere, she knew, she had a book that contained everything any gardener needed to know about light. What she really wanted was a battery of eight-foot VHO Gro-Lux light fixtures. That would make the plant grow at an astonishing rate. But it would also be expensive and Grace didn't want to think about that. She flipped through the rows of books. There were titles on subjects on everything from hydrangeas to hydroponics, but where was the one on light? Was it more blue light she needed for the cannabis? Or was it white? For the life of her she couldn't remember.

She was still debating the issue to herself when the doorbell rang. Grace ignored it. She wasn't expecting anyone, and if it was anyone local calling unannounced then they knew what to do. She continued scrutinising the books on the shelf. Then the bell rang again; this time for longer. Grace sighed. A little voice in the back of her head reminded her of the previous day's sense of foreboding but, like the doorbell, she ignored it. She had important work to do.

So did the person who was ringing her doorbell. After two

more rings her caller gave up, tried the door itself and was pleasantly surprised to find it unlocked. Grace's heart missed a beat as she heard a tentative and unfamiliar voice calling for her. Then, suppressing the urge to hide, Grace walked into the hall and found herself in front of an eager-looking young man in a cheap suit. He was holding a clipboard.

'Ah! Mrs Trevethan?'

'Ye-es.' Grace supposed she ought to smile. Someone to read some sort of meter, she told herself.

But then people who read meters didn't usually hold out a hand in greeting and personally introduce themselves. 'Nigel Plimpton,' he said, shaking her hand with vigour. Then he looked expectantly at Grace. But Grace hadn't a clue what he might be expecting. 'Oh,' was all she could say.

Nigel Plimpton gestured through the open front door to the driveway. 'Is it all right to park there?'

Grace looked at the blue Golf parked beside her own ancient Morris Minor. 'Er ... yes.'

'Good, good,' Nigel Plimpton made to step further into the house. Then, looking apprehensive, he checked himself. 'Dogs?' he asked, looking around.

'Dogs?'

'Yes. Dogs. Do you have dogs?'

'Oh I see what you mean. No. No ... I don't have any dogs.'

'Jolly good. Postmen and surveyors,' grinned her relieved visitor. 'Irresistible to our canine friends.'

Then, before Grace could stop him, he bounded past her and looked appraisingly at the hallway and the drawing room beyond. 'Oh yes. Yes, yes, yes! This is fabulous,' he said with unbridled enthusiasm. 'Gorgeous shutters.' He leaped towards the nearest window, extracting a tape-measure from his breast pocket as he did so. 'And rare to have such big windows in a house this old. '*Fabulous* view. I suppose that's why.'

Looking completely dumb-founded, Grace followed him into the room. Her mind hadn't quite registered what was happening. 'Can I help you?' she volunteered.

'No, no. I'm fine on my own.' Then, making a note on his clipboard, Nigel turned and, in his jaunty way, added that 'a cup of tea would be nice.'

Grace looked even more confused. 'I'm sorry,' she said, 'I have no idea why you're here. I think you've come to the wrong house.'

But Nigel prided himself on never making mistakes. He looked down at his clipboard. 'Liac House?' he asked.

'Yes.'

Nigel beamed again. 'Then there's no mistake.' He turned back to the window. 'I'll just get on with it, shall I? Oh … and it's …er … milk and two sugars.'

'There *is* a mistake,' said Grace. She was annoyed now and wanted the wretched man out of her house. And she certainly wasn't going to make him any tea.

Puzzled now, Nigel turned back again. This time he looked more carefully at Grace. She was pleasant-looking, he thought. Pretty, even, in a middle-aged sort of way. But what he noticed most was the fright in her eyes. The reality of the situation began to dawn on him. She had blocked the whole thing out of her mind. It wouldn't be the first time it had happened to him. 'Valuation for Ramptons re debts outstanding?' he prompted.

Grace shook her head.

Nigel began to feel embarrassed. 'It's, er, standard procedure before a house is put up for auction.'

'But this house isn't up for auction!'

'Ah.' Nigel sighed. 'Well … I'm afraid it will be.' Then,

noting Grace's look of sheer horror, he coughed and reached into his jacket pocket. 'I've got a, um, a duplicate of the letter.'

'What letter?'

'The letter from Ramptons.' He handed it to Grace.

But all Grace saw was a typewritten blur.

'People in your position,' continued Nigel, looking away from her, 'often stop opening their mail, so … so I'm the first real proof that it's, er, happening.'

'That what's happening?'

'The, er … the valuation.'

This wasn't too difficult: Grace simply could not allow herself to believe what the man was saying. So she didn't. Then she asked him to leave.

Nigel shuffled from one foot to the other. 'I'm sorry, but … well, I can't.' He looked half pleading and half apologetic. 'I really must do this.'

Grace took a deep breath. She didn't have the energy to fight with the man, but nor did she want him in her house a minute longer. She might start to believe in what he was doing there.

'I really would,' she repeated, 'like you to leave.'

Nigel Plimpton was about to answer back when a strapping six-foot vision wearing wellies and a thunderous scowl loomed suddenly behind Grace. He glared at Nigel. 'Didn't you hear what the lady said?' he barked in a deep Scottish burr. 'She wants you to leave.'

Nigel offered a weak smile – and no resistance. He had absolutely no intention of getting into a fight with someone who looked like that. 'Ah.' He delved into another pocket and produced a business card. Still with one wary eye on Matthew, he handed it to Grace. 'Yes. I can see that just now isn't the best time. Why don't you call the office to reschedule?'

Feeling numb, Grace took the proffered card and watched Nigel bolt through the archway towards the sanctuary of his car. Matthew looked in concern at Grace. 'Are you all right?' Grace nodded.

'What did he want?'

'He … well, he seemed to think the house was about to be put up for auction.'

'*What*?'

Grace wrung her hands and tried to smile up at Matthew. She failed. Her expression was one of pure anguish.

'There must be some mistake,' said Matthew.

'Yes,' said Grace.

Matthew scratched his head. 'Look, why don't you phone Melvyn Stott at the bank? He'll soon put you right.' But he didn't believe his words. Not really. And nor did Grace.

'Phone,' said Matthew, gesturing towards the instrument on the hall table. 'I'll go and … make us a cup of tea.'

'He wanted one of those as well,' said Grace.

'Eh? Who?'

Grace pointed to the card in her hand. 'The man from Ramptons.' She laughed; a brittle sound devoid of any humour. 'He wanted a cup of tea while he valued the house.'

Matthew's expression suggested that he knew exactly where the man from Ramptons could put his cup of tea. Nodding again at the phone, he then disappeared down the hall towards the kitchen.

Grace walked to the phone and, with a trembling hand, Grace dialled the bank.

'Good afternoon, Southern Bank.'

'Oh … hello. Um … I'd like to speak to Melvyn Stott, please.'

'May I ask who's calling?'

'Yes. It's Grace Trevethan.'

'Oh, Mrs Trevethan!' The voice, until now all brisk efficiency (mixed with affectation), relaxed into a familiar Cornish lilt. 'How *are* you?' It wasn't really a question; more an expression of sympathy.

Oh God, thought Grace. Is there no escape? For a mad, fleeting moment she felt the urge to slam the receiver down. But that would just make things worse. Wendy Treglowan, for all that she meant well, would have it around the village in no time that Grace was losing her marbles. Inwardly cursing the fact that she lived in such a tiny community, Grace took a deep breath and carried on talking. 'I'm fine, thank you, Wendy. How are you?' Then she bit her lip. That was absolutely the wrong thing to say.

'Well it's funny you should ask. I had this *pain* thing in my ear and, well, you know me. Never one to hang around in times of crisis, so I made an appointment with Dr Bamford and … and, well …!' On the other end of the line, Wendy lowered her voice. 'I know ears and noses are related but there's never been anything wrong with my sense of smell so you could have knocked me down with a feather when I smelled alcohol on his breath!'

'Wendy …'

'On *Dr Bamford's* breath. In the surgery!'

'Wendy. I'd really like to speak to Melvyn please.'

'Oh.' Where Wendy had earlier sounded affected, she now sounded annoyed as, reluctantly, she became brisk and efficient again. But she still made one last stab at gossip. 'I'll just put you through. I could have sworn he'd been smoking as well. *In the surgery.*'

This time Grace had the wit not to reply.

'I'll just put you through,' repeated Wendy.

After a moment, Melvyn's voice came down the line. 'Grace.' His voice, even when he uttered only a word, had something of the bedside manner about it. But then he was, after all, a sort of doctor. Or at least a counsellor.

Grace had had enough preamble from Wendy and dispensed with any formalities. 'Melvyn, I've just had a *man* ...' Oh God, she thought. I'm sounding like Wendy. 'I've just had a visit from this little man who told me the house was going up for auction. He said ... he said he needed to value it so I said there must be some mistake but he said no and gave his card thing and then dear Matthew threw him out and ... Oh God, Melvyn! What's this all about? Have you any idea?'

Melvyn did have an idea. More than an idea. He had all the facts. He also had a letter in front of him from Ramptons, detailing those facts. Grace had caught him in the process of writing to her about it.

'Grace. Calm down, Grace,' he soothed. 'Do you know what company the man was from? Have you got the card with you?'

'Yes.' Grace nearly dropped the receiver as she flipped it over to read the details down the phone. 'It's from a company called Ramptons.'

'Ah.'

Grace heard the resignation in Melvyn's voice. 'Who are they, Melvyn? And how can they possibly have anything to do with my house?'

Melvyn took a deep breath. 'Well, the thing is, Grace, it appears that John had some ... some interests that he, well, kept quiet about.'

Yes, thought Grace. Honey Chambers for one.

'I've only just had a letter from Rampton's myself. And ... well, I'm as surprised as you are, Grace.'

'Surprised about *what*?'

'Um ... Rampton's is an enormous investment trust in the city. John was part of a syndicate that ... took a huge tumble.'

Grace had thought she was through the worst. She wondered if Melvyn could hear her heart beating at his end of the line. She gulped. 'So ... so I owe them money, then?' A mad, scary part of her that she didn't recognise wanted to laugh. What was money? What was 'owing'? And so what, anyway? It was all water off a duck's back. She didn't have any money.

'Yes,' said Melvyn.

'How much?'

Melvyn was glad Grace couldn't see him. He looked down at the terms so clearly stated in the letter. 'If you don't pay them the money owing, then ... then they can claim any or all of your assets.'

Grace nearly did laugh. 'I don't *have* any assets, Melvyn.'

'Well, no. Not of the liquid kind.' Oh God, he thought. Grace really isn't going to like this. 'You've ... you've got Liac House.'

'But it's mortgaged! I have to find two thousand pounds a month to pay it!'

Melvyn sighed again. How he hated having this conversation. Especially with this woman. 'Yes but the mortgage John raised wasn't against the entire value of the house. Theoretically, you see ... well, actually ... that is to say, *legally*, Rampton's can claim the rest is theirs.'

Silence from Grace.

Melvyn assumed she didn't understand. 'There's still some capital tied up in the house, you see.'

Grace found her voice. A quavering voice. 'How much?'

'Well, I'd insist on getting a second valuation. We can't have Rampton's calling the shots here ...'

'No ... how much do I owe Rampton's?'

Melvyn cleared his throat and looked down at the letter again. 'Er ... three hundred thousand pounds.'

'Three ... hundred ... thousand ...'

'... Approximately.'

'Approximately,' repeated Grace in a tiny whisper. What had she vowed to herself the other night? That she would keep her house at all costs? The words rang hollow in her ear.

'Grace?'

Grace was still listening to the hollow ring.

'Grace?' he repeated. 'I know this is all a bit much to take in at once. Why don't I write to you with all the details and ...'

'... Three ... hundred ... thousand,' repeated Grace.

'I know it's a lot, but I'm sure ...'

'Melvyn, what am I going to *do*?' wailed Grace.

'Nothing.' Melvyn was adamant about that. 'You are to do absolutely nothing, Grace. If Rampton's call again, put them on to me. And Grace, don't worry,' he added with feeling. 'I'll sort something out. Trust me.' He replaced the receiver, wishing that he hadn't used the word 'trust' because he knew he was going to let Grace down. Her situation was hopeless and there was nothing he could do about it. The fact that her situation was so highly public didn't help either. What a pity he hadn't been able to keep it between Grace and himself. But then secrets were difficult to keep in St Liac.

He was amazed he had been able to keep his own little secret for so long.

Up in Liac House, Grace was also reflecting on the word 'trust'. It was a funny word, she thought. And a treacherous one. She had, after all, trusted John.

In a trance, she wandered through the hall and down the passageway towards the kitchen. Unaware of Matthew's presence when the entered the room, oblivious to everything except her thoughts, she made a bee-line for the photograph of John on the dresser. She picked it up and looked at it in detachment, as if seeing him for the first time. A handsome man, she thought. Smiling up at her from his deckchair in the garden, looking as if hadn't a care in the world. Then she shook her head. 'Bastard!' she spat, and slammed the photograph face-down on the dresser.

'Grace?'

Startled, Grace turned to see Matthew sitting at the kitchen table, his expression a mixture of worry, embarrassment and concern. 'Oh!' she said. 'Matthew … I'd … I'd forgotten …' Herself embarrassed that he had witnessed her uncustomary outburst, Grace looked away.

Matthew stood up. 'Grace? Would you like me to leave?' A sensitive soul, Matthew felt uncomfortable intruding on what was clearly a very private moment.

'Yes. No … I mean … that is to say …' But Grace didn't finish the sentence. Instead, she burst into tears.

Matthew reacted instinctively, pushing back his chair, rushing to Grace and enveloping her in his arms. She buried her head in his shoulder and wept. They stood perfectly still in the kitchen, Grace feeling vaguely pathetic – and pathetically grateful to Matthew.

Wishing he could think of something to say, but suspecting that words would be redundant, Matthew found himself looking at the opposite wall wondering, incongruously, why Grace had painted the room a strange shade of lilac. Then he remembered that it had been her attempt to brighten the room because, unlike the rest of Liac House, it never seemed to get any light. The attempt hadn't really worked, he thought: the kitchen was still gloomy.

After a moment Grace sniffed and pulled away from Matthew. 'Sorry,' she said. She looked up at him with a half-smile. She felt even more embarrassed now. Matthew was her gardener. And she was Grace Trevethan – not Lady Chatterley.

'S'alright,' replied Matthew, feigning nonchalance. Then he stepped back and looked into her eyes. 'It's bad, isn't it, Grace?'

She nodded. 'It's worse, actually.' Reaching for a tissue, Grace dabbed at her eyes and sniffed again. 'That horrid little man had every right to come in here with his tape measure and his clipboard ... I'm going to lose the house, Matthew.'

'No!'

'There's nothing I can do about it.'

Matthew scratched his head. The awful thing was, he suspected Grace was right. 'Look,' he said, 'let's sit down and ... and have a cup of tea.' He regretted the words as soon as he had uttered them. Tea. The great British cure-all. The ultimate panacea. He wished he'd said whisky instead.

'I don't want tea,' said Grace.

'No.'

'I want wine.'

Matthew couldn't help it. He laughed. 'Grace! It's four o'clock in the afternoon.'

Grace grinned. 'The sun must be over the yard-arm somewhere in the world. That's what my father used to say.'

'Oh ...'

'Open a bottle, would you Matthew?' Dabbing at her eyes again, Grace walked to the units at the back of the kitchen, opened a drawer and started rummaging through it. Not finding what she wanted, she slammed it shut and opened another. It took another two drawers for her to find what she was looking for. When she turned back to Matthew she was holding a packet of cigarettes in one hand and a box of matches in the other.

'Grace!'

Grace's hand was shaking as she struck a match. 'Women are allowed to smoke as well, Matthew.' The words came out far more sharply than she had intended. Grace rarely spoke sharply; rarely asserted herself. Perhaps that was her problem.

Matthew looked abashed. 'I just meant ... well, I didn't know you smoked.' Then he looked into the fridge he had just opened and, grimacing, looked at Gerald Percy's potato wine. Without enthusiasm, he picked up the bottle and gestured to Grace. 'This?'

'God, no!' Grace was appalled.

Matthew grinned with relief. 'Awful muck, isn't it?'

Grace drew deeply on her cigarette. It was a bit stale, but she didn't really mind. 'Dreadful. There's some decent red in the cupboard beside you. Let's have that.'

Matthew shrugged. If that would make Grace feel better then he most certainly wasn't going to argue.

Grace reached into another cupboard for glasses. The cigarette was making her feel slightly light-headed. She wondered if the combination of the wine and the horror of the last half hour would make her completely hysterical. Or maybe she would just fall apart. Then she turned back to Matthew and decided that she didn't want him to pick up the pieces. She didn't want anyone to pick them up. Sighing, she sat at the table and rummaged amongst the piles of paper.

'Are you sure that's wise,' asked Matthew, sitting opposite her.

'What?'

Matthew poured the wine. 'Trying to sort out your finances.'

'Oh I'm not doing that.' Grace took a sip and stubbed out her cigarette. Then she lit another. 'I'm making a list.' She reached for one of the brown envelopes, turned it over and picked up a pen.

Matthew was rather bemused. Here was the normally neat, perfectly coiffed and made-up Grace sitting opposite him with tousled hair, smudged mascara, chain-smoking and drinking wine in the middle of the afternoon. He wasn't sure whether he was shocked or amused. Worse, he didn't know if Grace was taking stock or cracking up.

It was the former. 'I'm making a list of things to sell.'

'To sell?'

'Yes, Matthew.' Grace looked at him from under her lashes. 'I'm broke, remember? I need money. To be perfectly honest, I need three hundred thousand pounds just to keep the house.' She said it with a look that said 'don't even ask'. 'Then there are the other debts,' she finished, drawing a brisk line under the word she had just written.

It was upside-down from Matthew's angle, but there was no mistaking that it read 'furniture'.

'Are you sure?' he said, nodding at the envelope.

Grace nodded. 'It's only bits of wood.'

'Yes, but … nice bits of wood. Some of it's been in the family for generations.'

Grace sighed and stubbed out her new cigarette. Chain-smoking didn't really suit her, she decided. That was the provenance of the fast and the loose. She bet Honey Chambers smoked. Picking up her wineglass, she looked at Matthew again. 'There *is* no family any more,' she said.

'No, but …'

'Anyway, the family didn't really like me.'

'Eh?'

Grace smiled, remembering. 'Oh they never *said* anything, John's parents. Or his sister. But I knew. Oh yes, I knew. They thought John was marrying beneath him.'

'You mean …?'

Grace nodded. 'They thought – well John's mother certainly did – that I wasn't quite the thing.'

'Eh?'

'Not from an old family. That sort of thing.'

'Well that's just daft. Anyway, all families are old, aren't they?'

Grace giggled. 'Yes, I suppose they are. I'd never thought about it like that before. I always knew,' she continued, 'they thought John could have done better than the daughter of a university lecturer.'

'That's what your father was?'

'Mmm.'

Matthew looked pensive. 'Mine was a brickie – when he could find the work.'

'And your mother?' Grace was intrigued. Matthew had never talked about his family before. Mind you, nor had she.

Matthew looked down into his wineglass. 'Oh … she died. When I was very young. I was … farmed about between uncles and aunts.'

'Oh.' Hence the restless spirit, Grace supposed. 'Anyway,' she repeated, 'there's no Trevethans left to inherit anything, so …'

'You said John had a sister. What happened to her?'

Grace giggled again. Then, guiltily, she put a hand over her mouth. 'Actually it's not funny. Poor Clare. She'd got it into her head – from her mother, I suppose – that she wouldn't settle for anything less than a rich Cornish landowner. Preferably one with a title.'

'So what happened?'

'Well the title part was forgotten pretty quickly. Then a few years passed and the land began not to matter as long as he was rich. A few years after that, it was decided that it didn't really matter about his being Cornish either.' Grace's lips were beginning to twitch.

'So?'

'So then it just became a desperate hunt for someone – anyone – just as long as he was …'

'… was what?'

'A man!' Grace bit her lip. It really wasn't funny. In reality, it had been quite sad. Then she saw Matthew's expression and burst out laughing.

So did he.

'Oh God,' moaned Grace, fighting to control herself. 'I really shouldn't have said that. Perhaps I'm becoming a bitch?' The thought amused her and she was overcome by another fit of the giggles.

No, thought Matthew. Not a bitch. Just slightly hysterical. Under the circumstances, he wasn't remotely surprised.

'Right,' said Grace when she had composed herself. 'Furniture. There are eight bedrooms crammed with furniture. I only need one bedroom. The drawing room's awash with antiques: do I need most of them? No. Do I need all the paintings? I don't. Then there's the dining-room suite. Sheraton.'

'Eh? Who's Sheraton?'

'The man who made the suite.' Grace chewed the end of her pen. 'I bet I could get twenty thousand for that.'

'Shame to see it go.'

'Matthew. When did I last have a dinner party?'

But Matthew didn't know – and Grace couldn't remember. Perhaps that had been another problem. Grace supposed Honey Chambers threw chic little dinner parties all the time in her elegant little pied-à-terre. Number 44, Wilberforce Street, she remembered from the letters written.

London SW3. Frowning, trying to banish that thought from her mind, she made a few notes on the envelope. 'You know,' she said when she had finished. 'I wouldn't be surprised if I could get about a hundred thousand for all the best bits. That's not bad, is it?'

'No,' conceded Matthew. 'Not bad at all.'

'Anything else you can think of?'

'To sell? Well ... hey! What about John's car?' If Matthew remembered correctly, John had driven a top-of the-range BMW.

But Grace already knew about John's car. 'I asked Melvyn about that.' She grimaced in distaste. 'Turned out it wasn't his. Leased. The hire company requisitioned it from the pound at Heathrow.'

'Oh.'

'Yes.'

Silence.

'I believe my orchids may be worth something.'

'Grace,' chided Matthew. 'You can't sell your plants. They're your life.'

'True – but they could be my livelihood instead.'

'Nah.' Matthew didn't like the idea at all. Pouring more wine, he said they'd soon think of something else to sell.

But Grace had already thought of something else. Plants, she thought. Livelihood. Grace the orchid-smuggler. Green-fingered Grace. Grace who possessed a manual on hydroponic gardening – and the seeds of a spectacular idea.

'Matthew?'

'Mmm?'

'You know that, um, plant I'm looking after for you?'

'Uh-uh.' Grace, he thought, was looking guilty.

'How much is it worth?'

Oh God. Grace *was* guilty. 'It hasn't died, has it? he asked.

That was all he needed.

'No. Not at all. It's, er … thriving. I was just wondering, you know … how much you'd get for it?'

Matthew reappraised his interpretation. Grace wasn't looking guilty, he realised. Sly would be a better word.

'Ounce for ounce,' he said, watching her carefully, 'the really good stuff's worth more than gold.'

'And that stuff's really good?'

Matthew nodded. She couldn't, he thought. Not seriously. He looked, wide-eyed, across the table. 'You're not … seriously … considering …?'

Grace shot to her feet. 'Greenhouse,' she commanded. 'Now!'

SIX

'Here's what I think.' Grace could barely contain herself as she looked at the cannabis plant. It had four spindly leaves, one tiny bud and, being a plant, no idea of Grace's ambitions for its meteoric development. 'I think we should take cuttings from the mother plant,' she hurried on, 'root the cuttings and grow them under lights hydroponically ...'

'... hydrowhatty?'

'Hydroponically. Growing plants without soil.' Grace's eyes were burning with the fervour of a zealot as she eyed her protégé, the mother plant. 'You can do it easily with cherry tomatoes. There's absolutely no reason why you can't do it with ... er ...'

'Weed?'

Grace's book held no truck with weeds. 'Marijuana?'

Matthew shrugged. 'Same thing. Cannabis, ganja, dope, shit ....'

'What?'

'Sorry?'

'Why did you say "shit"? Is something wrong?'

Grace, thought Matthew, had a lot to learn. 'No,' he said. 'Nothing's wrong. It's just that, well ... I can't believe you're seriously thinking about ...'

'... are you trying to tell me you'd never thought about it?'

'Well ...' Matthew looked sheepish. 'Of course I'd

thought about it. It just seemed a bit ambitious.'

'Nonsense,' said Grace the gardener. 'It's perfectly simple. It just means accelerating the growth of the most important bit of the plant. Which, in this case, means the bud.'

'Just like a cherry tomato, then?'

Grace shot him a warning look. 'It means,' she said, 'that we could have the first harvest in a couple of weeks.'

Matthew looked at the unsuspecting mother plant. 'How big a harvest?'

Grace mulled over that one for a moment. 'Twenty kilos?'

'*What?*'

'I don't see why not.' Grace looked at Matthew. 'You really don't know anything about hydroponic gardening, do you?'

'Grace. If I were to be really honest, I don't really know anything about any sort of gardening.'

'Oh you will, Matthew, you will.' Radiating confidence, Grace beamed up at him. 'Under my guidance, you'll become an *expert* on hydroponics.'

But Matthew was still looking doubtfully at the little plant in front of them. 'Do you realise what you're saying, Grace? Twenty kilos … a couple of weeks. That's enough to pay off your debts.'

Grace looked sceptical.

So she hasn't told me the extent of those debts, surmised Matthew. 'How long do you have to find that three hundred thousand?'

Grace was momentarily flummoxed to be catapulted back to reality. 'I don't know – but I can't imagine Melvyn can stall Rampton's forever. Let's just say I've got two weeks.'

Matthew nodded. 'If you can get twenty kilos in two weeks' time, then trust me – you can keep your house.'

'Matthew. I have absolutely no intention of losing my house.' The words were spoken quite calmly: the expression was steely. Matthew wondered if he had ever really known Grace. The real Grace.

'You know you can't tell anybody,' he said.

Grace looked at the cannabis. 'Tell anybody what? That I'm growing marijuana on an industrial scale? That I intend to profit from it?' Then, suddenly, she looked doubtful. 'Matthew, it's not bad for you, is it?'

'For *me*?'

'For *one*. For people in general' Grace tried not to look like a criminal in the making. 'I know it's illegal, but that's really because of a misunderstanding, isn't it?'

'Yes.' Matthew had no doubts about that. 'People think it can lead to hard drugs, but there's no evidence. And,' he added by way of reassurance, 'it's actually good for you. And it's a brilliant pain reliever for things like arthritis. My granny used to take it.'

'What? She smoked marijuana?'

'No ... my auntie used to bake it in cakes for her. She used to call them tipsy cakes.'

'I'm not entirely surprised.' Grace looked around the greenhouse. 'We'll have to make a lot of changes round here.'

'Oh?'

'Yes.' Grace looked sad for a moment. 'For a start, we'll have to get rid of the orchids.'

'*What?*'

'I'm afraid so. Only temporarily.' Grace's almost offhand manner belied the fact she was talking about her life's passion. 'And we'll need to make a list.'

'A list?'

'Of things to buy.'

Matthew raised his eyes. 'Grace, a moment ago, you were

making a list of things to sell. To raise money, remember?'

'Yes.' Grace smiled. 'Well now we'll have to put some of the money aside for things for the greenhouse.'

'Like what?'

Grace picked up an orchid and headed for the door. 'Hydroponic gardening,' she explained, 'is all about growing without soil – using sand or gravel. Or water.' She opened the door and dumped the orchid on the grass outside. 'And I think we should use water. It's the quickest method.'

Matthew looked in wonder at his employer. How had the bereft, penniless and helpless widow changed so quickly into this brisk, purposeful creature? It was as if she had found a switch inside herself, turned it on – and wasn't going to turn it off again.

'So,' she continued, picking up another orchid, 'we'll need a waterpump capable of at least fifty gallons per hour. And an airpump. We'll need hoses, pipes, tee-joints … and most importantly, we'll need a battery of eight-foot VHO Gro-Lux lights.' She beamed up at the bemused Matthew. Only hours before, she had been bemoaning the fact that she would never be able to afford the lights. Not any more. Not with her new plan. 'We're also going to have to restructure the electrics of this place. How are you with electrics?'

'Um …'

Grace grinned. 'Well, never mind. We'll learn together.' Humming to herself, she heaved the orchid outside and placed it beside its fellow evacuee. She allowed herself a brief moment of regret, a fleeting guilt, and then closed her mind to their fate. She would make it up to them later.

She went back into the greenhouse and looked in mock disapproval at Matthew standing beside the cannabis plant, scratching his head.

'Are you going to help me?'

'Eh?'

'Are you just going to stand there, or are you going to help me empty the greenhouse?'

'Oh … er, sure. Yeah.' Matthew shook himself out of his reverie and picked up an orchid pot. 'Grace?'

'Mmm?'

'Are you really, *really* sure you want to do this?'

Grace's set expression was answer enough.

'Okay, then.' Matthew grinned. 'There's an even quicker way.'

'Is there?' Grace paused at the door. 'What? I thought you didn't know anything about hydroponics?'

'Well, maybe not quicker. But a way to get more volume. The other plants,' he reminded her. 'In the vicarage garden.'

Grace nearly dropped the pot she was carrying. 'Oh my God, I'd completely forgotten.' Then she frowned. 'How many?'

Matthew shrugged. 'Ten?'

Grace sighed and then shook her head. 'We can't risk it, Matthew. I mean we *really* can't risk it. This isn't about rescuing dying plants any more. If anyone saw us …'

'Who on earth would see us?'

'Gerald? He nearly saw us last time.' Grace shook her head again. 'No. Matthew. I'm not going there again.' Then she noticed the wicked glint in Matthew's eyes. 'What? What are you thinking?'

'I'm thinking,' said Matthew, 'that we could go and get them when we're *sure* Gerald won't see us.'

'You mean in the middle of the night? No.' Grace didn't like that idea at all. 'Gerald has this really peculiar habit of wandering through the woods at night. Odd, for a vicar, don't you think? Perhaps he thinks they're haunted and need exorcising.'

Grace didn't know it, but she was right about the haunting part. Exorcising, however, was the last thing on Gerald's mind during his night-time forays. It would spoil his fun.

'No,' said Matthew. 'Not at night. During the day.' He paused. 'Sunday, to be precise.'

Grace looked at him with the air of a child who had stolen a sweet. 'Oh dear,' she sighed. 'I'm becoming a fallen woman, Matthew. Missing church is practically an offence in Liac.'

Matthew grinned. 'So we'll do it, then?'

Grace straightened her shoulders. 'Yes. If I'm going to embark on a criminal career, I might as well go the whole hog.'

———————————————

Three days later Grace and Matthew skipped church, rescued the rest of the cannabis plants from the vicarage garden and installed them in their new home. By that time they had totally transformed the greenhouse. What had once been a normal – if rather large – domestic hothouse now looked more like a factory. Having scrubbed the entire place from floor to ceiling, they painted it white, bought and then installed much of the hydroponic equipment. Where there had once been rows of orchids, there were now water pumps, great silver tubes of PVC – and, on the day after church, ten cannabis plants which had budded overnight. Until they in turn began to produce further cuttings, all Grace and Matthew needed was to install the Gro-Lux lights. Grace had bought them in Wadebridge on Saturday. She hadn't, however, bought enough electric cable.

Which was why, on Tuesday, she was rifling through the shelves at Jack's hardware shop in Liac. 'Shop' was, in fact, something of a misnomer: the place consisted of two garages and sold everything from fishing tackle to second-hand fridges. It was also on a promontory above Liac's harbour, and any car driving up to it was clearly visible to people looking up.

Nicky had seen Grace's little Morris Minor (Matthew called it a 'bap') chugging up the hill. She hadn't seen Grace for days. Nobody had seen Grace for days. There had been several knowing looks in church when her absence had been noted. Grace, it was assumed, was cracking up.

Nicky wasn't so sure. She had always suspected that Grace was more formidable than she looked; that she was one of life's survivors. She had assumed that Grace would find, possibly to her own surprise, that she could cope with widowhood – even impoverished widowhood.

Nicky had a horrible suspicion that Grace was actually coping rather better than she had anticipated and that she had found a new lease of life. Under normal circumstances, Nicky would have been delighted. Yet she was harbouring suspicions that the circumstances up at Liac House weren't at all normal. What was Grace doing all day? More to the point, what was Grace doing that required Matthew's presence all day – and half the night?

Nicky had dismissed the thought when it had first occurred to her. It was just too much of a cliché: the bored, lonely widow and the attractive young gardener. It was ludicrous, especially as the widow was Grace and the gardener Matthew. Nicky attributed her suspicions to her haywire hormones and her pregnancy. But that just made things worse: it was that very pregnancy she wanted to talk to Matthew about. She wanted to find the right moment to tell him but there hadn't been one over the past few days. There had hardly been any sort of moment.

So when Nicky saw Grace parking her car outside Jack's garage, she didn't hesitate. She threw aside the nets she was

107

mending and, still in her oilskins, began to trudge up the hill. She was oblivious to her surroundings; to the village she loved so much, the towering cliffs around her and the squawking, scavenging seagulls. All she could think about was her current predicament.

She and Matthew had never discussed marriage or children. Matthew, being Matthew, always managed to avoid that topic of conversation; to evade any discussion about responsibility. He even managed to avoid talking about the responsibilities of living together, yet he had been adamant that he wanted to move in with her. He had also declared that he never wanted to leave Liac. Nicky had taken that as an indication of the permanence of their relationship. Now she wondered if she had misinterpreted the situation. She was beginning to fear that she had misjudged him and that he was, in reality, more fly-by-night than happy-go-lucky: that he would take off the minute he heard about the baby they had neither planned nor discussed.

Grace did nothing to allay her suspicions. When Nicky reached the garage, she said 'hello Grace', and the older woman nearly jumped out of her skin.

'Oh! Hello Nicky.' Grace averted her gaze. 'How are you?'

'Fine.' Nicky looked at Grace. She was wearing wellies, baggy trousers and a tatty old jacket, but she was, as usual, immaculately made-up. True, Grace never seemed to wear much make-up, but she wore it exceptionally well. No matter what she was wearing, she always managed to look very feminine. Very Grace.

Nicky rarely wore make-up and spent her life on a trawler.

'Haven't seen you for ages,' she said. 'How are you?'

'Oh … you know. Busy.' Grace's smile couldn't disguise her unease.

Nicky frowned. Then she noticed the reels of cable that Grace, for some reason, was trying to pretend she wasn't holding in her hands. She nodded at them. 'What are you doing?'

Grace looked even more uncomfortable. 'Um, building a fence. You know ... keeping out the rabbits.'

'With electrical wire?'

'Er ... yes. It's an electric fence.'

Nicky shrugged. 'Oh. Okay. Actually, I'm looking for Matthew. Is he up at the house?'

Alarm flickered across Grace's face. 'No,' she said rather too quickly. 'He's out. He's ... looking for a transformer.'

Nicky didn't reply.

'For the electric fence.'

Nicky decided to drop the subject. If Grace didn't want her at Liac House then there was nothing she could do about it. Except wheedle the truth out of Matthew later on. 'Well, I really need to see him about something. If you do see him, could you tell him I'll meet him in the pub at nine?'

Grace nodded enthusiastically. 'Yes. Righty-ho. Better be off, then. Bye!' With that, Grace dashed off to her car and Nicky, feeling deflated and even more suspicious, ambled back down the street to the harbour.

In the driver's seat, Grace closed her eyes and waited for her heart to stop palpitating. Being a criminal, she thought, wasn't too bad: *feeling* like one was awful. She wondered if she was going to feel like one all the time – even when she wasn't doing anything wrong. Like just now. There was nothing illegal about buying several metres of electrical cable, but seeing Nicky had thrown her into a panic. And Nicky wasn't stupid; she must have suspected something was up.

Had Grace known what Nicky suspected, she would have

been mortified. She would also have been highly amused. The thought of her and Matthew having an affair was too ludicrous to be credible. So was the thought of a middle-aged widow growing industrial amounts of cannabis in her greenhouse. But to Grace, that was no longer a thought. It was a fact.

When she had calmed down, Grace started her car and pootled back to Liac House. The Morris Minor protested most of the way – something else Grace chose not to think about. The last thing she could afford right now was a new car. But at least she now had some money, or would have before the day was out. She had, as planned, arranged to sell most of her furniture and the main reason why she hadn't wanted Nicky at Liac House was because Matthew was currently supervising the removal of most of that furniture. Grace knew that she wouldn't be able to keep it a secret for ever, but, under the current climate (especially the climate in the greenhouse) she didn't want any visitors.

Ten minutes after leaving Jack's garage she turned into her driveway, swept past the bank of rhododendrons beyond the now uninhabited lodge, and down towards Liac House. She loved the fact that it was in its own tiny valley: apart from making the whole place intensely private, it provided ample shelter for her plants. And the sweep of drive in front of the house provided ample room for the vast removal van. When Grace saw it, she began to hyperventilate again. Reality was biting. Contemplating selling her furniture had been easy enough: witnessing its disappearance was something else altogether.

Grace drew up beside the van and got out of the car at the same time as two burly men appeared at the front door, struggling under the weight of John's beautiful Queen Anne secretaire. Grace felt a lump rise in her throat. True, it was too small to use as a desk and had stood in a corner of the study for as long as anyone could remember, but it was beautiful, the same age as the house itself, and had been in the Trevethan family for generations.

Then Grace reminded herself what she had told Matthew about the Trevethan family's attitude to her, squared her shoulders, and walked towards the man who appeared to be in charge of the struggling removal men.

'Mrs T?' he enquired.

Grace nodded. She hated being called 'Mrs T.' 'Nearly done?' she asked.

'Yes.' Oliver Spink patted his slicked-back hair and gave Grace the benefit of his most unctuous smile. 'Last few pieces coming out now, and very fine they are too.'

Grace looked in distaste at the double-breasted suit and what she interpreted as an insolent smirk. 'But not fine enough to fetch a decent price?'

Oliver Spink looked grave. 'Well, you know how it is, Mrs T. In today's market ...' He shook his head. 'To be honest, you're lucky we can take them off your hands.'

But Grace didn't want to hear about how lucky she was. They had already discussed that on the phone. It hadn't taken Oliver Spink long to realise that she was desperate for cash, didn't want anyone to know how she was obtaining it, and was, therefore, in a pretty poor bargaining position. Oliver Spink was not. He had become very rich bargaining with people like Grace. 'If it's all as good as you say, then I can offer twenty thousand,' he had said over the phone.

Grace had felt like weeping, but she had accepted. And now it looked like she was going to accept an even lower offer.

'Thing is, Mrs T,' the odious man was saying. 'That Sheraton dining suite isn't what you said it was.'

Grace bridled. 'It most certainly is! And what's more, it's authenticated.'

Oliver Spink scratched his chin. 'Ah, but it's also damaged.'

'Rubbish!'

'That is to say, it *was* damaged.'

'So what's the problem?'

'It was mended in … oh, I'd say in the early Victorian era. Five of the chairs and a leaf of the table bear the hallmarks of poor restoration. The walnut doesn't match … that sort of thing.'

'I don't believe you.'

'I'll show you, then.' Oliver knew he was onto a winner here. It was one of the rare occasions in his life when he had spoken the truth.

Then Matthew came sauntering up to them. 'Everything all right?'

'Fine, thank you,' said a thin-lipped Oliver. He didn't like the look in the Scotsman's eyes.

'This man,' said Grace, 'is trying to wriggle out of our deal.'

'Ah … Mrs T! That's where you're wrong. I'm not trying to wriggle out of anything. I'm just saying the Sheraton suite isn't worth what you thought it was.'

'Why?' barked Matthew.

'Because it's flawed. Look, I'll show you.' With that, he led Matthew and Grace into the van, indicated the table leaf and the chairs in question and stood, smirking, as Grace bent down to examine her dining-room suite for the first time in her life. Even her untrained eye told her that all was not quite right.

'So,' she said, rising to her feet. 'What does that mean?'

To his astonishment, Oliver Spink found himself feeling sorry for the woman. She was so patently obviously out of

112

her depth with criminals like himself – and so nice – that he hadn't the heart to reduce his offer by, as he had been intending, five thousand pounds. 'It means,' he said, 'that I'll have to make a reduction.'

'Of how much?'

'Three thousand.'

'One thousand,' interjected Matthew.

'Oh come on!' Oliver glared at the other man. He certainly didn't feel sorry for him. Didn't trust him either. He had encountered the type before. The type who seduced their employers, got them into all sorts of financial troubles but still, somehow, managed to hold the widows in thrall because the latter saw them as hunky bits of rough. Oliver knew all about rough. 'Two thou.'

'One thousand five hundred,' countered Matthew.

Oliver looked at Grace. 'Oh, all right then.' Then he laughed. 'You must have caught me on a bad day.'

'I really need twenty thousand,' said Grace.

Oliver looked at her. Her voice, like her hands, was shaking. 'I'm sorry,' he said. 'Eighteen thou. five hundred. That's my final offer.'

But Grace had calculated that twenty thousand was the very least she could accept. She needed at least two for the rest of the hydroponic equipment, another two for the equipment she had already bought on credit, three for the bills on her other credit cards, two for immediate bills, six for the outstanding mortgage payments and …'

'Unless,' said Oliver, interrupting her thoughts, 'there's anything else you can offer me?'

Grace looked down. 'No,' she said in a small voice. But she was looking down at her hands, and on her left hand her engagement ring caught a ray of sunshine and glinted up at her. She tried to pull it off.

'Grace!' protested a horrified Matthew. 'You can't do that?'

'Why not? I'm not married any more. I'm not engaged. And in the highly unlikely event that someone else is going to ask me to marry him, then I'll get another engagement ring, won't I?'

Oh dear, thought Oliver. That wasn't very subtle. And, he felt like saying aloud, if you want to keep this man, that's no way to go about it.

But Grace was still tugging at her ring. It had been used to being on her finger more or less constantly for twenty-five years and wasn't going to let go easily. But, eventually, Grace managed to dislodge it. 'There,' she said, thrusting it in Oliver Spink's face. 'That should get us back up to twenty thousand.' Sensing that Oliver was about to protest, she told him it was a Georgian heirloom.

'And how do I know that's true?'

'Because,' said Grace, 'of the way it's set.' She looked, without regret, at the ring. 'Unless you're really very stupid – and I don't think you are – you wouldn't ask any more questions. You would have to be *very* stupid,' she finished, 'to look a gift horse in the mouth.'

Oliver knew when he was beaten. He took the ring. A cursory glance told him it was probably worth five thousand pounds. 'Done,' he said. 'Twenty thou. for the lot.'

'Daylight robbery,' said Grace, watching as he extracted his chequebook. She knew she had been done and, in many respects, she didn't really care. But she did care about the ring. Not because she would mourn its absence – but because of Clare Trevethan. Clare who had married, aged forty, a pig farmer from Norfolk. Clare who had, like Grace, hoped for the children that had never materialised. Clare who, unlike Grace, had had the courage to take on foreign agencies and arcane customs and succeeded in adopting a child.

Grace had always intended to bequeath the ring to Clare. Years ago, she had realised that Clare's snobbery had been a front to disguise her shyness; that her rejection of Grace had been due to envy, and that her subsequent rejection of her entire family had been due to the misplaced notion that she had let them down. Grace had informed her of John's death and of the date of his funeral, but Clare had affected indifference, and so Grace had realised that any attempt to forge a friendship at this late date was doomed to failure. Clare clearly wanted nothing more to do with the Trevethans.

But Clare had always admired the Georgian ring and Grace had wanted to bequeath it to her. Now, that option was no longer open to her.

'You've done the right thing, Mrs T,' smirked Oliver Spink.

'Oh shut up,' said Grace, turning away.

Matthew looked at her in astonishment as she exited the van. Then, shooting a particularly nasty look at the removal man, he too left the van and followed Grace to her car.

'Are you okay?' he asked as she delved into the back seat for the electrical cable.

'Fine.' But Grace looked doubtful. 'Matthew?'

'Mmm?'

'Do you think I've made a horrible mistake?'

Matthew considered that one. 'No,' he said after a moment. 'Under the circumstances, you didn't really have much option.'

Grace watched as Oliver Spink's men closed the tailgate of the van. 'No,' she sighed. 'I didn't, did I?'

'So,' said Matthew, determinedly changing the subject. 'You got the cable?'

115

'Yes.'

'It's all systems go, then?'

'I think so.'

But that turned out not to be the case. Half an hour after entering the greenhouse, Grace discovered that she had underestimated the amount of fertiliser, that they would need more lights and that she hadn't enough garden hoses to suit their purposes. 'We'll have to go back to Wadebridge,' she said. 'There's no other way.'

'What about Jack's?' suggested Matthew.

Grace shook her head. 'These are specialist lights, Matthew. There's no way he'd have them.' Nor was there any way Grace was going back to Liac for her supplies. Far too close to home. Then she remembered her encounter with Nicky. 'Oh, Matthew, I nearly forgot.'

'What?'

'I ran into Nicky this morning. She was looking for you.'

'Eh? Why? I live with her. She knows where to find me.'

'Yes, well … Anyway, she asked if you would meet her in The Anchor at nine.'

Matthew shrugged. 'Sure.'

Grace fumbled in her pocket for her car keys. 'Look, Matthew, I know we swore we couldn't tell anyone about this, but I really think you ought to tell Nicky.'

'Why?'

Men, thought Grace, could be so dim. 'Because isn't not fair on her. Here you are, spending all day and half the night here – she's got every right to wonder what you're up to.'

'Is that what she said? She was "wondering what I was up to"?'

'No. She didn't say that at all. But I could read between the lines. Besides, it made me feel very uncomfortable having to lie to her.'

'About what?'

Grace sighed. 'She was going to come up here to look for you, so I panicked and told her you were out buying a transformer. For the electric fence.'

Matthew was lost. 'What electric fence?'

'Precisely. I had to lie to her, Matthew. It wasn't nice.' Grace reached in her pocket for her car keys. 'So I suggest we go to Wadebridge right now, come back and finish installing the equipment, and then you can go and meet Nicky and tell her the truth, all right?'

'Okay.'

SEVEN

Melvyn Stott had long been wondering if the time was right to tell the truth. Not that he had ever *lied* – he had just grown accustomed to being evasive when people asked questions. Especially people like Margaret and Diana in the post office. They were always probing, always asking when he would find a lovely Cornish lass to settle down with. It wasn't right, they said, that a nice young man like Melvyn should be all alone. But, at fifty, Melvyn could hardly be called young. And nor, for the past six months, had he been all alone. He had found someone with whom he was blissfully settled: not a lovely Cornish lass but a gorgeous, strapping Scandinavian with blonde hair, blue eyes, rippling biceps, a washboard stomach and a pert bottom which looked particularly fetching in skin-tight jeans.

He was wearing those jeans when Grace bumped into him in the garden centre outside Wadebridge. 'Sorry,' she said automatically. Then she looked up, realised she was in the presence of a Nordic god, and found herself blushing. The god stayed mute and motionless. Then he flashed Grace a smile of such brilliance that she felt weak at the knees. Grace told herself to get a grip and be on her way – but her trolley seemed to have forged a bond with that of the god. She tried to pull it away but it wouldn't budge. 'If you could just …' she began, nodding in the direction of the god's companion. 'If … Oh!'

For at that moment, the companion turned round, revealing himself to be none other than Melvyn Stott. Grace hadn't recognised him from behind. But then Melvyn Stott was usually clad in a sober suit; not jeans, a leather jacket and a baseball cap. 'Oh!' he said as well, blushing slightly. 'Grace.'

Grace didn't quite know what to think. Part of her was intrigued; but the part that hated lies wanted her to hurry on because she didn't want to talk to anyone from Liac; didn't want anyone to know that Matthew was in the adjacent aisle buying equipment that she couldn't possibly pass off as the components of an electric fence. Melvyn, of course, was absolutely the last person she wanted to meet here: he would want to know why she was spending hundreds of pounds on gardening supplies when she was over half a million pounds in debt.

Melvyn was also in two minds. One of them wanted to pass this off as a perfectly ordinary encounter. The other, rather more persistent one, suggested that Grace was extra-ordinarily interested in the six-foot scion of Norway pressed against him. No Wadebridge store attendant, this, her expression seemed to say.

'Er ... have you met my friend Tony?'

'No,' said Grace. 'Hello.'

The tall Norwegian bowed. 'My name is Tony. I'm from Scandinavia.'

'Oooh! Congratulations.' Grace turned to Melvyn, appraising him in a new light.

Embarrassed by the mischievous twinkle in her eyes, Melvyn turned to Tony. 'Um ... could you go and get one of those giant bags of kitty litter, Tony?'

Tony nodded gravely and walked away from them.

Grace and Melvyn watched him parade down the aisle.

'He … he, um, doesn't talk much,' said the latter.

Grace looked at the exquisite derriere and then, impishly, at Melvyn. 'Does he have to?'

Momentarily non-plussed, Melvyn fingered the amethyst brooch on his collar. As ever in times of crisis, he reverted to bank-manager mode. 'Grace … have you read the letter I sent you.'

'Um, no. I'm sorry, Melvyn. I haven't had time. I've been too busy working on a little plan.'

'Oh?' This was the sort of thing Melvyn wanted to hear.

'It's a bit soon to talk about it just now.' Grace offered a coy smile. 'I don't want to jinx it, you see.'

Perhaps this wasn't the sort of thing he wanted to hear after all. 'Look Grace,' sighed Melvyn. 'I really can't hold them off for much longer. It's gone up to head office now. They don't know you, Grace. All they see is a middle-aged woman with huge debts and … and no income.'

But rather than looking upset, Grace was grinning.

'What,' finished an exasperated Melvyn, 'are you going to *do*?'

Grace leaned closer. 'I'm becoming a drug dealer,' she whispered.

But that just made Melvyn cross. 'Grace,' he chided, 'I'm serious.'

Before Grace could reply, Tony reappeared, biceps rippling under the weight of an enormous bag of kitty litter. Melvyn beamed. 'Thank you, Tony.' Then, distracted by the rippling, he turned back to Grace. 'We really have to go now. Grace, you *will* phone me, won't you?'

'Yes. Righty-ho.'

Melvyn sighed. 'Come on, Tony.'

'Bye!' said Grace. Then, when the two men disappeared from view, she breathed an enormous sigh of relief. Melvyn hadn't asked why she was spending money she didn't have. Nor, thankfully, had he seen Matthew. Grasping the bar of her now-mobile trolley, she sped off down the aisle.

She found Matthew surrounded by coils of garden hose. 'Matthew!' she hissed.

'Oh, hiya. Where've you been?'

'You'll never guess!' Grace glanced covertly around to make sure they were alone. 'I've just run into Melvyn Stott ... and you'll never guess who he was *with*!'

Matthew shrugged. 'The six-foot Swede?'

'Wha ... how did you know?' Suddenly deflated, Grace was also slightly annoyed. If a secret was out, how come she hadn't known about it?

Matthew grinned at her expression. 'Nicky and I saw them walking along the beach together and, er ... they weren't exactly kicking a football around in a blokish sort of way.'

'Ooooh!'

'But,' added Matthew, 'I think it's still a secret.'

'Not now. Melvyn seemed a little embarrassed – but he didn't try to hide it.'

'Difficult to hide a six-food Swede in Wadebridge.'

'Actually,' corrected Grace, 'he's Norwegian.' Then she sighed. 'Poor Melvyn. As if anybody really cares what you get up to in private.'

Matthew shot her a warning look. 'Oh they do, Grace. Everybody cares. Everyone wants to know.' Then he looked down at the lengths of hose, the extra Gro-Lux lights and the vast quantities of fertiliser in Grace's trolley. 'And if anyone sees this, they're going to want to know what *you're* getting up to in private.'

'They won't see,' said Grace, supremely confident.

But Matthew's next words severely dented that

confidence. 'Er, Grace … how are you going to pay for this?'

'Oh.' Grace blinked. She hadn't thought about that. She forced a smile. 'I'm going to hand over my credit card and hope for the best. And you, Matthew, are going to cross your fingers and hope for the best.'

To their mutual astonishment, the best happened. But not before Grace nearly fainted from lack of oxygen, as she held her breath at the till while the credit card machine took forever to process her transaction. And she didn't dare look the cashier in the eye. She was back on a guilt trip; feeling like a criminal. And the cashier *knew*. She knew he knew.

'He knew,' she said to Matthew when they reached the sanctuary of the car-park.

'How knew what?'

'The cashier. I could tell from the way he looked at us. He knew we were up to something.'

'*Grace!* It's your imagination. Of course he didn't know. Nobody knows. You've got nothing to worry about.'

But Matthew knew. Back at Liac House, he became so engrossed in the hydroponic machinery that, like Grace, he lost all track of time.

Martin Bamford tried, and failed, to engage Nicky in conversation. 'Drink?' he offered when she entered the pub.

Looking distracted, Nicky shook her head. 'Not drinking.'

'Ah.' Martin remembered the pregnancy.

Nicky looked at her watch. Ten past nine. 'Matthew here yet?'

But the question answered itself. Save for Martin, Charlie and Harvey, the pub was deserted. And Harvey didn't really count. He was sitting at a table in the far corner, blowing smoke into a cup. Nicky knew what that meant.

'Soft drink?' suggested Martin.

'Oh ... yeah, why not? I'll have a coke, thanks.'

'Good.' Martin turned in his bar-stool. 'Coke, please, Charlie.'

'I heard.' Charlie reached under the counter for a bottle of coke.

'Quiet,' said Nicky, looking around.

'Yes. Join me?' Martin indicated the stool beside him.

'D'you mind if I don't, Martin? I've got ... well, I'm not feeling very sociable. And I really want to talk to Matthew alone.'

'But he's not here yet.'

'No. But he will be.' Nicky took her coke, thanked Martin and went to sit at a table in the corner.

Martin shrugged. He suspected Nicky had earmarked tonight as the right moment to tell Matthew about the baby. Although quite why she had to tell him in the pub rather than at home was something of a puzzler. Still, it was none of his business. He shrugged and pulled a book out of his jacket pocket.

Behind the bar, Charlie pursed his lips. Martin was deliberately – even ostentatiously – not talking to him. He thought it incredibly childish. But then Martin *was* incredibly childish sometimes. Tonight he was sulking because of Charlie's miles-off-the-mark tip for yesterday's race at Doncaster. And Charlie was annoyed – it wasn't as if he had been *riding* the bloody horse. But that didn't seem to have occurred to Martin.

Charlie looked around the pub. He supposed a stranger would find the atmosphere a little strange: four people, all of whom knew each other incredibly well, not talking to each

123

other. He supposed it *was* a little strange. But then Harvey and Nicky spent all day in each other's company: just because they happened to be in the same place of an evening was no reason why they should strike up a conversation. He looked over to Harvey: there was actually no reason to suppose they *could* strike up a conversation. Harvey was plastered.

Charlie turned his attention to Nicky. She had her back to him. That, he thought, really was strange. Nicky was normally so sociable. Obviously she had something on her mind: something she wanted to unburden to Matthew.

Charlie looked at his watch. Nine fifteen. He sighed. Then, unable to bear the silence any longer, he looked at Martin, head bowed over his book. 'Good book?'

Without replying or looking up, Martin showed him the cover.

'Ah,' said Charlie. '*Hollywood Wives*.'

But Martin's attention was firmly focussed on Jackie Collins and her shenanigans in La-La Land .

'I enjoyed *Being Dead*,' continued Charlie.

He might as well have been talking to a blank wall. He *was*, in fact, talking to a blank wall.

'Reading a Kafka at the moment,' he said. 'Not very funny. Except,' he mused, 'the story about the bloke who turns into a beetle. That's a bit wacky.'

Still without looking up, Martin sighed and took a slug of his beer. But Charlie was not to be deflected. 'Wouldn't get anyone turning into a beetle in Jackie Collins. Mind you, you might get someone *sleeping* with a beetle.' He pondered that one. 'Yes,' he said, now resigned to the fact that he was talking to himself. '*He wrapped her up in his stick-like arms,*' he imagined, ' *... all six of them. Then he tapped her sensuously on the head with ... with his wiggly wobbly ariel ...*'

'Oh for Christ's sake!' yelled Martin, finally looking up. 'Will you just *shut up*!'

But before the startled barman had a chance to reply, Nicky leaped to her feet, scraped back her chair and flounced towards the door. 'That's it,' she said, glaring at Charlie.

Charlie was more than a little non-plussed by this double assault. He had only been trying to make conversation – and not with Nicky.

Then he realised her anger wasn't directed at him. 'If he comes in now,' she said as shrugged into her jacket, 'tell him I left in a huff.'

Charlie grinned with relief. 'All right, love.' Yet, worried by how upset Nicky looked, he tried to reassure her. 'He's probably fast asleep on your couch at home.'

'Yeah. Yeah, you're right.' Nicky looked far from convinced. 'Bye, then,' she said, leaving the pub.

Silence prevailed for a moment. A silence broken, as usual, by Charlie. 'Where were we, then?'

'*We*,' said Martin, 'weren't anywhere. You were wittering in an extremely annoying fashion and I was ignoring you.'

'Oh. Well … are you going to talk to me now?'

Martin picked up his book. 'No.'

'Oh.'

Nicky wasn't worried: nor was she in a mere huff. She was extremely angry. Shoving her hands deep into the pockets of her jacket, she was on the point of stomping off down the hill to the cottage when she became aware of footsteps behind her. Hoping to see Matthew, she turned back towards the pub.

It wasn't Matthew. It was Harvey.

'Leaving already? She asked. 'Bit early for you, isn't it?'

In the darkness of the car park, Harvey had difficulty

focusing on Nicky. A difficulty that, in truth, had nothing to do with either the darkness or Nicky: everything to do with Harvey's general focusing abilities.

'Not leaving,' he mumbled. 'Just come out to take a leak.'

Nicky snorted. 'For heaven's sake, Harve, there's a loo in there, you know.'

'Not the same,' replied Harvey, fumbling with his flies. 'Better to do it outside. Call of nature. Best to be at one with nature.' Then he hiccuped, raised an arm in a salute and tottered off towards the low wall at the end of the car park.

Nicky watched him for a moment. Then she looked beyond him to the hill on the horizon. Liac House lay just behind that hill. Seething now, Nicky turned her back on Harvey and trudged down the hill. She looked at her watch again. Nine thirty. What could Matthew possibly be doing there at this time of night?

'It's going to be very, very bright,' said Grace.

'That's fine,' said Matthew. 'We want it to be bright, don't we?'

Grace looked around the greenhouse. It now bore no resemblance at all to a normal greenhouse – nor to a factory. It looked more like the set of the film *Alien*. There were tubes everywhere; great gurgling pipes, funnels full of hydroponic nutrient solution and cables criss-crossing the walls and the ceiling. Grace was slightly apprehensive about the latter: Matthew's knowledge of things electrical had indeed proved rudimentary. She looked up at the Gro-Lux lights and bit her lip. 'You're sure it'll be okay?'

''Course it'll be okay.'

Then Grace looked at the cannabis cuttings. It would have to be okay, she thought. Bathing the little plants in ferocious light every few hours was the only way to accelerate their growth. The existing lights weren't nearly powerful enough for what she hoped would soon be a happy hoard of hash.

'Right.' Grinning, Matthew pointed to the switch. 'You do the honours.'

Grace curtsied as Matthew picked up a screwdriver, pretending it was a microphone. 'It gives me great pleasure,' he boomed, 'to ask Dame Reggae-Spliff of Port Liac to switch on this year's illuminations!'

'Thank you.' Grace curtsied again to the audience of cannabis. 'Thank you.' Then she reached for the switch.

Down in the village below, Harvey's little bonding session with nature came in for a rude awakening. One minute he was happily relieving himself against the low wall, idly looking at the faint lights of sleepy Cornwall. The next he was blinking furiously at the blinding white flash illuminating the sky in front of him. 'Christ!' he yelled, instinctively shielding his eyes with both hands. Then he peeked through his fingers. The light was still there; an unearthly constellation of pure white beams, emanating from the hill at Liac.

'Shit,' breathed Harvey. 'Armageddon.' Then, vaguely sensing that something was amiss in the trouser department, he looked down. 'Shit, shit, shit!' Too late, he realised that communing with nature required the constant supervision of a guiding hand. 'Bugger!' he seethed, shaking one leg and hastily buttoning his flies.

Then he blinked at the light again. It was definitely not of this world. It was part of the omen: a man falls from the sky; Matthew loses his job; all the plants die; Armageddon. He was witnessing a Close Encounter of the Third Kind. Or perhaps the Fourth. He turned and ran back into the pub.

'Hey!' he yelled. 'You've gotta come outside. Something terrible's happening. Grace's house it all lit up. It's like a spaceship has landed … it's all glowing and white and other-worldly.' Wide-eyed with terror, he stared at Charlie and Martin. 'Grace,' he announced in apocalyptic tones, 'is being abducted by creatures from another planet!'

'Oh do shut up,' said Martin. 'Look at you; you're the one from another planet. Planet Alcohol.'

'No, really.' Harvey had been shocked into sobriety. 'There really is something there! Come and see.'

Martin raised a sceptical eye to Charlie. 'Do we believe him?'

Charlie shrugged. Believing Harvey was probably insane, but it was bound to prove more entertaining than not talking to Martin. 'Why not?'

'C'mon!' yelled Harvey. 'We've got to go and save Grace.'

Martin snorted in derision. 'Load of nonsense,' he said, following him out of the pub. Then, when they reached the car park, he snorted even more loudly. 'Well,' he said, sarcasm dripping from every syllable. 'Extra-terrestrials aren't what they used to be, are they? I wonder if Steven Spielberg knows that they can only afford forty-watt bulbs?'

He had a point. Where Harvey had been convinced he had seen the terrible blinding flash, there was now near-darkness, broken only by a few feeble pinpoints of light emanating, respectively, from the phone box on the outskirts of the village, Vivienne Hopkins' cottage, and the Vicarage.

'It was there … I swear it. It was a ….'

'… a blinding flash of light. Yes, yes, yes.' Martin turned back towards the pub. 'I suppose I ought to be jealous, really. There I was, admiring Jackie Collins' imagination when all the time I was in the presence of … *Jesus Christ*!' Almost blinded by the sudden flash, Martin stumbled and, fighting to regain his balance, fell against the wall. 'What in God's name …?

'I told you,' said Harvey, pointing. 'See?'

Martin slowly rose to his feet, vaguely wondering why the wall was damp on a dry night like this. Wiping his hands on his Jermyn Street trousers, he looked in amazement at the hill beyond. Harvey hadn't been exaggerating. Something was deeply amiss at Liac House.

'That's a lot of light,' said Charlie. 'Reminds me of that Peter Ackroyd book. Now, what was it called? *First Light*. Yes, I remember. It was all about the discovery of ...'

'Let's call the police!' interrupted Harvey. 'And the RAF. They'll want to be included.'

'No,' said a suddenly sombre Martin. An intelligent man, he had just put two and two together – and come up with something rather more prosaic than Close Encounters of the Fourth Kind. And he had just remembered Nicky's response to his query about the cannabis plants. Nicky had told him that Matthew had called in an expert. Shielding his eyes, Martin looked again at the comet-like lights. Yes, he thought, they were definitely coming from Liac House. And he would put money (more than the amount he had lost at Doncaster) on a bet that they came from the greenhouse.

'No,' he repeated. 'Let's just go back into the pub. There's ... er ... something I want to discuss with you two.'

A horrified Harvey rounded on him. 'Are you out of your fucking mind?' he screamed. 'We've gotta get up to the house. We've gotta save Grace.'

Martin held out a hand to restrain him. 'Er ... no. I, um, well I know what's going on up at the house.'

'Eh?' This from the flummoxed Charlie. 'What d'you mean?'

'Just come back inside,' said Martin.

'But Grace is going to die!'

'Harvey. The only thing Grace is in danger of dying of is

over-exposure to ultraviolet light. I can't think of anything else up there that might kill her. Unless you believe that an excess of dope can be fatal.'

'*What?*'

But Martin had retreated back into the pub. Harvey looked at Charlie. Charlie shrugged. Clearly Harvey wasn't going to get an answer unless he followed Martin indoors.

'Dope, you said?' asked Harvey when they reached the bar.

'Yes, Harvey. Grace is growing dope.'

'But Grace is ... well, she's a *widow*.'

'So? Widows can break the law as well, you know.' Martin knew a lot about widows. A large percentage of his patients were widowed – and a very large section of that percentage found that they bloomed rather than wilted in their new incarnation. Admittedly, few of them bloomed in the same way as Grace, but that was probably due to ignorance. 'Being widowed,' finished Martin, 'doesn't mean that you're condemned to knit pointless sweaters until you die of boredom.'

'No ... but, well ... Grace growing *dope*. I don't believe it.'

'This calls for serious measures,' said Charlie, reaching behind the bar.

'Of what?' Martin peered at the bottle Charlie was uncapping. 'Lagaboollen. Oh *good*.'

Charlie looked in reverence at the amber liquid. 'Nothing like a classic malt.'

Harvey, however, was far more interested in Grace than in whisky. 'How do you know? How can you be so sure that she's growing cannabis?'

Martin shrugged. 'Oh ... I've seen lights like that in Amsterdam. Er ... years ago. When I was on a medical study.'

'Studying what?'

'Oh … something medical.'

'Right.' Harvey wasn't really interested in medical studies – but he was riveted by Grace's supposed new occupation. 'So, let's get this clear. Grace is growing dope – huge amounts of dope – in order to please Matthew?'

'I guess that was the original idea. But from what Matthew's been saying, from putting two and two together, and from what we saw tonight then, no, I think she's got other ideas.'

'Like what?'

'Oh come on, Harvey! You saw the lights. She must be growing vast quantities. However much she may like the stuff herself, no dope-head is going to …'

'… did you ever try the stuff yourself?' asked Charlie, pouring the malt.

Martin coughed. 'Er … once. At university. Didn't inhale of course.'

'Of course.'

'Like Clinton,' said Harvey.

'Yes.'

'He didn't impale, either.'

'Eh?' Irritated, Martin looked at Harvey. 'What are you on about?'

'Monica Lewinsky.'

Martin's lip curled in disgust. 'Don't be so revolting, Harvey.'

'But why,' asked Charlie, returning to Grace and the lights, 'is she growing it?'

'Distribution? I don't know. Remember, Grace is hard up, she wants to keep her house.' Martin sipped his whisky. 'I say! Jolly good stuff, Charlie.'

'Are you actually talking to me?'

'Of course.'

'Good. About time too.' Charlie grinned and poured a hugely generous measure for himself. 'Kind of warms the heart, doesn't it?'

'What? Conversation? The whisky?'

Charlie smiled. 'No. The fact that Grace is carrying on the local tradition of complete and utter contempt for the law.'

'The law? Who mentioned the law?' Sergeant Alfred Mabely, with his knack for appearing in the right place at the wrong time, came striding through the door. He looked in disapproval at the three men – especially at Charlie, who was standing with his customers at the bar, holding a bottle of whisky.

'Ah, Sergeant,' said Martin 'All right?'

Alfred nodded. 'You're on the wrong side of the bar, Charlie. It contravenes the licensing act to serve from there.'

Charlie was nothing if not quick. 'I'm not technically serving, Sergeant.'

'No?'

'No. We're ... we're having a private party.'

Alfred looked at his watch.

'Early closing. We closed early to have a private party.' Charlie raised the bottle of malt. 'Care to join us?'

Alfred sighed. 'Oh ... just a small one, then.'

Charlie poured him a large one.

Alfred sipped and nodded in appreciation. 'Anyone noticed those lights up at Liac House?' he asked suddenly.

'No!' The three denials were immediate, simultaneous and vehement.

'No, no,' repeated Martin, slowly shaking his head. 'Haven't seen any lights. How's your car, Sergeant?' he added, failing to sound casual.

'Any luck with those poachers?' asked Charlie, also failing in the same endeavour.

The policeman looked reflectively over the rim of his glass. 'Oh, I'll get them. It's just a matter of time. Crime never pays.'

'I should think not,' said an indignant Martin Bamford. 'Never.'

It was well past ten o'clock by the time Matthew returned to the cottage. Slightly tired, he was also supremely elated. Somehow he had managed to coax the fuse box back into life, and he had left Grace secure in the knowledge that the timers would, from now on, automatically ensure that the greenhouse was bathed for much of the night in the sort of light normally reserved for celestial manifestations. He had also left her wearing sunglasses.

'Nicky?' he said, closing the cottage door behind him. The door led straight into the sitting room, and a cursory glance told Matthew that it was empty. He craned his neck round the partition wall. She wasn't in the kitchen either. Upstairs was the only other option. Matthew frowned. Nicky didn't normally go to bed this early. That meant she was probably stripping wallpaper. And if Nicky was stripping wallpaper at this hour that, in turn, meant she was in a bad mood.

Then Matthew remembered her request to meet in the pub. 'Shit!' he said to himself, and bounded upstairs.

'Nicky?' He stood in the tiny landing that led to the only bedroom and the tiny bathroom. Nicky was in the former, standing halfway up a ladder, wielding a stripping knife with alarming force. Shreds of dark blue wallpaper lay scattered on the floor.

'Where have you been?' she asked without looking round.

'Nowhere.'

Nicky sighed. 'What have you been up to?'

'Nothing.'

Nicky nodded. 'Well, I'm glad we got that cleared up.'

The sarcasm wasn't lost on Matthew. He walked towards the ladder. 'Sorry. I was working up at the house. I lost track of time.'

Nicky still didn't look at him.

'Sorry,' he repeated.

Nicky climbed down the ladder. 'I waited for ages in the pub. Didn't Grace tell you?' She spoke very deliberately, with no trace of accusation in her voice.

That, Matthew knew, meant trouble. 'She did. I was really, *really* busy. I'm really, *really* sorry.'

Nicky couldn't help grinning. At last she looked at him. He looked like a naughty boy who had been caught playing truant. More importantly, he didn't look as if he had a guilty, shaming secret. If anything, he looked excited. She stepped forward and pecked him on the cheek.

'Look,' he said, taking her by the shoulders. 'I've got something to tell you.'

'Good. 'cos I've got something to tell you too.' Nicky stepped back and sat on the edge of the bed. 'Sit down.'

Matthew *was* excited. Grace had been right; it wasn't fair to keep their activities a secret from Nicky. Anyway, she would be thrilled about the money. It would mean that Matthew wouldn't have to leave St Liac to find work.

'Let me tell you my thing first,' he pleaded. ''Cos it's really quite good.'

Nicky smiled. 'So's mine.'

'Right, you go first, then.'

'No.' Nicky laughed at Matthew's over-eager expression. 'You go first.'

'All right.' Matthew took her hands in his and looked into

her eyes. 'I've moved all the plants up to Liac House. We're gonna grow them up there really, really quickly. See ... there's this special way of growing them. It's called hydroponics.' Matthew rushed on, failing to notice that Nicky's expression had changed. 'You know how Grace is a really good gardener? Well, it's gonna get us out of all our money problems.'

Nicky stiffened. 'Us?'

'Yeah ... me and Grace. It's perfect, Nicky. And it's so simple. The first crop'll be about twenty kilos ... we sell it, and anything we make over what she needs to pay her debts we split fifty-fifty.' Then Matthew noticed the way Nicky was looking at him. He squeezed her hands. 'Look, I know it's extreme, but it's *smart*. I don't want to leave here to get work, and this way I get to stay.'

Nicky pulled away. 'Until, that is, you go to jail.'

'I'm not going to *jail*.'

'Matthew, smoking weed is one thing – large scale cultivation is another.' She shook her head. 'I'm surprised at Grace. It's really stupid.'

Matthew was more than a little surprised at Nicky. And annoyed. 'It's *not* really stupid. It's really smart. Of course, I bet you'd think differently if it was *your* idea.'

Nicky looked at him as if seeing him for the first time. 'Yeah,' she drawled. 'Yeah, you're right. When you're being chased around your prison cell by a sixteen-stone bank robber with a stiffy, I'll be sitting in here thinking "why couldn't it have been me? Why couldn't I have had that brilliant idea?" Christ, Matthew,' she continued, 'you've been bleating on about how unhappy you are. About losing your job. And what's your solution? *Crime*,' she spat.

Matthew reacted as if he had been slapped.

But Nicky hadn't finished. 'You'll get in deeper and you'll drag Grace down with you.'

'Nicky ....'

'Matthew, you are such an *idiot*.'

They locked eyes again, across the chasm that had brutally replaced their intimacy.

Then Matthew shrugged. 'What's your news, then?'

Nicky looked down. 'Nothing. It doesn't matter.'

EIGHT

St Liac soon became used to Grace's lights. People like Martin who knew exactly why they were there spent much of their time disabusing the ignorant amongst them of the notion that anything was wrong. There weren't, in truth, many people who didn't know what Grace was growing in her greenhouse. Diana and Margaret didn't know, but seemed happy with the idea that Grace was growing a special Himalayan tea. Vivienne Hopkins didn't know, but assumed that Grace was pulling out all the stops for the W.I. tea party. Gerald Percy didn't know either but he suspected the lights only existed in his imagination; relentlessly tormenting his sleep; torturing his soul. The Almighty was finally exacting his revenge against Gerald for all those nights when he had willingly lain awake, invoking all manner of spine-tingling ghouls and ghosties.

After three nights of the imaginary lights, Gerald could stand it no longer. Telling himself they *had* to be real, he made one of his midnight flits through the woods to Liac House, and crept towards the greenhouse. When he returned to the Vicarage, it was with a spring in his step and a weight off his mind. The lights, he thanked God, were real. Gerald had never realised you needed so many to cultivate marijuana.

It didn't occur to Grace that the lights might be the talk of the neighbourhood. No-one mentioned them to her, and she, naturally, didn't mention them to anyone else. As far as she was concerned, they were her and Matthew's secret. And, of course, Nicky's. She never asked Matthew what Nicky's reaction had been to the cannabis crop; just assumed that she felt the same way as Matthew did. But she always asked Matthew how Nicky was and every day Matthew said 'fine' and Grace said 'good' and then they went back to tending their plants.

Matthew didn't want to tell Grace that his relationship with Nicky was slowly dying; that every night he got home later and Nicky rose correspondingly earlier and, as a result, they barely saw each other. To ease his pain, Matthew repeatedly told himself that their venture would soon be over; that they'd have their first crop within a week and the final harvest before the end of the month.

He wasn't fooling himself about that. Under hydroponic cultivation, the plants were growing at a dizzying rate. Matthew and Grace took cutting after cutting, grew them with light and water, and watched as they obligingly sprouted buds. Buds which, in turn, blossomed and bloomed. Grace was delighted, and swore that she would join the campaign to legalise cannabis. Not, she had to admit, because she had particularly strong feelings about its use as a drug. She just thought the plants were terribly pretty.

So life, for Grace, was looking up. Most of the time she forgot she was more than half a million pounds in debt, and when she was reminded of the fact, she dealt promptly and briskly with the reminders. Martin Stott's came in the form of letters – and they went straight into the bin. The more alarming ones came by telephone from Rampton's Head Office; from a man called Quentin Rhodes. Initially, Grace dealt with him by pretending to be a Chinese maid. Subsequently – and rather more effectively – she coped with his demands by not answering the phone. At all.

Grace was feeling so upbeat about life that she even found herself reassessing her feelings about John. She was glad about that: it had been difficult reconciling his status as a complete bastard with the fact that she had been married to him for nearly twenty-five years. If John had been a truly terrible man, that didn't reflect terribly well on her. No, she thought: latterly, John had been a very stupid man. He had made mistakes and compounded them with other mistakes. His business methods may have been flawed, but his intentions, surely, had been honourable.

But there were two things Grace could not forgive him for. One was the lawn mower. The other she banished from her mind. Nevertheless, she began to visit his grave again; going for long, bracing walks along the clifftops and then turning back to the graveyard on the promontory with a handful of wild flowers to lay on his tombstone.

It was probably inevitable – and cruelly appropriate – that the subject she had banished from her mind should return to haunt her in the graveyard. Nearly a week after Grace's lights became the topic of conversation in Liac, Grace opened the gate of the churchyard, dutifully closed it again behind her, and headed towards John's grave. She was surprised to find that she wasn't alone: even more surprised to see that the other mourner seemed embarrassed to be found there. The woman took one look at Grace and hurried towards the gate at the rear. Then Grace realised why. There was a fresh bunch of flowers already on John's grave. She closed her eyes, willing herself to recapture the fleeting figure on the day of John's funeral. Then she opened them again. It was the same figure – fleeing this time. Not even thinking about what she was doing, Grace called out to her.

'Honey Chambers?'

The woman hesitated.

'44 Wilberforce Street?'

Slowly, the woman turned round. The dramatic, turban-like headscarf was as Grace remembered. So were the sunglasses behind which she hid. But this time Grace wanted to see her.

'London SW3?' Grace finished, slowly walking towards the other woman.

Honey Chambers looked like a rabbit caught in car headlights. Her stance told Grace she wanted to bolt. Her intuition *was* to bolt. But she couldn't. She was rooted to the spot. As Grace approached, Honey reached up and took off her sunglasses. Grace wondered fleetingly if she was an actress. There was something studied about the gesture; something dramatic and rehearsed. Then Honey took a few steps towards her and Grace looked into her eyes. They were dark brown, almost black. And, thought Grace, as impenetrable as the sunglasses.

'He had me post his letters,' said Grace. She's older than I thought, she said to herself. In her forties. But very well-preserved. And very expensive-looking.

And her voice, when at last she spoke, was rich as well. Confident and quite deep. Actressy, thought Grace. But she obviously hadn't rehearsed this line. Grace's words had taken her completely by surprise.

'I ... I never got any letters,' she said.

Grace raised her eyebrows.

'Oh,' said Honey, realising.

What, thought Grace, happens next?

What happened next was that Grace found herself asking Honey to come back to Liac House for a drink.

Grace began to feel that she was two people. One of them was sat in the passenger seat of Honey Chambers' Mercedes convertible, politely giving directions to Liac House. That person smiled a polite acknowledgement at Honey's declaration that the house was magnificent, ushered her through the front door, made a few inconsequential remarks about the interior of the house (not noticing Honey's surprise at the paucity of furniture), invited her to sit down at the kitchen table and asked if red wine was all right because the only white she had was the vicar's potato wine which was, basically, undrinkable.

The other Grace said *what am I doing?* and tried not to look too hard at Honey; at the sleek bobbed hair, the sensuous mouth and the fashionable clothes with their perfect accessories. It was only after two glasses of wine that the two Graces met each other, took a proper look at Honey and realised that while she was intimidatingly elegant, she was just as uneasy as Grace.

The truth was that Honey Chambers had been so wrong-footed by Grace that she was in far greater need of the wine. Here she was, in Grace's stunningly beautiful house, accepting Grace's hospitality, trying to pretend that this was an ordinary social situation and not a fateful encounter between John Trevethan's wife and a mistress who, if Grace's covert scrutiny was anything to go by, had already been dismissed as a superannuated trollop. Honey felt horribly ill-at-ease in her smart London clothes, being granted a brief glimpse of the side of John's life that he had never let her see. The part of his life that she knew had been more important to him than anything else.

Grace had surprised her. She had expected a frump, not an extremely pretty woman not much older than herself. A woman radiating good health and confidence and who,

Honey suspected, was being so frightfully nice because she wanted to lull Honey into a false sense of security before ripping her to shreds. It was only after two glasses of wine that she realised Grace was spouting niceties because she couldn't think of anything to say.

Steeling herself, Honey made the first move. 'Look,' she said, 'this is all a bit … unusual.'

'I'll say.' Grace didn't mean to sound sharp. She had meant to imply that she was floundering just as much as Honey was.

Honey took a deep breath. 'Why did you ask me here, Grace?'

'I … I don't know.' Grace brushed a strand of hair from her forehead. 'I really don't know.' Then she took another sip of wine. 'Why did you agree to come?'

Honey grinned. 'I don't know.' She looked closely at Grace. 'Curiosity?'

'Yes. Yes, I suppose that's it. I knew about you – you knew about me. I suppose it's only natural that if we met we would be … curious. Why did you come to the funeral?' she added suddenly.

Honey spread her hands in front of her. 'I don't know – but I wish I hadn't. When I saw you there, surrounded by all those people who were part of your and … well, your life … I felt I shouldn't have come.'

'No,' said Grace. 'You shouldn't.'

'I'm sorry.'

The two women looked at each other over the table. Honey noticed the white band of flesh on Grace's finger where there should have been a ring. Grace noticed Honey's expensive jewellery.

'Nice address, SW3,' said Grace. 'Chelsea, isn't it?'

Honey sighed. 'I know what you're thinking: and you're

wrong. John never gave me a penny. I have my own money. Quite a lot, actually.'

'In the business, are you?'

'*What?*' Honey recoiled in horror.

Grace, too, was horrified. 'I didn't mean that … I *really* didn't mean that. I meant are you an actress? That's what they say, isn't it? They call it "the business"?'

Honey laughed. 'I don't know. No, I'm not an actress. I'm an interior designer.'

'Oh. Nice.'

'Yes.'

'I'm a gardener,' said Grace, gesturing to the window where the greenhouse abutted the kitchen. Too late, she realised her mistake.

'Goodness,' said Honey, admiring the endless rows of cannabis plants. 'You most certainly *are* a gardener.' Then she frowned. 'What sort of plants are they?'

'Orchids. Rare orchids.' Grace looked in desperation through the window. '*Very* rare orchids.'

'Oh.' Honey lost interest in a polite sort of way. 'I know nothing about plants.'

Thank God, thought Grace. Then she looked back at Honey and giggled.

Honey looked uneasy again. 'Why are you laughing?'

'Because it's so ridiculous, isn't it? You and me sitting here, drinking wine together when … when …' Grace leaned back in her chair. 'When what I really want is for you to tell me about you and John.'

'Are you sure?'

Grace nodded.

So Honey told her. She told her how they had met in the Tate Gallery ('The London one,' she said, acknowledging the existence of the Cornish branch); how they had struck up a conversation; how the conversation had led to a drink, drink to dinner and … well … that it was more of a companionship than anything else.

'Yes,' said Grace, looking wistful. 'That's what the letters said.'

Honey was dying to know about the letters but had the sense not to ask.

'The Tate Gallery,' said Grace, reflecting. 'I never really shared that with John – his love of art. He was very knowledgeable about paintings, you know. And furniture.'

'Ye-es.' Honey remembered that John had told her Liac was crammed with antiques. But it wasn't. Not now. 'Look,' she said. 'I hope you don't mind me asking, but this house seems a little … well, empty. Of furniture.'

Grace sat bolt upright. 'Oh! Yes. Yes. I … um, well, I had to sell some of it.'

Honey was intrigued. 'But I thought John was wealthy?'

'Oh he *was*. But he died … he died at a very unfortunate time. His affairs were all over the place, I was in the middle of setting up a business and, what with probate taking so long and all that, I needed to raise some cash.' Grace realised she was beginning to hyperventilate again, feeling like a criminal. In time, she supposed, she would get used to it.

'What sort of business?' asked Honey.

'Smug … er, export. Exporting orchids. Rare orchids. Very rare orchids.'

'You must be very gifted,' said Honey, meaning it.

'No, not really.' Grace was feeling slightly desperate again. It was nearly dark outside: the Gro-Lux lights would come on soon and she didn't want Honey to see the greenhouse lit up like a spaceship. On the other hand, she wanted to know more about this woman. She was intriguing. Even more intriguing was Grace's realisation that she was beginning to like Honey. And that was wrong. She should hate this woman.

'Do you have any children?' she asked, meaning 'do you have children by John?' and thereby kindling hatred. But even as she asked the question, she knew the answer.

'I'm not very maternal, I'm afraid.'

'I couldn't have any,' said Grace.

Honey looked up. 'No, I know.'

'Gosh, you know a lot.'

'I don't, really. I only ever knew the … the basics of John's life.' Honey regretted the words as soon as she had uttered them. It made Grace sound like a basic: like a washing machine or a sink.

'Well … talking of basics,' replied Grace. 'Can I ask you another question?'

Honey shrugged. 'If you want.' Suspecting she knew what was coming, she replenished both their glasses.

'How did you cope with sex?'

'Sex?'

'Yes. Sex.'

Honey bowed her head. She knew Grace had been dying to ask, and she supposed she shouldn't have been so disingenuous as to expect Grace to believe that it had all been about companionship.

'Sex?'

'Yes,' said Grace. 'Sex.'

Honey's lips twitched. She took a sip of wine to try to disguise her smile. She failed. 'It was a nightmare,' she said.

Grace's expression was unfathomable.

Honey couldn't help it. She giggled. 'It was so exhausting!'

Then Grace, too, started to chuckle. 'Oh God, it was so frustrating! Talk about flogging a dead horse!' She put a hand to her lips. Really, she thought, she shouldn't be talking about this. She shouldn't be laughing with her husband's mistress about John's lack of …

Then she saw that she wasn't laughing with Honey at all. Honey wasn't looking remotely amused any more. She was looking at Grace with a mixture of guilt, shame and pity.

Grace's hand was trembling as she picked up her wine glass. 'No,' she said, almost inaudibly. 'It wasn't like that, was it?'

Honey shook her head and looked away. 'No. Not really.'

Suddenly Grace needed to know. She didn't know why: she knew it would hurt her – but something in her needed to know. 'What did you do, then?'

Acutely embarrassed now, Honey shook her head. 'Look, I really don't think we should be talking about this …'

'No. Please. I'd … I'd like to know.'

Honey looked across the table. Why was Grace doing this, she wondered? Why was she insisting on hurting herself? 'I …' But she, Honey, couldn't do it. She shook her head again.

'I'd like you to tell me,' said Grace.

Honey leaned back in her chair. 'Ice cream,' she sighed.

'Pardon?' Grace didn't understand. 'What did you say?'

'Ice cream. I … I sucked it from his fingertips. It drove him wild.' Honey couldn't stop herself smiling at the memory. 'I had to pretend to pass out to get any rest at all. He was insatiable.'

Grace blanched and fiddled nervously with the collar of her shirt.

Honey coughed. 'I think,' she said as she leaned forward again, 'he thought you weren't interested.'

Grace wondered if she was visibly shrinking into her seat. It certainly felt like it; as if half of her was disappearing. 'He was wrong,' she said in a small voice.

Honey couldn't look her in the eye any more. She glanced around the kitchen, desperately searching for something; anything to say. 'It's a beautiful house.'

'Yes,' said Grace automatically. 'I … I think I'd like you to leave now.'

Honey nodded. But she couldn't leave Grace looking as she did. 'He did love you, you know,' she said in a clumsy attempt to alleviate Grace's misery.

Grace took another sip of wine. 'Don't patronise me.'

Honey nodded. It was a fair comment. But she did genuinely want to help Grace. 'Look,' she sighed. 'If you ever want to talk …

'Yes. I know the address.'

Honey knew a firm dismissal when she heard one. She rose to her feet and reached for the scarf. Grace continued to stare at the chair she had vacated. '44 Wilberforce Street.'

Head bowed, Honey left the room.

'London,' said Grace. 'SW3.'

NINE

Grace looked at the cannabis cutting in her hand and wondered if the drug would help her sleep. She certainly didn't want a repeat of last night when she had lain in bed, a stranger to sleep, bombarded by visions of John, Honey, fingertips and ice cream. Companionship, she had thought. So that was what companions did with each other: lick ice cream from their fingertips. She had made a mental note to remind herself of that, should she ever find a companion. The sheer improbability of such an eventuality had made her laugh. At least that was what she had initially thought she was doing. It took her a few minutes to realise she was actually sobbing inconsolably because of the terrible, aching loneliness and the realisation that she had indeed been married to a bastard. In the end, utterly exhausted, she had cried herself to sleep.

In the morning, Grace woke up with a blinding headache, a depression that began to lift as soon as she saw the sunshine, and vowed to herself that life was going to get better. It had to: yesterday she had hit rock bottom. And she hadn't liked it there. Yet, an hour after Matthew arrived, and when they were well into the day's hydroponic cultivation of cannabis, Grace began to feel exhausted again. Maybe marijuana was the answer; maybe it would help her sleep. And even if it didn't, it was high time she acquainted herself with the legendary medicinal properties of the drug. She cupped the cutting in her hand and turned to Matthew.

'Matthew?'

'Mmm?'

'Will you give me one?'

Matthew nearly dropped the watering can. He was glad he had his back to Grace and that she couldn't see his expression. It was that of a startled animal. Perhaps, he said to himself, he hadn't heard correctly.

But he had.

'I want to know what it feels like.' There was no mistaking the coquettish little ring to her voice.

Matthew's heart sank. Then he wondered if he had been wilfully stupid; deliberately ignoring the signs. He made a rapid mental inventory – and didn't like what he saw. Grace weeping in his arms; Grace not reminding him of his appointment with Nicky; Grace continually saying she didn't know where she'd be without him. Grace basically altering her whole lifestyle so that she could spend all day and half the night with him.

'*Please*,' she said.

Matthew sighed, put the watering can back on the table and drew himself to his full height. He supposed he was partly to blame. He had made no secret of the fact that he loved being with Grace. And she was, after all, only human (Matthew meant female), and had made the natural assumption that he loved her.

Oh boy, he said to himself. This is going to be really, really difficult. 'Um … Grace …' he began, still with his back to her.

The Grace touched him in the shoulder. The gesture was easy. Familiar. Intimate. Matthew stiffened.

'I mean,' said Grace. 'If I'm growing it and selling it, I really should know the effect it has. Don't you think?'

Matthew nearly collapsed onto the trestle table.

'Are you all right?'

'Yeah, yeah … fine. Lost my footing, that's all. Sighing with relief, Matthew turned and beamed at Grace.

Goodness, she thought. He really is *terribly* attractive. She wondered why she had never noticed before. A handsome couple, she thought. Matthew and Nicky.

'Anyway,' she said, looking down at the cutting in her hand. 'I just thought it would be a good idea. Makes sense, don't you think?'

'Yeah. Perfect sense.' Matthew reached into the pocket of his boiler suit for his tobacco tin. ''Course you should know what it feels like.' Aware of the sudden rush of blood to his head, he hoped he wasn't blushing. How *embarrassing*, he thought. Trying to dismiss all thoughts of Grace as sex-starved widow, he opened the tin and extracted his cigarette papers, his tobacco and the small lump of dope that he had told Martin he didn't have. It was for emergencies only.

Grace looked on in horror as he started to roll a joint. 'No!' she gasped. 'Not in here!'

'Eh? Why not?'

Grace leaned close to him. 'Someone might *see*!'

'Grace!' In a sweeping gesture, Matthew indicated their cannabis nursery. By his calculations, there were already in excess of five hundred plants.

'Oh I know,' said Grace, easily dismissing the potential for a five-year jail sentence. 'But nobody knows what they *are*. But if you light up here, somebody might come and then they'd smell it wouldn't they? I'm not daft, you know,' she added with a conspiratorial grin. 'I know you can smell it a mile off.'

Matthew cast his mind back to the numerous occasions when he had been sitting on the lawn mower, chatting to

Grace and smoking a joint. Wisely, he forbore to mention that to her. 'Okay,' he shrugged, closing the tobacco tin. 'If you want to go outside – we'll go outside.'

'Come on , then!' Grace grabbed her jacket and walked briskly out of the greenhouse. Matthew didn't know whether to laugh or cry when he saw her heading towards her car.

'Grace,' Matthew said ten minutes later. 'Where exactly are we going?'

'Pentyre.'

'*What?* Why?'

'Because no-one will see us there.' Grace gunned the protesting engine and then switched down into third.

'But Pentyre's ten miles away!'

'Exactly.' Grace thought her plan eminently sensible.

Matthew groaned and leaned back in the cramped passenger seat. Grace really was a mass of contradictions, he thought. Happy to grow cannabis by the hundred-weight in her greenhouse; terrified to be seen smoking it. Still, Pentyre was beautiful; great rocky cliffs leading like giant steps down to one of the most glorious beaches in North Cornwall. Given that you had to be fairly fit to trudge back up the cliffs, it was a safe bet that the beach would probably be deserted.

It was – but still Grace panicked.

'Look, Grace,' said Matthew when they had nearly walked down to sea level. 'There's no-one around.' This was indubitably true. There was nobody on the beach; they hadn't encountered a soul on their way down and there were no walkers on the headland. There wasn't even a trawler in sight.

Matthew sat on a grassy knoll and patted the ground beside him. 'Calm down, relax. It's safe here,' he assured Grace.

'Sure?'

'Sure.'

Grace sighed and sat down. 'Oh well, might as well get this over and done with.'

Grinning, Matthew rolled a spliff.

Admiring his dexterity, Grace asked if he smoked a lot.

'Not really,' he mused. 'Couple a day, maybe?'

'Does it help you sleep?'

'Yeah. Definitely.' Matthew could swear by that. Then he looked at Grace in concern. 'Why? Aren't you sleeping?'

'Not very well. Sometimes. Well, you know ...' Grace trailed into silence. She wasn't going to tell Matthew about John and Honey. She wasn't going to tell anyone. That was all in the past. Firmly in the past.

'Well ...' Matthew handed her the joint. 'Try this. All your worries will just ... go up in smoke.'

Grace grinned. Then, as she took the joint, Matthew saw the flicker of doubt. Go on,' he urged. 'Just pretend it's a cigarette.'

Grace knew she was good at pretending. Inhaling deeply, she let the smoke filter deep down into her lungs, let it sit here for a moment and then watched it waft in the sea breeze as she slowly expelled it.

Matthew expected her to cough. Grace, however, was expecting something far more exciting.

It didn't happen. After a few seconds she looked at the joint between her fingers and turned to Matthew. 'Nothing,' she said with a shrug. 'Can't feel a thing.'

Matthew smiled. Grace of the quick fix. 'Give it time,' he said. Then, 'Hey!' He looked in alarm as Grace took another drag, inhaling so deeply that the end of the joint began to crackle. 'Hey, hey, hey! Slow down!' He reached out for it, waited for it to cool down and then put it to his own lips.

Grace exhaled and watched him, wondering if she had been doing it right. But Matthew seemed to do exactly the same as she had done and looked for all the world as if he were smoking an ordinary cigarette. As he exhaled, he looked out to sea, then closed his eyes. He looked the picture of contentment.

Grace was itching for another go, but wasn't sure of the etiquette. Did one ask – or was one offered?

Matthew answered the unspoken question by handing her the joint again. Determined that she too would look contented, she took a feverish drag. Nothing happened. She turned, disappointed, to Matthew. 'It's not working.'

'Just wait.'

Grace looked suspiciously at the joint. A new, rather worrying thought had just occurred to her. 'It's not addictive, is it?'

Matthew coughed and shook his head. 'No. It's not crack.'

Grace handed it back to him. 'Are you absolutely sure this works?'

He grinned. 'Oh yes. It works.'

Grace watched him smoking. Maybe her metabolism was just different, she thought. Maybe it affected some people and not others. She looked out to sea. Even though the dope wasn't affecting her, it was difficult not to feel mellow. There was something so satisfying about the sound of the waves crashing against the rocks below; something so rewarding about looking at the azure sky and the little white clouds drifting lazily by. She loved Cornwall. She loved it with a passion. No matter that she had been married to a Cornish bastard, she still adored her adopted county. Smiling contentedly, she looked round at Matthew. She adored him as well, she decided. Not with passion, of course. The thought made her want to giggle. Then she leaned further towards him. Still staring straight ahead, seemingly beyond the horizon, he was unaware that she was studying his profile.

Grace blinked. There was something really peculiar about Matthew's profile, something she had never noticed before. For the life of her she couldn't think what it was. She frowned. There was something really peculiar about Matthew as a whole. Then she remembered what it was. This time she couldn't help herself. She started to giggle.

Matthew turned round. What enormous pupils he has, thought Grace. That was probably because he was peculiar. She giggled again.

'What?' said Matthew, grinning widely.

'Nothing.' Grace tried to control herself. 'Nothing. Nothing at all. It's just that ...'

'What?' Matthew looked completely bemused. 'What is it?'

Grace couldn't decide if Matthew sounded paranoid or just amused. And that, in itself, was highly amusing. She laughed at him. Then, feeling guilty, she put a hand to her mouth. Her eyes, however, were dancing with merriment.

'What *is* it,' asked Matthew.

Grace hadn't realised how funny Matthew looked when he was puzzled. 'It's you,' she said.

Matthew handed her the joint and looked at her in a lopsided sort of way. Grace decided she might as well take it because you never knew: it might start to have some effect if she tried hard enough.

'You ...' she began. 'You're ... you're ...'

'What?'

Grace screamed with laughter. 'You're Scottish!'

Matthew grinned. So, he thought. It works. 'Er ... thanks,' he said.

But Grace was off. She could hardly smoke because she was shaking so much and, inhaling again, she began to splutter. That, too, was hysterical. She howled, passed the joint back to Matthew and collapsed against the rock behind her.

Matthew began to laugh as well as Grace wiggled her wellies in the air. Then he, too, howled because he had just had a vision of Grace at a W.I. tea party, stoned out of her tree.

'Oh God!' screamed Grace. 'It's really not funny, is it?'

'No!' roared Matthew, collapsing as well.

'Feeling any better?' asked Matthew over his shoulder.

A little moan floated up to him.

Matthew nodded to himself. Then he turned back to the sea and shaded his eyes against the sun. It was lower, much lower in the sky than when they had arrived. He looked at his watch and realised with a start that they had now been at Pentyre for three hours. The first two had been a riot: the last he had spent in peaceful, solitary contemplation while Grace had gone for a 'little lie down.'

Behind him, Grace tried to get up. Then she realised she couldn't because her feet had stopped working. She moaned again, rested her head back against the grass, closed her eyes and tried to cast her mind back to the few occasions in her life when she had been drunk. What sort of idiotic behaviour had her drunkenness induced, she wondered? She vaguely remembered feeling happy and being a bit silly – but not *that* silly. She also remembered that the hangovers had been pretty nasty – but nothing as catastrophic as this. Her head was thundering, as if someone was pressing large objects – wardrobes, perhaps – against her eyeballs. And she felt incredibly sick. To her horror, she remembered that she *had* been sick; prior to collapsing in a heap she had weaved off and thrown up behind a rock. Oh God, she thought. What would the women at the W.I. think if they could see her now?

Grace made a mental inventory of the rest of her body and moaned again. She was dying. Of that she was sure. Even her legs were sore. Then she remembered the reason for that: she and Matthew had been dancing; cavorting about on the rocks and being screamingly funny. Grace frowned. What had happened after that? Oh yes – they had put the world to rights. They had sat down again and achieved what politicians in every corner of the globe had been trying, and failing, to do for the last few thousand years. Grace dimly recalled that it had been so frightfully *easy*: so terribly obvious. Admittedly, she couldn't quite remember how they'd done it, but they had. It hadn't even taken them long. Or maybe it had. Grace had rather lost track of time.

Then she remembered that Matthew had asked her if she felt any better. When had that been? And had she replied? She rather thought she hadn't. She opened her eyes and looked around for him. 'Matthew?'

'Mmm?'

'Where are you?'

'Here,' said Matthew. He leaned back. 'I'm here.'

'Oh.'

Matthew grinned and looked down at the prostrate Grace. She still looked very pale. Ashen, even.

'I ... I still feel a bit dizzy,' she replied.

'Oh. D'you think you can stand up?'

With a monumental effort, Grace dragged herself backwards, trying to gain leverage against the rock behind her. Then she hauled herself to her knees. 'Nearly there,' she said, heroically clutching at tufts of grass.

'Are you hungry?'

'*Hungry?*' Food was the last thing on her mind. Then, to her intense surprise, she realised it wasn't. For some strange reason she was famished. 'Oh, God, yes. I hadn't thought of that. I'm ravenous.'

Matthew smiled. 'You've got the munchies.'

'The what?'

'The munchies.' Matthew stood up, reached out and helped her to her feet. 'It's what happens sometimes. You get really hungry afterwards.'

'Oh.'

Matthew put an arm round her shoulders. 'C'mon. Lets go and buy some chocolate.'

'Matthew?'

'Yeah.'

'I don't feel very well.'

Matthew gently patted her on the back. 'You'll feel better soon.'

But Grace was still feeling like death when they got back to the car. And she sat slumped in the passenger seat while Matthew drove the little Morris to the newsagent's at Constantine Bay where he bought obscene amounts of chocolate.

After three Mars Bars Grace perked up a bit. She looked at Matthew with a rueful smile. 'Feeling better now,' she said. 'I'm sure I'll be as right as rain after another little sleep. I don't think,' she added, 'I'll do that again in a hurry.'

'Well, at least you know what it feels like now.'

'Yes.' Exhausting. She closed her eyes and leaned her head against the window.

'Grace?'

'Yes, Matthew?'

'Why did you do this?'

'I told you. Because I wanted to know what it was like.'

'No. I mean, what really made you decide to the cannabis thing?'

Grace looked bleakly through the window. '44 Wilberforce Street, London SW3,' she whispered.

'Eh?' Matthew hadn't a clue what she was talking about.

'Oh … nothing.' Grace was tired now. Terribly, terribly tired. 'I just want to stay here,' she said. 'I love it here. It's so beautiful, so peaceful.'

'Yeah,' said Matthew as Grace drifted off to sleep. 'I love it here as well. And,' he added to himself, 'I love Nicky. And I never, ever want to leave.'

'I love it here,' said Nicky. 'It's so quiet.'

Gerald Percy smiled. It was good to see the young people in church, he thought. Although rather surprising to see Nicky on her own on a weekday afternoon. He had been in the vestry when she had entered a few minutes previously, and, sensing that she wanted to commune with God rather than God's mouthpiece in St Liac, he had left her to her prayers. But then Nicky, seeing him through the half-open vestry door, had called out to him.

'If you think this is quiet,' said Gerald, sitting beside her in the pew, 'you should see Evensong.'

Nicky grinned. She liked Gerald Percy. What she really liked about him was that he didn't take himself too seriously; didn't come over all heavy about religion during his sermons. Nicky knew that some of the more elderly inhabitants of St Liac thought Gerald verged on the flippant sometimes, but Nicky and her friends rather enjoyed it when Gerald got carried away and talked about the devilry in a Hammer House of Horror sort of way.

They sat in silence for a moment; Gerald sensing that Nicky wished to talk to him about something specific. He wasn't going to push her. He knew from considerable experience that prompting people wasn't the best way: it was much more effective to sit quietly with them, waiting for them to find the moment.

It came rather more quickly than Gerald expected.

'I wish I were a Catholic sometimes,' mused Nicky.

'Really?' Gerald tried not to sound excited. Then, sensing that Nicky would be amused, he grinned at her. 'Incense,' he said. 'Nice costumes. Lot to be said for it, really.'

But Nicky wasn't amused. 'They have confession too.'

'Ah.' He should have known from her expression. What, he wondered, had Nicky done? Then he remembered his midnight foray to Grace's greenhouse. No, it wasn't herself she was here to talk about.

'I've got some friends,' she said after another silence. 'I think they're going to get into a lot of trouble.'

Yes, thought Gerald.

Nicky stared straight ahead. 'They're doing something that's illegal. I think something terrible's going to happen and I don't know what to do.'

'I don't suppose you could go to the police?'

Nicky shook her head.

So, thought Gerald. It's definitely Grace and Matthew. 'Thought not,' he said.

Nicky looked anguished. 'I don't know if I'm worried for them or worried for myself.'

Gerald sighed. This was a tricky one. 'If one has a problem that seems to be unsolvable, then perhaps one shouldn't try to solve it. Maybe,' he said, looking closely at Nicky, 'one should just accept it.'

Nicky turned to him. 'What do you mean?'

'God grant me,' quoted Gerald, 'the serenity to accept the things I cannot change, the courage to change the things I can, and the wisdom to know the difference.'

Nicky looked down into her lap. 'The wisdom's the hard part,' she said with a sad smile.

Don't I know it, thought Gerald. Then he stood up, kissed Nicky on the head and walked back towards the vestry.

Oh God, thought Nicky, what do I do? Deep down, she knew that if she tried to change what Matthew was doing, she would be trying to change Matthew himself. And she couldn't do that. The only person who could change him was Matthew himself. Nicky had a horrible feeling that Matthew wasn't going to change and that, as a result, he was going to end up in jail.

TEN

'Mrs Trevethan! Please don't put down the phone!'

Grace put down the phone. Cursing herself for having answered it in the first place, she took a few deep breaths. This was the third time she'd made the mistake of picking up the receiver – and the third time she had hung up on Quentin whatever-his-name-was from Rampton's. Grace knew she couldn't carry on like this. She also knew that she wouldn't have to. Their first crop was all but ready. Twenty kilos of cannabis.

Calmed by that thought, Grace applied herself to her morning ritual of throwing her post in the bin and going to the kitchen to make tea. Cursing to herself, she saw that last night's washing-up was still in the sink. Even by the late evening, Grace had still felt slightly spaced out, and it had taken all her energy to cook herself some supper. Washing-up simply hadn't featured on the agenda.

She sighed, turned on the radio and then started on the dishes. It wasn't on, she told herself, to let standards drop. She never left dishes until the morning – and she would never do it again. Nor would she smoke dope again. Although she couldn't deny that it had been enormous fun at the time, the aftermath had been appalling. She was not destined to be what Matthew called a 'dope-fiend'. Nor was she going to become a slattern and leave dirty dishes all over the place.

Grace squirted an excessive amount of washing-up liquid into the sink and attacked a pan with vigour.

Then a radio announcer who she particularly detested came on and informed her in his smarmy voice that he, 'Fun-boy' Buxton, would be entertaining her for the next two hours with his sophisticated wit and repartee. Oh God, she thought. She turned to get rid of Fun-boy at the same time as he announced that, boring though it was, the news would have to come first.

Grace went back to the sink. She supposed she ought to listen to the news. She was now so out of touch that she wouldn't have known if a spaceship had landed in St Liac and abducted half the residents. Grace made a mental note to be more sociable; not to spend all her time growing cannabis in the greenhouse.

The news, however, was deeply dull. The stock market had plunged (Grace didn't want to know about that), there was a war in a country she'd never heard of, and the Prime Minister had kissed a baby. The only remotely interesting snippet in the national headlines was that the Minister for Domestic Violence had shot his male lover at point-blank range. Grace was still grinning about this when the West Country news announcer came on air. 'Police,' he announced, 'are celebrating a major victory in the war on drugs today.'

Grace went rigid and dropped her pan.

'Two men and one woman were found guilty at Bristol Crown Court after police discovered marijuana with an estimated street value of half a million pounds hidden in a barn on their family farm ...'

Grace wiped her hands and turned towards the radio.

'Sentencing them to fifteen-year jail sentences ...'

Grace turned off the radio. Then she went back to the

sink. But she couldn't concentrate on the dishes – only on the enormity of the crime she was about to commit. She, too, had half a million pounds of marijuana on her property. She, too, could go to prison for fifteen years. And so could Matthew. She couldn't do that to Matthew. He had found his first true home and his first true love; his life was just beginning. Hers, on the other hand, was nearly over. Or so it felt.

Grace was still fretting about what to do when Matthew sauntered into the room.

'Hiya,' he said. 'Feeling better?'

Grace turned round. Matthew was grinning widely. His slightly bronzed face gleamed with good health, his eyes sparkled with enthusiasm, and he looked as if he hadn't a care in the world. Grace summoned a smile from somewhere and said she was fine, thanks, and would he like a cup of tea?

Matthew said he would, sat down at the kitchen table and picked up the paper. 'Any news?'

'No. Nothing.' Grace prayed that the Bristol story was too new to have made it into a paper printed last night. 'Just the usual.' Then she told him about the Minister for Domestic Violence and Matthew laughed. Looking at him, Grace made the resolution that if the police came to call at Liac House she would vehemently deny that Matthew had anything to do with her activities. Matthew would protest but the police wouldn't care. The case against Grace would be too strong. She was heavily in debt; she was an expert gardener; she had a large greenhouse; she grew cannabis plants; she paid her creditors. Simple.

Grace handed Matthew his tea and wished that she could hand him his notice at the same time. For his own sake, she didn't want him around any more. But she had to have him. He was the one with the expert knowledge. She couldn't reap a harvest without Matthew.

'Do you really think it'll be ready in two days' time?' she asked as, still in her dressing gown, she sat with him at the kitchen table.

'Sure.'

Two days. Grace could keep the smile on her face for two days. She was good at pretending. 'How's Nicky?' she asked, as she always did.

Matthew sighed. He had had enough of pretending that all was well. 'To be honest, Grace, she's been really moody recently. She doesn't want to talk to me, she gets up at really weird hours, she … well, I think she disapproves of what we're doing.'

'Oh?' Grace tried to remain calm. 'Er … why?'

Matthew shrugged. 'She seems to think we'll get caught – *as if!*'

Grace responded with a weak grin.

'But,' continued Matthew, 'desperate times call for desperate measures. I'm unemployed …'

'… I know, I'm really sorry.'

'No! Not your fault! It's … er … well, just circumstances. Anyway, it was my decision as well.'

No, thought Grace. It was mine. All mine. And I'm going to take all the blame.

'I mean,' continued Matthew, unaware that anything was wrong, 'the only other option was me going back to Glasgow. I didn't want that and she didn't want it either. Last thing I want is to be back at Uncle Willie's building site …'

'… building site. Oooh. What does he build?'

'Er … houses?' Matthew looked at Grace. Perhaps she wasn't, after all, as fine as she thought. Perhaps she still had a hangover. 'Anyway,' he finished. 'I think Nicky feels that we're being a bit extreme.'

Grace cradled her mug in both hands and looked over the

rim to Matthew. 'Does she?'

'Yeah.'

Grace could cope with the thought of going to prison. What she couldn't cope with was the thought of Nicky and Matthew's relationship faltering and then dying a messy death because of her. 'Matthew. Have you talked about this? Properly, I mean? I don't mean to pry but ... well, I always thought you and Nicky were going to be ... you know ...'

'Yeah,' said Matthew. 'So did I. But I get to bed in the wee small hours and she gets up about five minutes later and ... well, we don't seem to have any time to talk.'

Grace reached out and took his hand in hers. 'Matthew, why don't you surprise her?'

'I already have.' Matthew looked like the dour Scot he wasn't.

'No. I mean, why don't you go and see her during the day? Go to the boat ... bring her a present ... I don't know. Just *talk* to her.'

'Y'think?'

'Yes, Matthew. I think.' Grace had been on the point of adding that she knew about relationships, but realised she didn't. She hadn't even known about her own relationship with John. She wondered what it must feel like to know beyond the shadow of a doubt that a relationship was right, or to fall in love at first sight. She hadn't loved John at first. Love had been something that had grown with time. Or so she had thought.

'Why don't you go and see her on the boat?' she repeated.

'I get seasick on boats.'

'So ... she'll know you're making an effort. A big effort...'

Matthew grimaced. In theory it was a good idea. But he didn't relish the practice. 'What about,' he suggested, 'I arrange to meet her in the pub instead?'

165

Grace shook her head. 'Look what happened the last time you two agreed to meet in the pub. Anyway, it's hardly intimate.' Men, she thought. 'And it's not as if it requires any effort…'

'True.' Matthew stood up. 'Okay … you're right. I'll go to the boat. But why don't we all meet in the pub anyway? You never get out, Grace.' Matthew's eyes lit up as he warmed to his theme. 'We could have a celebration.'

'Of what?'

Matthew nodded towards the greenhouse. 'Our first harvest.'

'A bit premature, don't you think?'

'Nah! Anyway, it would be fun. You, me, Nicky, Harve, Martin … we could have a bit of a get-together.'

Grace pondered that one for a moment. It would, she thought, be fun. And a change of scene. And she had, moments before, made a mental note to be more sociable. 'You've got a deal,' she said. Then she stood up. 'Come on. We've got work to do.'

Matthew went to see Nicky at lunchtime. He knew the *Sharicmar* would be back in harbour by then. He also rather hoped she would be moored at the quayside and not in the middle of the harbour. This was not the case. He saw from the cliff above Liac that Nicky's boat was tied to a buoy some two hundred yards out at sea. That meant he would have to row out to her – a prospect he didn't relish. Still, Grace had been right: it would mean that Nicky would realise he was making a huge effort. Grinning, he walked down the high street to the harbour, stopping on the way to buy Nicky a little present.

Reaching the harbour, he borrowed old Jack Dawkins' rowing boat and headed out to the *Sharicmar*. He didn't mind the rowing; the activity kept him from feeling seasick. It was the rolling about, especially on a so-called stationary vessel, that really got to him.

'Ahoy!' he yelled as he approached Nicky's boat. He could see her, resplendent in her oilskins and red-spotted scarf, expertly gutting a fish on deck.

Nicky looked around. 'Hey! What on earth …?' she cried.

Grace had been right, thought Matthew. Nicky looked extremely surprised – and very pleasantly so. He rowed right up to the hull of the trawler, bounced against the tyres and tied his own little boat to the ladder. Nicky crossed the deck and looked down at him. 'What on earth are you doing here?'

Matthew held up a white plastic bag. 'I've brought you something.' Then he climbed up the ladder and vaulted onto the deck, trying to think about how nice it was to see Nicky in daylight rather than about how sick he was going to feel in a minute.

Nicky took the proffered bag.

'It's lunch,' said Matthew. 'I've brought you lunch.' Well, it was a present of sorts. Nicky and Harvey didn't usually bother with lunch. 'Cornish pasties.'

But Nicky was now looking into the bag, wrinkling her nose at the smell. 'Fish,' she said. 'You brought me fish.'

Matthew shrugged and pecked her on the cheek. 'Well, they'd run out of pasties, and anyway I thought it would be a nice change.'

Nicky sighed and went back to her fish: the newly dead ones as opposed to the newly-battered ones. She really wasn't in the mood for Matthew's jokes. 'What are you doing here?' she asked. 'You never come on the boat.'

Matthew looked at her set expression. The fish had been a mistake, he told himself. 'I was beginning to wonder what you looked like,' he said. 'I go to bed ... five minutes later you get up.'

Nicky shrugged and hacked the head off a fish. 'It's the tides.'

Matthew came closer. 'It's not the tides,' he said softly.

Nicky sighed. 'No, it's not the tides.' Looking more pained than angry, she turned to him. 'I *really* don't like what you're doing, Matthew.'

Matthew looked down. 'Yeah. I know.'

'I really don't want to be in a relationship with someone who's irresponsible.'

'Yes you do,' countered Matthew. 'I've been irresponsible all my life.'

But the levity was misplaced, and he knew it. Nicky was deadly serious. 'Well,' she said. 'It's time you changed.'

'Why?'

'Because you're getting old.'

Matthew bellowed in mock-outrage and tapped his forehead. 'I'm not getting old! These are laughter lines.'

'Nothing's that funny.'

Matthew sighed. 'I don't understand this. I thought you liked me the way I am?'

'I do.' Nicky peeled off a heavy rubber glove and cast her mind back to her conversation with Gerald Percy. 'But things change, Matthew, and you have to change with them.' She studied him carefully as she spoke, looking for a sign that he had taken her words on board.

'Look,' he said. 'I *will* change – but after this.' The lines that he had attributed to laughter looked more like the hallmarks of bullishness. 'Okay?'

Then Harvey appeared from below decks and saw the

open plastic bag. 'Fish and chips!' he yelled. 'Fantastic!' He looked appreciatively at Matthew. Nicky glared at him.

'Okay?' repeated Matthew.

'If you say so,' said Nicky. She put her glove back on, picked up her hatchet and decapitated another hapless mackerel. The look she gave Matthew left him under no illusions as to whose head she really wanted to sever.

Sensing an atmosphere, Harvey shrugged and retreated below decks.

'Look,' tried Matthew. 'I really don't want this to ruin our relationship.'

'No.' Another head flew into the basket at Nicky's feet.

'Things'll get back to normal soon.'

'Yes.'

'And ... look ... can't we just *be* normal? Can't we go to the pub of an evening like anyone else?'

'If you like.'

Matthew sighed. 'Tonight, then. Eight o'clock?'

'How did it go?' asked Grace.

'Oh ... fine.'

Oh dear, she thought.

'She was a bit tied up,' said Matthew, not wanting Grace to know just how much Nicky disapproved of their activities. 'Still, she's coming to the pub tonight, so that's good.'

'Ye-es.' Grace snipped a few more blossoms and hung them up to dry. If we don't get these out of here soon, she told herself, that relationship is going to hit the rocks.

Matthew was thinking along exactly the same lines. Yet he couldn't disguise his excitement as he looked at the plants.

'Our mutant buds,' he said, imitating a Dr Who Dalek, 'will soon be ready, Great One. We can release them into the atmosphere and take over the entire planet.'

Grace giggled.

'D'you realise,' said Matthew in his normal voice, 'what we've done here, Grace? It's fabulous.'

Yes, thought Grace. And fabulously dangerous.

'It's time,' continued Matthew, 'for me to go to London. Get a dealer.'

'Ah.' Grace looked up from the plant she was snipping. 'No. No, you're not going. You're staying here. I'm going.'

'What?'

'That's my decision.'

Matthew scratched his head. 'Grace … I don't think you realise what's involved here.'

Grace picked up another plant.

'Look, the last time you were in London was five years ago for the Chelsea Flower Show.'

'So?'

'So you can't sell this stuff through a florist.'

Grace picked up a humidifier and started to spray a row of younger plants. 'So what's your master plan, then?'

'Well, I was going to go to Portobello Road … or Notting Hill or something like that. Find a dealer. Sell it.'

'That's it? That's your plan?'

Matthew scowled. 'Yeah. What's wrong with it?'

'It's rubbish.'

'Grace!' Matthew was beginning to get annoyed. 'You've got to blend in. Look at you. A drug dealer will take one look at you and know there's something fishy going on.'

Grace ignored him and carried on spraying.

'With the greatest respect, *I'm* the hip one. You're a wee bit more hip replacement.'

Now it was Grace who was annoyed. And hurt. He had never spoken to her like that before. When she finally turned to him, she looked, and sounded, uncharacteristically fierce. 'One more word out of you, Matthew, and I'm going to throw the whole crop into the sea.'

Realising he had over-stepped the mark, Matthew tried another tack. 'I don't think you're thinking this through. If you seriously think …'

'… I mean it, Matthew.' She looked at him as if he were a very small, obstreperous child. She must, thought Matthew, have been taking lessons from Nicky.

Matthew nearly lost his temper. 'You are not my boss! We're partners.'

Grace didn't reply.

'Your cheque bounced, remember?' Matthew glared at Grace. The subtext was clear. He was working for free; doing her an enormous favour.

Grace sighed. 'Look, can we discuss this later? When we're actually ready?'

'Huh.'

'We're supposed to be celebrating, remember? We're going to forget about this and go down to the pub and have a jolly evening and … and, discuss this tomorrow.'

Matthew turned and snapped off a blossom with rather more force than was necessary. He would see about that. He wasn't going to be told what to do by a middle-aged widow. The middle-aged widow, however, had already made a plan.

'Grace! What a surprise.' Martin Bamford looked more than surprised: he was thunderstruck to see Grace in The Anchor. 'What brings you here?'

Grace laughed. 'Well … I just thought I hadn't seen anyone for ages. Matthew asked if I wanted to come down for a drink and so … here I am.'

'And jolly nice to see you it is. Drink?' he offered.

'Please. Gin and tonic.'

Martin leaned over the bar. 'Where's Matthew, then?' he asked as he tried to attract Charlie's attention.

'Oh … he just nipped home to change. Martin?' added Grace in a near-whisper.

'Yes?'

'Can I ask you something?'

'Of course.'

'It's … it's a bit of a secret.'

Oh God, thought Martin. Something medical, then. He didn't know why he didn't just transfer his surgery to the pub. Which would, now that he thought about it, be rather a splendid idea from everyone's point of view …

'Well,' continued Grace. 'Not really a secret. It's just that I don't want Matthew to know.'

'Oh?' This sounded interesting.

'Yes. You see, I've got to go to London in the morning.' Grace looked conspiratorial. 'Solicitors. That sort of thing.'

'I thought Melvyn dealt with your solicitor?'

'… Other solicitors. John's affairs were terribly complicated, you see.'

'Yes. So I'd heard.'

'Well the thing is … I've got to go and see one of the London solicitors, and I don't want Matthew to know.'

'Er … why?' Martin handed Grace her drink and took a sip of his beer.

'Because he'd want to come with me.' Noting that Martin was looking completely bamboozled, Grace hurried on. 'You see, I haven't been to London for years, and Matthew's worried that I'll get lost and be hopeless and that I'll need a minder.' And, she remembered, a hip replacement. Grace laughed – but not about the hip replacement. 'You know how protective he is, Martin.'

Martin shrugged. He didn't know.

'So,' finished Grace. 'You won't tell him, will you?'

'No. Not if you don't want me to. But, um … why are you telling *me?*'

'Oh!' Grace giggled and put a hand to her mouth. 'Because I'd like your help in getting me to London.'

Ah, thought Martin. So that was it. Grace didn't have enough money for one train ticket, let alone two.

Martin reached into his jacket pocket. 'Of course I'll help you. If you could just …'

Grace looked apologetic. 'It's just that I've been having such problems with it lately. I don't really trust it to get as far as Bodmin.'

'Er … what?'

'My car,' said Grace.

'Grace …'

'I know it's an imposition, but I'd be ever so grateful.'

Finally Martin realised what Grace was on about. 'You want me to give you a lift to the station?'

'Yes.' Grace looked surprised. She thought she'd already told him that. 'You don't mind, do you?'

'No. Not at all.' Martin smiled at her over the rim of his glass. 'It would be a pleasure.'

'Thanks.' Grace breathed a sigh of relief and took a sip of her drink. That, at least, was one small hurdle surmounted. She didn't care to think how she was going to broach the others.

She didn't, anyway, have the opportunity. Matthew and Harvey walked into the pub. 'Hi Grace,' said the latter.

'Hello, Harvey. How are you?'

'Fine. Matthew told me you've come to celebrate.'

'Er … did he?' Grace looked in alarm at Matthew.

He winked back. 'Yeah. Spring. A gardener's holiday.'

'Oh if *only*,' said Grace with a laugh. 'But it *is* nice to be out.' She looked around her, feeling that she was, after all, going to enjoy the evening. Especially as she and Matthew had successfully buried the hatchet of their earlier altercation. Neither had referred to it for the rest of the afternoon, and they had spent a happy few hours imitating Daleks and, of course, growing cannabis.

Then Grace noticed that Nicky wasn't there. 'Where's Nicky? I thought you said she was coming?'

'She is,' said Harvey. 'She's be a little late. Still on the boat.' He looked at Grace with his mournful eyes. 'We had a ripped net. Bad omen.'

'Oh, surely not.'

'What about a game of pool,' suggested Martin. He was damned if he was going to spend the evening listening to Harvey banging on about omens.

'I don't know how to play,' said Grace.

'Oh, it's very easy.' Harvey headed towards the table. 'Come here and I'll show you. My balls,' he said, 'are stripey and the Doctor's have spots.'

Martin looked thunderous.

'Oh dear,' said Grace, giggling. Then, following the others, she asked Matthew if Nicky played pool.

''Course she does.'

Grace nodded. 'Good. It would be horrid if she couldn't join in later.'

But Nicky didn't join in. When, half an hour later, she appeared at the door of the pub, she took one look at Grace laughing delightedly with Matthew as she successfully potted a ball. Nicky turned on her heel and slowly retraced her steps; that one brief glimpse had been enough for her. There was something about the way Matthew and Grace reacted together; something almost chemical that transcended the physical. Nicky knew beyond a shadow of a doubt they weren't having an affair. For a mad moment, she wished they were: she would at least be able to identify with that sort of relationship. This was far worse. They were engaged in a game that was going to have terrible consequences – but they thought it was child's play. Nicky could tell that from their faces. And Nicky blamed Grace.

Shoulders hunched, hands thrust deep into her jacket pocket, she turned away from the pub and ambled down the hill towards the cottage. She didn't get very far.

'Nicky?'

Surprised, Nicky turned round again. It was Grace's voice.

'Grace!' Oh God, she thought. They saw me and they sent Grace to coax me back. She felt even more excluded.

Grace walked towards her. As if reading Nicky's thoughts, she told her she'd told the others she was popping to the loo. 'They didn't see you,' she said, trying to sound as if nothing was wrong. Her eyes, however, betrayed her worry. 'But I did. Why didn't you come in, Nicky?'

Nicky shrugged. 'I'm not drinking at the moment. Didn't want to be surrounded by drinkers.' Aware that she sounded truculent – pathetic, even – she forced a grin.

But Grace knew there was more to it than that. 'Are you angry with me?'

Nicky sighed. 'No. I'm angry with Matthew. It's his fault.'

'It was *my* decision, Nicky.' Grace looked imploringly at Nicky. 'Really, it was. I'm trying to save my house.'

'Grace, everybody knows what you're doing. Pretty soon you'll have the police up here.'

Grace's expression told Nicky she thought that was plain ridiculous. Nobody knew. It was her and Matthew's secret. 'Nonsense,' she said. 'They'll never find out.'

'Grace! Your whole house lights up like a spaceship. People aren't stupid.' Except, she felt like adding, you and Matthew.

Grace was rather shocked to realise that people had noticed the lights from afar. But she wasn't going to voice her surprise to Nicky. Another two days, she told herself. Another two days and we'll have the first batch ready. 'We're nearly done now,' she said to Nicky.

'Yeah.' Nicky was less than impressed. 'Matthew could be in jail by tomorrow.'

Grace knew that. Grace didn't want to think about that. Grace was, in fact, thinking about something else. Something that had just occurred to her.

'Why,' she asked suddenly, 'aren't you drinking?'

The question took Nicky by surprise, and she hesitated before replying. 'I ... I just don't feel like it.'

But her momentary pause and the evasive look in her eyes told Grace all she wanted to know. Oh God, she thought. So that's it. And that's why she's so upset.

Grace nodded. 'He doesn't know, does he?'

Nicky averted her eyes.

'Nicky.' Grace wanted to reach out her, to take her in her arms and tell her that everything would be all right. Then she remembered how she had snapped at Honey Chambers about being patronising. She resisted her impulse and stood where she was. 'How can I help?'

This time Nicky's expression was imploring. 'Just don't let him go to jail, Grace.' Then she turned away, a small forlorn figure in the darkness, and made her way down the hill.

Grace stared after her. What was she doing to these people's lives, she wondered? What was she doing to her own? Then she shook her head. They were too far gone now: she *couldn't* turn back. She was too close to saving her house. And too near to finding a solution for Matthew to stay in Liac and live happily ever after. Unless, of course, he went to jail.

Assaulted by her conflicting thoughts, Grace turned back towards the pub. She really didn't feel like playing pool and laughing and pretending all was well with the world. So she went back into The Anchor, stayed for half an hour, made her excuses and left again. As she went, she saw the way that Matthew was looking at her. She waved back, pretending she hadn't seen. She wanted to believe that Matthew had been looking pensive, but she knew this wasn't true. He had been looking suspicious. Grace slunk off home, feeling like a criminal.

But Grace had been wrong. Matthew was feeling neither pensive nor, indeed, suspicious. He was annoyed with Grace. And with Nicky. Asking Grace to the pub had been a mistake. She had swanned in, charmed everyone and behaved as if she owned the place. She had even displayed a natural aptitude for pool.

As far as Matthew was concerned, he and Grace had not buried the hatchet about going to London. True, he had pretended that all was well – but that was because he hadn't yet made a plan. Now, on Grace's departure from the pub, he realised he had better make that plan. And quickly.

'You all right?' asked Harvey, noting his expression.

'Yeah. Sure.' Matthew wasn't going to admit to Harvey

that he wasn't particularly all right. He wasn't even going to admit to himself that he was, in fact, feeling thoroughly emasculated.

'Drink?' asked Martin.

'Thanks.' Matthew held out his pint glass.

'No Nicky,' said Harvey as Martin went off to the bar.

Matthew sighed. 'No. No Nicky.' Then he sat down on the pew beside the pool table and lit a cigarette. 'Women like cuddly toys, don't they?'

'Eh?'

'They like to hug them and squeeze them and poke their eyes out and rip off their fucking limbs.'

Harvey looked, wide-eyed at his friend.

But while Matthew spat out the words with vigour – even venom – he appeared to be talking to himself. 'I avoid confrontation. I know it. But if you grew up in Glasgow in the 1970s, you'd avoid confrontation too.'

Harvey supposed he would, but didn't get a chance to reply. Matthew continued with his tirade, the words tumbling out at high speed.

'All I want is an easy life. I want to grow some vegetables, smoke some reefer, sing some carols at Christmas time and,' he added, his voice rising, 'who knows, one day I'd like to be a dad and raise a couple of calm fucking children!

'But that's it! I've had it. I've fucking had enough. I'm gone. No more Mr Cuddly Toy!' Matthew took a feverish drag of his cigarette. 'I'm not hanging around here to be a whipping boy for Ganja Grace and Nicky the fucking lobster queen!'

Harvey nodded.

'I'm fucking gone,' repeated Matthew, nodding to himself. 'I'm gone. I'm gone! I'm fucking out of here. And before I go, I'm gonna see both these women and give them a piece of my mind.' Primed for confrontation, he looked up at Harvey.

'Are you done?' he asked, turning back to the pool table.

Matthew sighed. He *would* give them a piece of his mind. Tomorrow. When he was feeling calmer.

ELEVEN

Grace had spent much of the previous evening standing in front of the full-length mirror in her bedroom. It had been nothing to do with vanity; everything to do with self-doubt. She hadn't bought any new clothes in ages, and didn't have a clue what might be suitable for London. She had no idea what the smart set was wearing – much less what widowed, middle-aged drug dealers wore to sell their wares in Portobello Road.

For a while, Grace had scoffed at Matthew's less-than-sophisticated plan; she had then adopted it. She hadn't been to London for five years, had lost touch with most of her old friends in the city, and those who were still on her Christmas card list were not the sort to be able to devise a strategy for off-loading twenty kilos of cannabis. Matthew's plan was her only option.

But, rifling through her wardrobe, she had been stumped about the question of her attire. Wellie boots and Barbours were definitely out. The dress she had worn on her last foray to London screamed 'Chelsea Flower Show' and made her look like a herbaceous border. Grace remembered enough about Portobello to know that she would stick out like a sore thumb in that.

Then she had tried on her black suit, but, rather than making her look like a mysterious sophisticate, it made her look dowdy and funereal. (Had she really looked dowdy in it at John's funeral?) Still in front of the mirror, she had tried to jazz it up with a jaunty little boater, but that had made her look like a gondolier in drag. No, she had thought, it has to be something timeless yet elegant; something that suggested she was a woman on a mission.

Frowning, she had cast her mind back to what Honey Chambers had been wearing. Honey was clearly an up-to-the-minute sort of person. She had looked as if she knew all about clothes. Grace had remembered a loose-fitting, taupe-coloured trouser suit and a floaty headscarf. She, Grace, tended to go for the more tailored look and didn't have anything in taupe, but she *did* have a trouser suit. And while she was lacking in the floaty scarf department, she had a hat that matched the trouser suit. A hat, she remembered, that had received many an admiring glance when she had last worn it. So Grace had tried on the ensemble, been pleased with the result, and had retired to bed secure in the knowledge that she would look the part. Acting it would be a different matter.

The hat, she had been pleased to notice, still drew admiring glances. When Martin Bamford had picked her up at eight-fifteen, he had gasped in wonder.

'I know,' Grace's response had, she thought, been appropriately kittenish. 'Rather splendid, isn't it?'

Martin had continued to gaze and Grace, settling happily in the passenger seat of his Jaguar, had attributed his reaction to the fact that she so rarely dressed up. She resolved to make more effort in the future. When she had money. When she had sold the cannabis. That thought preyed on her mind for much of the journey and now, as they approached Bodmin Parkway, Grace was beginning to feel distinctly nervous. Her hands, she noticed, were clenched tightly round the bag in her lap. She took a deep breath and told herself to relax. Then she turned to the driver's seat. 'Martin?'

'Yes?'

'I'm not really going to see a solicitor.'

'No.' Martin looked at her with a half-smile. 'I didn't really think you were.'

Grace nodded, 'I didn't think everybody knew.'

'Not everyone. Just … um … those of us who put two and two together.'

'Nicky told me my house lights up like a spaceship.'

Martin laughed. 'Yes, it does.'

'So what do other people think?'

Martin shrugged. 'That you're trying a new type of orchid? That you're growing a special tea?'

Then Grace realised. 'You've been trying to protect me, haven't you?'

Martin went slightly pink, and Grace, immensely touched, felt like weeping. She hadn't known; hadn't, as others had done about a different sum, put two and two together.

'So,' she said after a short silence. 'I'm now going to London to sell it.'

'And you don't want Matthew to know because he'd insist on coming with you?'

'Yes. I don't … I really don't want him involved, Martin. There's too much at stake.'

Martin wondered if Nicky had told her about the baby. 'There's a lot at stake for you as well, Grace.'

Grace sat up in her seat and tried to look purposeful. A woman with a mission. 'Not really,' she said with a coy smile. 'I know what I'm doing.'

'Do you really?' Martin was intrigued.

'Oh yes. I've got … contacts.'

'You do?'

Grace nodded. 'I do. I haven't gone into this lightly, you know.'

Martin grinned. 'No.' He looked at Grace, the hat, and the trouser suit. You're a woman of many surprises, Grace.'

'Thank you, Martin.'

But when the pulled up outside the little station five minutes later, Grace had another attack of the nerves. She had no plans beyond going to Portobello Road. And no contacts. Steeling herself, she fumbled for the door handle. 'Thank you, Martin. Thanks so much.'

'My pleasure. But, Grace?'

'Yes?'

'What's Matthew going to think when he sees you're not there?'

Grace had thought of that. 'I left him a note. Told him I had to go to Wadebridge and then to lunch with the Penraths.'

Martin looked doubtful. 'Do you think he'll believe that?'

'Probably not.' Grace got out of the car. Then she bent down and grinned back at Martin. 'But it won't matter, will it? I'll be in London – and he doesn't know where I'm going.'

Martin responded with a wink, a wave and, as Grace closed the passenger door, he eased off the brake and the car purred back towards St Liac.

Grace felt suddenly bereft – and horribly apprehensive. What on earth, she told herself, do you think you're *doing?*

Grace managed not to answer this question until she reached London. For most of the four-hour journey, she buried herself in the magazines she bought at Bodmin, kept a firm hold on the handbag in her lap, and, occasionally, looked up to admire the view. It might, after all, be the last view she would be able to appreciate in many years.

At Paddington, she made her way to the taxi rank and waited patiently in the queue for a black cab. Stations always made her feel uneasy: she knew they were the hangouts of the unscrupulous and the unsavoury, so she kept her head down and clutched her bag to her breast. As an ex-Londoner, she knew people ignored each other here anyway. She was well aware that it simply wasn't done to smile and say hello to a stranger the way one did in Liac. So Grace, not looking at other people, remained blissfully unaware that they were looking at her.

After ten minutes, she found herself at the head of the queue. Jumping gratefully into the cab that pulled up in front of her, she leaned towards the glass partition and asked to be taken to Portobello Road.

The driver looked at her through his mirror. 'Going to a party then, luv?'

'Er … no. Just a little shopping. Antiquing, you know.' There had been antique stalls at Portobello in her day. Surely they must still be there.

'Oh,' said the cabbie. 'American, are you?'

'No.' Grace looked puzzled. Since when had she sounded American? 'No. I'm from Cornwall.'

'Ah. Cornwall.' The driver looked disapproving. He didn't know anything about Cornwall. 'We go to Tenerife,' he said.

'Oh.'

'For our holidays.'

'Ah … nice.' Grace didn't really want conversation. She wanted to concentrate on what she was going to do.

'It's the weather, you see.' The cabbie wagged a finger at

her in the mirror. 'Now you can take your Cornwalls and your Whitstables ... they're all very well. But there's no getting away from the weather, is there?'

'Er ... no.'

The cabbie nodded. 'Four of us. That's the wife and my mate Jim and his lady. Every year. Regular as clockwork. Two weeks in Tenerife.'

Grace sighed, leaned back in her seat and, for no reason other than to pretend she was busy, began to rummage in her handbag.

'You'll want to be careful of that, luv.' said the driver.

'Of what?'

'Your bag. 'Specially in Portobello. You mark my words, that place isn't getting any better. Now the last thing anyone could accuse me of is being racist, but you can't say I didn't tell you.'

'Er ... tell me what?' Grace looked into the driver's mirror.

He tapped his nose and winked. 'Just you keep that bag close to you, that's all I'm saying. Take your eyes off it for one second and it'll be gone. It's the drugs, you see.' He nodded in a knowing fashion.

Grace's heart missed a beat. How did he know she had drugs in her handbag? '*What*? What did you say?' Hands trembling, she closed the bag.

'Drugs. They'll whip it away and, before you know it's gone, they'll have taken your money. And, mind, anything else they fancy. Money for drugs, see?'

'Oh I *see*.' Grace slumped back in her seat. Her hat went askew and her heart was still palpitating, but she supposed she ought to be grateful to the driver. She was obviously heading to the right place. She took a few deep breaths and then leaned forwards again. 'Lot of drugs around there, are there?' she asked, readjusting her hat and trying to sound only vaguely interested. 'Hash, ganja, spliffs … that sort of thing?' she added casually.

The driver looked completely non-plussed. 'Er … yeah. Yeah. Lots of drugs.' His eyes narrowed. He'd had all types in his cab, but this was a peculiar one all right. Not quite all there, if you asked him.

'Are we nearly there?' asked Grace after a moment's silence. 'I'm in rather a hurry. Any chance you could go … just a little faster?'

The driver shook his head. 'Oh no. Not in this traffic. Not a chance, luv.'

'Oh.' Grace looked at the traffic. It was hardly bumper-to-bumper. Then she noticed the street sign on her left. Westbourne Grove. She frowned, trying to remember. She was sure Westbourne Grove led to Notting Hill, and that Portobello Road was in the heart of Notting Hill.

'You'll be wanting the top end, then?' said the driver.

'I beg your pardon?'

'The top end of Portobello. That's where the antique shops are. Mark my words, you don't want to go to the bottom end. Seedy. Stay up with the antiques and you should be all right.'

'Oh …. Thank you.' Grace made a mental note to bolt to the seedy end as soon as possible.

Two minutes later, the driver turned right into a short road of elegant terraced houses. 'This is Elgin Crescent, see?'

'Oh.'

'It's, like, the boundary. I'll drop you at the end and you turn *left* up Portobello, right? You'll not be wanting to go *down* the road.'

'Right,' said Grace, opening the door. 'Down is the seedy end?'

'That's right.'

Grace closed the door behind her and popped her head through the side window. 'Thank you. How much do I owe you?'

The driver pointed at the meter. 'Seven eighty.'

'Goodness!' Grace opened her bag and rummaged for her purse. 'That's a lot.'

'You just mind that bag of yours, right?'

'Yes.' Grace handed him a ten-pound note. 'Righty-ho.'

'Oh come *on*,' said a languid voice behind her.

'I beg your pardon?' Grace whirled round to see a young man dressed entirely in black glaring at her.

'Haven't got all day you know.' The man ostentatiously tapped his foot on the pavement.

The driver winked at her and handed her the change. 'Oh,' she smiled, handing back twenty pence. 'Keep that. Please.'

The driver shot her a look. Then the man behind elbowed her aside and stepped into the cab. Grace glared at him. 'Moron,' she said under her breath. Then, as the cab swung round, she walked to the end of the street and turned right into the seedier end of Portobello Road.

From what the driver had been saying, she half expected to be catapulted straight into Sodom and Gomorrah. Instead, she found herself on a perfectly ordinary, bustling street lined with vegetable stalls, second-hand clothes racks and other stalls selling strange bits of bric-a-brac. The shops behind the stalls, she noticed as she walked through the throng, sold mainly records and CDs. And even those that didn't, like the little cafés selling ethnic food, had loud music blaring from them. Or at least Grace assumed it was music.

She walked on, forcing herself to look at the people around her. She knew she would have to make eye contact soon, but wanted to get a feel for the place before she started doing that, wanted to blend into her surroundings. She felt her confidence begin to soar as she walked. There were all sorts of people here; people from all walks of life. Some of them were bound to be drug dealers.

After a few minutes, she felt brave enough to make her first approach. Out of the corner of her eye, she noticed a young couple, idly flicking through some shirts on one of the clothes stands. Her intuition told her they weren't interested in the shirts. They were waiting for something. Or someone.

She sidled up to them. 'Psst!'

The girl, who had bright orange hair, a ring through her nose and a leather jacket peppered with studs, looked at her in alarm. Grace winked and looked at her companion. His pink hair was standing on end. So were his antennae.

'Can I show you something privately?' whispered Grace. She opened her handbag and beamed at them. 'It's ever so nice.'

The man looked at her, raised his eyebrows and then grabbed his girlfriend. 'Come on. Let's go.'

Giggling, they sauntered off.

'*Well*!' said Grace to herself. Then, as she watched the retreating pair, they turned round and giggled again.

Grace sighed and told herself that she mustn't get downhearted. Not *everyone* here could be a drug dealer. Still, it wasn't exactly flattering to be laughed at.

She decided to adopt a new tactic. She would flick idly through the clothes as the young couple had been doing, and wait for people to come to her.

Just as she was looking in amazement at a multi-coloured chiffon skirt, she felt a presence beside her. She stiffened, then turned to see a large Rastafarian man standing at her side. She smiled.

He didn't.

'Would you like …?' she began.

The man shook his head. 'No. I don't know who you are.'

This looked promising, thought Grace. He obviously knew what she was offering him. 'Can I show you?' She opened her bag.

The Rastafarian looked down and shook his head. 'No. I'm not interested.' Then, too stoned to realise what he had seen in the handbag, he walked away.

Grace snorted. What on earth *was* he interested in, then? Perhaps she was being too subtle. Maybe a more brazen approach was called for. She sauntered down the street again, swinging her handbag and, even though she felt rather self-conscious about it, her hips. A moment later she saw another man staring at her. She stopped and beckoned him towards her. 'Come on,' she urged. 'Come here. I've got,' she added as the man approached, 'something really tasty for you!'

The man looked at her in amusement and walked straight past.

Exasperated, Grace swung her handbag again and continued down the street. Then she noticed the cars. Some of them were parked beside the stalls. Others were inching their way through the throng of pedestrians. Cars, she thought. Yes, the dealers would be in cars.

With renewed confidence, she sashayed up to a Volvo estate and bent down at the open driver's window. 'Are you looking for something?' she asked the paunchy individual slumped in the seat.

He looked up at her, seemingly undecided as to whether he was looking or not.

Grace winked at him. 'Know what I mean?'

'Yeah,' he said, not altogether ecstatically. 'All right, then. Hop in, love.'

Grace went bright pink, turned on her heel and walked

briskly away. Oh dear, she thought. So that's what they think. Had Grace stopped to consider the fact that she was making a very poor job of blending in with her surroundings, she might not have been so surprised. Grace was wearing a huge, formal and terribly out-of-date white hat with a broad brim, a black band and a white feather trailing – she thought fetchingly – down her neck. Equally startlingly white, and just as outmoded, was her trouser suit which, in turn, matched her shoes and bag.

Grace stuck out like a sore thumb. Worse, she was beginning to be noticed by everyone, not just by those she approached. People were nudging each other, sniggering as, in desperation, she tried tactic after tactic. She leaned nonchalantly against a lamp-post; she whistled, she nudged and she nodded in encouragement. Occasionally a car tooted at her, but she would always turn away. It was no use, she thought eventually. Doing it in the open air was obviously not the way.

She was reconsidering her options when she noticed the pub. That was it, she thought. Far more intimate. She could sidle up to people and show them the contents of her bag before they even had time to mistake her for a prostitute. Twenty minutes after entering the Market Tavern, Grace was charged and arrested for soliciting in a public place.

'Oh Christ! Matthew looked up from the plants as he heard the scrunch of footsteps on the gravel. Then, seeing Martin Bamford looming at the open door of the greenhouse, he breathed a sigh of relief. 'Thank Christ it's only you.'

Martin looked affronted. 'What do you mean, "only you"?'

'I mean only you as opposed to Alfred Mabely. Only you as opposed to the riot squad. Only you as opposed to Customs and Excise. That sort of thing.'

'Oh,' said Martin, entering the greenhouse. Then, taking in the forest of cannabis plants, he said 'oh' again – this time investing the word with several syllables and a look of pure joy. As if unable to believe his eyes, he blinked rapidly. 'Is this ... it all ...?'

'Yep,' grinned Matthew. 'Every single last leaf. Pure *Cannabis sativa* ... well, crossed with *indica*.' He gestured up to the racks where the blossom was drying and hardening. 'And that's the first crop. Twenty kilos.'

'Bugger me rigid,' said Martin.

'Rather not.' Matthew went back to watering the latest cuttings. 'What're you doing here anyway?'

But Martin didn't answer the question. He was still looking in awe at the incredible sight before him. Then he smiled. 'And to think it's all mine.'

'Eh?' Matthew looked up and glowered at him. 'What d'you mean "all mine"?'

'I mean,' said Martin, 'that because I paid for the seeds, all this belongs to me.'

'Oh get real.' Matthew didn't even consider taking Martin seriously and went back to his watering.

Martin shrugged. He hadn't been serious; he was aware of what Matthew and Grace were risking – and what they were trying to save – by cultivating cannabis. Still, it was true, he *had* paid for the seeds. He thought it ungracious of Matthew not even to offer him a couple of ounces.

'I just meant ...' he began.

'... You can have a pound,' said Matthew.

'A pound?' Martin was astounded. 'Well ... that's ... that's very kind of you. And, of course, of Grace.'

Matthew scowled again. 'It's my decision – not Grace's. I'm allowed to take decisions on my own, you know. We're partners. No-one's the boss.'

Ah, thought Martin. So he hasn't suspected. He wondered how to broach the subject. Then Matthew asked him again what he was doing coming to Liac House.

'I'm … well, I'm worried about Grace.'

'Eh? Grace is having lunch with the Penraths. Over Bodmin way.'

Martin fingered his collar. 'Well, actually … now that you mention it – she's not.'

'Yes she is.' Matthew gestured to the notepad on the corner of the trestle table. 'She left me a note.' Then he drew himself to his full height and gave Martin the benefit of a superior smile. 'To be honest, Martin, she's avoiding me.'

Yes, thought Martin. That much is true.

'Y'see,' continued Matthew, 'we had a wee bit of an argument yesterday. I said it was time to go to London to find a dealer and Grace tried to pull rank and said that she'd go 'cos she'd had a better idea and …well …' Matthew stalled. 'She can't have,' he finished lamely.

'Why not.'

'Because she doesn't *know* anyone in London. She's buried herself here for years, lost touch with all her old friends.'

'Ah.'

'What d'you mean?'

'I mean that's what I suspected … after I took Grace to the station this morning.'

'Eh?' Matthew looked up again. He looked suspicious – and alarmed. 'You … took Grace … to the station?'

'Yes.'

'Why?'

'Because she was going to London.'

Matthew dropped the watering can. 'Oh ... oh Jesus!'

'She said she was going to see a solicitor.'

'She doesn't *have* a solicitor in London!'

Martin looked at the floor.

'She took a sample, didn't she? She's gone to find a dealer?'

Martin remained mute.

'Bloody hell! You *idiot*!'

'She must know someone in London,' said Martin, looking highly embarrassed.

'No.' Matthew was adamant. 'She knows no-one – at least no-one who can help her with drugs.'

'She must,' repeated Martin. 'She told me she had contacts. Think, Matthew, *think*.'

Matthew thought. Then he remembered Grace's curious remark the other day: her strange reply to his question about what made her decide to grow cannabis.

'Yes,' he said, nodding to himself. 'Maybe she does. Maybe ...'

'Maybe what?'

'Have you got your car here?'

'Yes.' Martin looked surprised. 'Why?'

'Because you and me are going to get into it. Right now.'

Martin gestured to the plants. 'But we can't just leave them here. Untended.'

'Shit!' Matthew surveyed the greenhouse. 'I know,' he said after a moment. 'We'll get Harvey. He's not working today. Harvey can look after the plants. C'mon!' Matthew grabbed his jacket and hurried out of the greenhouse.

'But where are we going?'

'44 Wilberforce Street,' said Matthew. 'London SW3.'

'44 Wilberforce Street,' said Grace to the police officer. 'SW3.'

'Name?'

'Honey Chambers.'

'Is she your lawyer?'

Grace shook her head.

'A relation?'

Grace looked up. 'No,' she said in a small voice. 'Just a … friend.'

Pen poised, the police officer looked down at Grace again. 'Number?'

'I told you … 44 …'

'No, I mean the phone number.'

Grace shook her head again. 'No. I … I've forgotten it.'

Barely able to disguise her disgust, the police officer looked down again. She'd seen it all before. Countless times. And where did this woman think she would get by asking this Honey person (and Honey was a working name if ever she'd heard one) to vouch for her? With any luck 'Honey' would be on their books and they could kill two birds with one stone. She looked at Grace. Two middle-aged birds. Two old boilers.

Honey's voice, admittedly, was a surprise. WPC Henderson dialled Directory Enquiries, then Honey, and was surprised by her husky, sophisticated voice. A kept woman, she decided. She told Honey Chambers that they had arrested one Grace Trevethan for soliciting in a pub on Portobello road and listened, amused, at the sharp intake of breath at the other end. Honey had obviously done much better than Grace; she was set-up in her posh pad while Grace was still trawling the streets. Honey, she suspected, wouldn't want to know.

But Honey did want to know and, half an hour later, she

bowled up in a taxi outside Ladbroke Road police station, wrong-footed WPC Henderson with her Armani clothes, corroborated Grace's story that she was up from Cornwall for the day, claimed total responsibility for her and even said that if the case came to court then she would post bail. However much it was.

WPC Henderson knew when she was beaten. The wretched Grace Trevethan was released: lock, stock and appalling outfit to boot.

'What on earth,' asked Honey as they left the police station, 'did you think you were *doing*? For God's sake, Grace, you can't just go hanging around nasty pubs like that. You're bound to get into trouble.'

Grace didn't reply. Honey looked at her dreadful clothes and felt nothing but pity for her. Poor woman. So sex-starved she has to come all the way to London and ply her wares in seedy pubs.

Honey wished she hadn't mentioned the ice-cream. That was what must have pushed Grace over the edge. 'Look, Grace,' she said, oozing sympathy. 'If you really want to meet a man, I know of some much better places.'

Grace looked at Honey as if she were an imbecile. 'I wasn't trying to meet a man!'

'What? What were you doing, then?'

Grace beckoned for Honey to come closer. Then she opened her bag.

'Bloody hell!' Honey saw the dope, looked guiltily around, put a hand on Grace's shoulder and steered her smartly away from the police station. 'Grace! You must be mad! You've just been in a police station – with a bagful of marijuana! What on earth do you think you're *doing*?'

'Not trying to be a prostitute, that's for sure.'

Honey was appalled to see Grace smiling. 'Keep walking!' she hissed. 'You don't want to get arrested. Again. Have you any idea …?' she began.

'Yes!' said Grace as the hurried along the road. 'Look, I'm really grateful that you came.'

Honey was beginning to regret that she *had* come. Grace had obviously flipped.

'Remember you said that if I ever wanted to talk?' said Grace as Honey hailed a taxi.

'Yes.'

'Well, I think we need to talk.'

Honey shrugged. Then she bent down at the window of the cab. '44 Wilberforce Street,' she said to the driver.

———————————————

'Well,' said Honey half an hour later. 'I have to say I'm impressed.'

'Are you?'

'Yes. It's very … er … enterprising of you.'

Grace nodded. She had told Honey the whole story, but she didn't want her to be impressed. She wanted her to help. Grace looked around Honey's large, elegant drawing room with its white walls, Art Deco furniture and the two full-length windows overlooking the leafy square below. It was, she thought, an incongruous environment in which to be discussing drugs. Then she looked back at Honey, elegant in another loose-fitting trouser suit and floaty scarf. She looked down at her own outfit. It wasn't, she had to concede, quite the thing. She was out of touch.

Honey, however, was not. Of that she was sure.

'Look,' she said, as Honey leaned forward on the leather sofa and replenished their tea. 'I don't know what to do. I told you I can't involve Matthew ... there must be some way you can help?'

Honey frowned. 'I don't really see how.'

Grace raised her eyebrows. 'Call a dealer for me?'

Honey sighed. 'No, Grace. It's mad. I can't. You'll end up in jail. Oh, Grace ... give up the house. Go to India. Take up yak farming.'

'I'm not going to give it up.' Grace was resolute. 'Call a dealer. Please.'

Honey looked away. She felt highly uncomfortable. Unspoken between them was the fact that she owed Grace a favour. True, she had rescued Grace from Ladbroke Grove police station, but if she really wanted to help, if she could save Grace from the predicament that her husband – Honey's lover – had landed her in, then she could do more.

She sighed and looked under her lashes at Grace. 'How do you know that I know a dealer?'

Grace didn't respond. She merely raised her eyebrows again.

Honey stood up. 'All right – but on one condition.'

'What's that?' Grace wasn't sure she liked the sound of that.

'That you let me lend you an outfit that's ...' Honey looked down at Grace's hopeless suit and the now-crumpled hat lying on the floor. 'Well, that's not *that*.'

'Oh.' Then Grace looked up and smiled. 'All right.'

Five minutes later, and for the second time in less than twenty-four hours, Grace found herself standing in front of a full-length mirror trying on various outfits. She blocked out of her mind the possibility – indeed the near-certainly – that her own husband had also frequented Honey's bedroom in various states of undress. Eventually she settled for a navy-blue suit with dark pink collar and cuffs. It conveyed exactly the right impression. It made her look like a businesswoman: sleek, stylish and confident. She walked through the double-doors of the bedroom back into the drawing-room.

'What do you think?' she asked.

Honey looked up. 'Perfect,' she said with an admiring smile. Neither of them mentioned the fact that it fitted like a glove: that Honey and Grace were exactly the same size. Even the shoes Honey had suggested fitted like gloves.

Grace sat down beside her. 'When will he be here?'

'Any minute.'

'Is there … well, anything I should know about him?' asked Grace. The enormity of her undertaking was beginning to unsettle her again.

'What do you mean?'

'Well … I don't know anything about drug dealers. Is he ruthless? Will he be armed?'

Honey burst out laughing. 'Vince? No! He's a pussycat. He's really quite sweet – in a hippyish sort of way.'

'Oh.' A hippyish pussycat wasn't at all what Grace had been imagining.

Honey peered at the dope Grace had lain on the table. It looked like a giant lollipop made of weeds. 'Are you sure this is ready to smoke?'

Grace looked as well. 'Ye-es. Matthew said it really needed another day to dry out. But, well … it had to be today.'

'Yes.'

Then the doorbell rang. Honey sprang to her feet. She didn't want to admit it to Grace, but she was also feeling nervous. She had never tried to sell the stuff before: she had only bought it, and in very small quantities. She strode across the room, into the hallway, and buzzed the intercom for Vince to enter.

Grace stood up, squared her shoulders, and told herself

that she was a businesswoman. Then the hippyish pussycat loped into the room. The first thing that surprised Grace about him was his age. She didn't know why, but she had been expecting someone much younger. And someone with a little more ... presence. Vince looked like a student who had got lost in campus in the seventies and had only just found his way out.

Honey came into the room behind him. 'Grace,' she said. 'This is Vince.'

Vince stepped forward to shake hands.

'Hello,' said Grace, taking in the greying beard, the lank pony-tail, the leather jacket and the tatty jeans.

'Hi,' he said. 'Nice joint.'

Grace looked puzzled. 'But you haven't even tried it yet!'

Vince gestured around the room. Grace noticed that his fingernails were dirty. 'No. Nice pad.'

'Oh, I see. It's Honey's. I'm just here on ... business.'

'Yeah.'

'I've got some ... stuff.'

'Yeah. Cool. She said.'

Grace picked up the cannabis. 'So ... shall we get down to business?'

Vince shrugged. Then he sat down, pulled a tin out of his jacket pocket and extracted a penknife and some papers. He cut a small amount of cannabis from the bunch and, excruciatingly slowly, began to roll a joint. The process, to Vince, was like a religious ritual. It could not be hurried.

Grace and Honey stood beside him, silently egging him on.

Then Vince began to nod to himself, as if reciting a mantra. 'Draw,' he said. 'Spliff ... puff ... shit ...'

'Yes,' snapped Grace. 'Thank you.'

But Vince was unperturbed. 'Call it what you will,' he continued in tones of awe. 'But it is my belief … my firm belief … that this is the door to enlightenment.'

Honey and Grace exchanged a look. 'In your own time,' said the latter.

But sarcasm was lost on Vince. He finished rolling the joint and, again with exquisite slowness, licked the paper to seal it. 'And now,' he said, 'for the acid test.' With that he lit a match and drew on his creation.

Vince's eyes were anyway slightly protruding. As he smoked, they seemed to get wider and more bulbous, as if they were about to pop out of his head.

If Grace and Honey couldn't believe the change in his eyes, Vince himself couldn't believe the strength of the life force that had entered him. A great wave of something soothing, something all-consuming yet utterly peaceful surged through his body, washing away doubt and care and leaving pure, unadulterated contentment.

He stopped smoking after the third drag. 'Jesus!' he said to the wall in front of him. 'Jesus H Christ!' He looked at the joint. This wasn't weed. This was a short-cut to Nirvana.

'I'll give you sixty quid for it,' he said to the wall.

Behind him, Grace laughed. 'Don't be silly.'

'Seventy?' He supposed, really, it was worth a hundred.

'No,' said Grace, stepping closer. 'That's just a sample. I've got twenty kilos.'

'What?'

'Yes. Twenty kilos at the moment.' Suddenly worried, Grace added hastily that she could get more. A lot more.

Vince stood up and turned to face the women. He looked ashen.

Grace knew that feeling.

But she had attributed Vince's appearance to the drug – not to her words.

Vince was terrified. This was way out of his league. If he were to be perfectly honest, he wasn't even a drug dealer. Just a failed musician turned supply teacher who loved his wife and kids, and, occasionally, did a little dealing on the side. The last thing he wanted to do was get involved with the sort of people Grace was after. They were ruthless. Armed. 'No, no, no,' he said. 'No. You've got the wrong man here.'

Grace looked appalled. Vince interpreted the look as one of disapproval. He didn't want her to think that he was some sort of ex-hippy who merely dabbled. 'I mean,' he said. 'I run a limited operation here. You're talking big league. Really big league.'

But that was exactly what Grace wanted to hear. 'Well,' she trilled. 'You've just got promoted, then.'

Vince shook his head. 'I don't have that kind of money.'

'Well,' Grace was not going to give up now. 'Do you know someone who does?'

Vince looked distinctly uneasy. 'I've … I've heard of someone.' China Macfarlane, he told himself. Ruthless. Armed. Then he thought of what sort of percentage he could cut himself on a deal with him; thought of the new bicycle he had promised his daughter and the trip to Glastonbury he had promised his wife. Then he thought of his beloved motor: the TransAm that so badly needed overhauling. He began to waver.

Grace noticed. She nodded to Vince and then pointed to the telephone. 'Call him.'

Vince looked from Grace to Honey. They looked as if they never went further than Harvey Nichols. But here they were, intimidating him with their smart outfits and their steely expressions, propelling him into the seedy underbelly of gangland London. Then it occurred to him that brittle Chelsea women like this were probably far more ruthless than the likes of China Macfarlane. He couldn't lose face in front of them. Vince nodded at Grace and picked up the phone.

Ten minutes later, the unlikely trio were on the pavement outside 44 Wilberforce Street, climbing into Vince's TransAm with the painted eagle on the bonnet, en route to a decrepit warehouse in the badlands of King's Cross. Vince was shaking with nerves. Honey was doubtful. Grace was ecstatic. None of them noticed the two men sitting in the Jaguar parked across the street. Martin Bamford's Jaguar.

The minute Martin saw Grace emerge from the house, he reached for his doorhandle. 'That's her! There she is! Let's go and rescue her!'

'No!' shouted Matthew, reaching across and preventing him from opening the door. 'No, no, no. Wait a mo.' He peered through the windscreen. It was dusk now, and the man climbing into the driving seat of the TransAm was difficult to make out. But he looked thoroughly dodgy. And he had a ponytail.

'We don't know who that guy is,' he said to Martin.

'So? I don't care who that guy is. We can't just watch …'

'But he might be a drug dealer or something! You can't just go wandering into something like this.'

Martin looked at his friend. 'Why have you got so bossy all of a sudden?'

'Jesus! You're so fucking insensitive. This could be dangerous!'

Martin snorted. He hadn't realised Matthew was a wimp. *They* weren't in danger. Grace was.

Then the TransAm pulled away. 'Shit!' seethed Martin. 'Now look what you've done! They're getting away now!'

Matthew rolled his eyes. 'Yeah, well follow them, you dozy quack.'

'Fuck off,' said Martin, easing the sleek machine out into the street.

No-one in the TransAm noticed they were being tailed. None of them knew about the two bickering men in the Jaguar, united only in one purpose: that of saving Grace.

As the sun settled behind the hill at Liac, Harvey Sloggit slumped to the ground behind one of the trestle tables in the greenhouse. He was bored now of tending the plants; bored of priming himself to fend off any unwanted intruders; bored of watching more marijuana than he'd ever seen in his life growing almost before his eyes. So bored that he felt he needed a little lift. Something to perk him up. Knowing that Grace and Matthew wouldn't mind, he cut a small amount off one of the dried plants and rolled a joint. Just a small one. He knew how powerful it was.

Even so, it was stronger than he expected and, after five minutes, he felt at one with the world and floated off into a happy daze. A daze that was in the process of taking him into an even happier world when he heard the voices.

'Grace?' called one.

'Coo-ey?' went another. 'Grace? Are you there?'

Shit, thought Harvey. He sat bolt upright. Diana and Margaret. He scrambled to his feet, determined at all costs to keep the women out of the greenhouse.

But he was too late. The women, wearing woolly hats like tea-cosies, were already through the door.

'Ooooh!' said Diana, looking at the riot of cannabis. Then she sniffed. 'Funny smell.'

Then Margaret saw Harvey. 'Harvey! Where's Grace?' She looked around. 'We tried the house, but she's not there.'

'She's … um …'

'We've come to finalise the details of the W.I. tea party. Grace invited us for supper.' Then, disappointed, she looked around again. 'It was organised ages ago.'

Harvey practically leapt on them. He didn't like the way Diana was sniffing at the plants. 'You've got to get out!' he all but shouted.

'Oh no.' Margaret peered through the forest of plants. 'We've got to see Grace.'

'Er … no. You have to leave. It's the plants, you see. They're very delicate.' Harvey braced himself against one of the table, preventing them from coming any further. 'They're very special orchids, you see. From Peru.'

But it was no use. Both women were sniffing again. Then Margaret picked up one of the pots. Her tea cosy quivered as she shook her head. 'Oh no. These aren't orchids.'

'Aren't they?' said Harvey, the picture of baffled innocence.

Margaret touched a leaf. 'Oh no.' She frowned. 'More like tea.'

'Tea!' yelled Harvey. 'What a good idea!' He grabbed Margaret and propelled her out of the greenhouse. 'Let's go to the kitchen and I'll make us tea.'

Margaret looked doubtful. 'But we were expecting supper …'

'There's some ham,' said Harvey in desperation. 'Grace left some ham. I can knock you up a sandwich. 'Come on, Miss Skinner,' he said to Diana over his shoulder. 'Let's go and have a nice cup of tea.' Like everyone else in St Liac, he knew about Diana's almost religious devotion to tea.

But he had forgotten about Diana's equally strong

propensity for petty theft. As he and Margaret left the greenhouse, Diana held her breath, picked up one of the smaller plants and popped it into her handbag. Then she followed the others into the kitchen for a nice cup of tea.

TWELVE

'I really don't like this,' said Vince. 'I don't like this *at all*.' He turned to Grace in the passenger seat. 'This *really* isn't my scene.'

It really wasn't Grace's scene either. Her ecstasy at finding a dealer had begun to evaporate as they drove to north London. Now it had vanished. As Vince drew to a halt, she stared at the derelict warehouse in the industrial wasteland behind King's Cross. She shuddered and, summoning a smile, looked at Vince. 'It'll be fine,' she said. 'Not everyone lives in a nice house in Chelsea, do they, Honey?'

In the back seat, Honey shrank deeper into the comfort of her Armani suit. In the normal course of events, she balked at the prospect of venturing north of Hyde Park. King's Cross was utterly beyond the pale – but *this* place was a different planet. 'No,' she said to Grace, not trusting herself to say any more.

Grace turned back to Vince. 'What's the name of your friend, again?'

Vince was horrified. 'He's not my *friend*.'

'Your contact, then.'

'China Macfarlane,' whispered Vince.

'Oh. Scottish-Chinese. What a funny mixture.'

'Er … no. He's English. An ex-military policeman.'

'Why's he called China, then?'

Vince decided it might be politic not to inform Grace of the ex-military policeman's particular talent of smashing china into the faces of people he didn't like. 'Dunno,' he said miserably. Then he opened his door. 'Look, let's just get this over with, shall we? I've got things to do, you know.' The last sentence was gruff: designed to indicate that he had a backlog of nefarious activities to catch up on. The truth was infinitely more prosaic.

'Come on, Honey,' said Grace. 'It'll soon be over.' With a confidence she didn't feel, she sprang out of the car and walked towards the warehouse.

A short, wiry and pugnacious-looking individual was waiting for them at the small door in the wall.

'Vince?' he said to Grace.

'Er ... no.' Grace wondered whether or not to introduce herself. Then she took another look at the man's expression and decided not. 'That's Vince.'

Vince nodded to the other man. 'China Macfarlane?'

'Yeah. C'mon. He's in here,' he said, entering the warehouse.

'Who's in there?' whispered Grace to Vince.

Vince shrugged. ''Dunno. His partner I suppose. This thing's too big even for someone like China to handle on his own. Look, are you really sure ...?'

But Grace had already stepped through the door into the cavernous interior. She had expected it to be a vast, empty hangar. To her surprise, it was anything but: it was festooned with giant inflatable objects, hung with strange multi-coloured lights and, on her left, a giant inflatable pig. In the depths of the slightly smoky interior, she saw what looked like a children's paddling pool on the floor.

Behind her, and despite her fear, Honey looked admiringly at the décor. 'It's just like a window display at Harvey Nicks.'

China Macfarlane snorted. 'There's a rave tonight. We hold 'em here.'

'What's a rave?' asked Grace.

'Oh *Grace*.' This from Honey. 'It's a big party with lots of young people dancing.'

'That sounds nice. Is it someone's birthday?'

'Someone's birthday!' China laughed and nodded to himself. 'Very nice. Very funny.'

Then, as they progressed into the middle of the warehouse, Grace saw a tall man, half-shrouded in the gloom, casting a fishing line into the pond. She looked round to Honey. Honey shrugged. Behind them, Vince tried to pretend he wasn't there.

'*Merde!*' Shouted the man with the fishing rod. '*Loupé de nouveau.*'

Intrigued, Grace stepped towards the pool. From her new position, she had a better view of the man. He was tall, around her own age, with a regal bearing, a fine patrician face and – but she already knew this – a commanding voice. So, she thought, this is Mr Big. Trying to intimidate us by speaking in French. She'd soon wipe that superior smile off his face.

But before she could say anything, the tall man looked over to China. 'So,' he said. 'What have you brought me?'

Oh, thought Grace. He really *is* French.

Beside her, China Macfarlane snorted again. 'Two ladies – and a fucking hippy.'

The tall man pondered that one in silence for a moment. Then he re-cast his fishing line – and missed again. Grace stepped even closer to the pool and looked at the fish he was trying to catch. They were, in fact, yellow plastic ducks. She looked up at the tall man. '*Si vous détendiez votre poignet,*' she suggested, '*je crois que ça irait mieux.*'

The tall man smiled back, showing a glittering set of perfectly even teeth. Then, without a word, he cast his line again, and sank the hook into the head of one of the ducks. '*Eh voilà!*' he cried. Stepping down from the dais on the other side of the pond, he made a formal bow to Grace. '*Merci, Madame. Je suis reconnaissant de votre avis.*' Grace wanted to sneer at him, but all she could do was stare. He noticed her discomfiture.

'You like to fish?' he asked, sounding, but not looking, exactly like Gérard Depardieu.

Grace hoped her face was as expressionless as her voice. 'Yes. Where I live the fishing's wonderful.' She was quaking inside. Both from nerves and from something she couldn't quite identify.

'I hate it here,' said the Frenchman with venom. 'The fishing is terrible.' He smiled again. 'I should visit you. Where do you live?'

Oh no you don't, thought Grace. She knew all about French men. Well, she *had* known all about French men. Her year as an au pair in Paris seemed like a lifetime ago. She stayed silent. Silent but smiling.

'What is your name?'

The way he said '*ees*' made Grace want to go weak at the knees. The last thing she had expected a hardened criminal to do was to flirt with her. She told herself that it was just one of many weapons in his arsenal of lethal approaches. 'Grace,' she said.

The Frenchman smiled. '*Parfait. Grace,*' he repeated, pronouncing it in the French way. Trying to seduce her, she thought, with one little word.

'I am Jacques.' He bowed again. 'Jacques Chevalier.' There was merriment in his eyes when he looked up again. 'You have something you wish to sell me?'

Grace nodded.

'You will show me, yes?' Jacques came very close to her.

Grace nodded again, this time with less assurance. She wished this Jacques Chevalier would stop looking at her as if he'd never seen a woman before. She glared at him and extracted the cannabis sample from the handbag Honey had lent her.

Jacques took if from her and sniffed it in what Grace thought was rather an ostentatious manner. Then she saw that he was looking at her, not at the cannabis. She steeled herself for some sort of Gallic claptrap about the scent of English roses. It wasn't forthcoming. Jacques looked interested. Extremely interested. Grace was delighted. She wanted Jacques to be interested. In her cannabis. Not in anything else.

'Where did you get it?' he asked.

Grace didn't flinch as she looked him straight in the eye. 'The people I represent,' she said grandly, 'wish to remain anonymous.'

Jacques grinned. 'Ah ... yes. The people I represent wish to remain anonymous as well. Maybe they are the same people, yes?'

Stop it, thought Grace.

Behind her, Honey and Vince exchanged a worried glance. Honey was well past her Harvey Nichols phase – she wanted out of there. But not as badly as Vince.

'Look,' said the latter, stepping forward. 'Can I go now? I've got to pick me daughter up from her flute practice and ...'

And, on cue to Jacques Chevalier's almost imperceptible nod, China Macfarlane stepped out from the shadows, grabbed Vince by the shoulders and put a knife to his neck. Jacques nodded again. Honey stifled a gasp. Grace stared straight ahead at the only man who could save her.

'How much do you have?' he asked her.

'A lot.' A small smile played at the corners of Grace's mouth. Two could play at this flirting game, she thought.

'Why don't I just take it?' teased Jacques.

'You don't know where it is.'

Jacques sighed and shook his head in mock-disappointment. 'Ah ... yes. But I am sure I can get you to tell me.' Grinning broadly, he reached for Grace's hand. Then he began to stroke her palm with his own manly, yet surprisingly delicate fingers. 'What if I cut off your fingers, one by one, until you change your mind?' There was evil in his voice; a luscious, luxurious evil that held Grace transfixed. Honey's reaction was far less complicated. She moaned and, as befitted a well-bred girl from Chelsea, fell into a dead but supremely elegant faint. China Macfarlane belied his status as a brutal, crockery-smashing sort of person and bent to catch her before she hit the ground.

And then Matthew Stuart belied his recently-earned reputation as a wimp, burst through the warehouse door and, waving his arms in an authoritative manner, ran up to them. 'All right,' he yelled. 'Nobody move! I'm the police. The whole place is surrounded!'

The stunned silence didn't last long. China Macfarlane knew a policeman when he saw one, and this most certainly wasn't one of the species. He dumped Honey on the floor, sprang towards Matthew and extended his flick knife. Matthew's eyes widened as he saw the lethal blade glinting inches from his neck. 'Ah,' he said.

With a feline grace, Jacques Chevalier moved away from Grace and addressed Matthew. 'And who,' he enquired, 'would you be?'

Before Matthew could reply, Martin Bamford appeared

from the shadows. He had witnessed the failure of Matthew's entrance. Charm, he decided, was the thing. Disarm them with charm. Play for time. Resplendent in his three-piece suit, he sauntered up to them. 'Hello everyone,' he beamed. Then he nodded to Jacques. 'Martin Bamford. Are we too early … for the rave?'

Even Jacques was non-plussed.

'I can't wait,' continued Martin. 'I just love … er, raving.'

Vince was beginning to hyperventilate. This was surreal. He wanted out. Now. Xanthe would kill him if he was late collecting Flower from her flute lesson. 'Look,' he pleaded to Jacques. 'This has nothing to do with me. It's …'

'Shut up, weirdy-beardy! snarled China, waving the knife at him.

Vince shrank back into the shadows.

Jacques looked at Martin and then turned to Grace. 'Who,' he asked in his quiet, caressing voice, 'is this guy?'

'That's my doctor,' said Grace.

'And this one?' Jacques pointed to Matthew.

'He's my gardener.'

Jacques had come across his fair share of oddballs in his lengthy and hugely successful criminal career, but this woman with her posse of minders took the biscuit. He looked appraisingly at her. Unlike the others, she seemed perfectly calm.

'Oh,' he said. 'Nice. Are we expecting anyone else?'

'No.'

'Your cleaning lady, perhaps?'

Grace smiled and shook her head. 'No. No-one else. No.'

Jacques sighed. 'Very well.' He looked at the unlikely little band of intruders and nodded towards China Macfarlane. 'This is China,' he told Grace. 'He beats people up for me.'

For the first time since she entered the room, Grace began to tremble.

Jacques raised his eyebrows. 'Shall I … er …?'

'No! No. No … please.' If anyone was going to get beaten up, thought Grace, it's me. She took a deep breath. 'Matthew. Take Martin and Honey and wait for me outside.'

Matthew still had a flick knife at his throat and wasn't, really, in a position to take anyone anywhere. Especially when, as Grace spoke, China moved the knife even closer.

Grace turned to Jacques. 'Please?'

Jacques shrugged. He couldn't see why not. They couldn't go anywhere: not if he sent China out with them. He turned and blew a kiss to the scowling ex-policeman. 'Okay. Take them out, China.'

Back on her feet and brushing out the creases in her Armani suit, Honey looked horrified at the prospect of Grace being left alone with this hoodlum. Even if he was, she had to confess, a rather handsome hoodlum. 'Grace …'

Grace shook her head. 'Wait for me outside.'

'Shall I go too?' asked Vince, perking up somewhat.

'Yeah.' China gestured with the flick knife. 'Outside – but no further.'

Vince sighed; poor little Flower. As China escorted them outside, Jacques turned back to Grace.

'Come. Let us go to my office.'

'Righty-ho,' said Grace, picking up her handbag. She was frightened again – but determined not to show it. She wasn't terribly sure if she was going to like being on her own with Jacques Chevalier. She certainly didn't like his office. 'Oh,' she exclaimed when he escorted her into the ladies' loo.

'I know, I know.' Jacques looked genuinely embarrassed as Grace took in the folding chairs and the trestle table. 'I'm sorry. It is not nice.' He flashed her a smile. 'It is, however, only temporary.' Then he pulled out a chair for Grace and asked her to sit down.

Grace sat, handbag firmly clutched in her lap. 'You ... you move around a lot, do you, then?'

Jacques smiled. 'Yes. I suppose you could say that.' London; Paris; Nice; Buenos Aires ... Jacques had bases in many cities. That, like the fishing in London, was a source of increasing annoyance to him. Jacques loathed urban living: he was a country boy at heart.

He sat down opposite Grace, sighed heavily and clasped his hands in front of him. Then he looked at Grace again. What a very pretty woman, he thought. Spirited, too. And, he reckoned, passionate under that repressed exterior. A very unlikely criminal. Grace looked at Jacques. He looked like a film star. A French Al Pacino. Sexy in a thrilling and highly inadvisable way. Definitely a criminal. It was Jacques who broke the silence.

'All the people I deal with,' he told her, 'are scum.' He frowned at his perfectly manicured fingernails. 'I am a little scummy myself.' Then he leaned forward. 'But you, I think, are not scum. That worries me.'

Grace wasn't having any of this. She glared at him across the rickety table. 'I take exception to that,' she said, bristling. 'I come from a very long line of scum. My dear late husband was one of the scummiest men to walk the face of the earth.'

Jacques grinned. 'Oh. My apologies.' So: she was a widow. And not an altogether un-merry one.

'Look,' said Grace, unnerved by the way he was looking at her. 'Let's just get to it, shall we?' Jacques raised an eyebrow.

'Three and a half thousand a kilo. Twenty kilos in the first week and then ten kilos two weeks later.' Grace knew she was speaking far too quickly, that she was being criminally

214

uncool, but she couldn't help herself. The words just came tumbling out. 'After that we can do twenty kilos every four weeks.'

Jacques suppressed a smile and looked at the breathless woman. 'Three grand a kilo,' he offered. 'And no more deals until I see the first batch.'

Grace gulped. 'Three and a quarter.' Then she saw Jacques's expression. Oh God, she thought, I'm pushing it too far.

Where, wondered Jacques, had she got her figures from? This was ludicrous. She was fleecing him. He nodded. 'Done.'

Grace couldn't believe it. 'Oh thank you. Thank you. Thank you *so* much.' She knew this was uncool as well – especially the tears she was trying desperately not to shed. But she had done it: she had saved her house.

Jacques inclined his head. '*Je vous en prie.*' Then, in English, he asked her how come she spoke French.

'Oh … it's a long story.'

'A pity.'

'I beg your pardon?'

Jacques shook his head. 'It's a pity that there's no time to relate long stories. That, I suppose, is the curse of modern commerce.' Then he leaned down, reached into the cardboard box at his feet and extracted a bottle of wine. 'But there is time for a little drink to celebrate our deal, yes?'

Grace nodded. 'Yes. That would be lovely.' Composed now, she looked at the label on the bottle and realised it would be very lovely. It was Chateau Léoville Barton 1986.

'What are you smiling at?' asked Jacques, opening the wine.

'The contrast,' said Grace. 'Here we are, in a ladies' loo in a warehouse behind King's Cross, drinking wickedly expensive claret.' Then she thought that the claret part was probably rather fitting. She was feeling wicked. She had just clinched a wicked deal.

'You know about wine, then?'

'No. Not really. My husband did, though. I suppose … I suppose I learned a bit from him.'

'Ah.' Jacques reached into the box for two glasses. 'Yes. Your late husband. The scum.'

'I suppose you know a lot about wine,' said Grace. 'Being French.'

'It is not the being French that counts,' said Jacques, pouring the wine. 'It is the being sophisticated.'

'Oh.' Grace accepted a glass. 'Yes. Thanks.'

'Part of me is sophisticated,' said Jacques, examining his fingernails again.

'Yes. Yes.'

'I can't believe your friend fainted.'

'Who? Honey?'

'Yes. Do I really look like I would cut someone's finger off?'

Grace looked at him. 'Oh yes.'

Jacques nodded. 'Thank you.'

They drank in silence for a moment. Companionable silence, Grace thought. She remembered the night she had cried herself to sleep because of the terrible loneliness of not having a companion. Then she looked again at Jacques, and the other Grace, the one who sipped tea at W.I. gatherings, took over and told wicked Grace that she was mad to be drinking claret in a King's Cross warehouse with a criminal who dealt in drugs and removed fingers.

Grace stood up. 'I really must be going now.'

'Yes.'

'I'm, er … sorry about my friends.'

Jacques shrugged. 'Not at all. It must be nice to have people who care about you.'

Oh, thought Grace. 'Yes,' she said.

'Now you must go with your Honey and your doctor and your gardener.'

'Yes.'

'And your hippy?'

'Oh … he's not mine.'

'Ah.' Jacques was rather pleased about that. He had plans for the hippy. Opening the door of the ladies loo, he escorted Grace back through the warehouse and through the little door at the back where the others were waiting.

'Grace!' Matthew ran towards her. 'Are you all right?'

'Of course I'm all right, Matthew. Why wouldn't I be?'

Behind her, Jacques smirked.

''Bye, then,' said Grace, giving Jacques a little wave. 'We'll deliver in a week. Come on boys,' she added to Matthew and Martin. 'Let's get cracking.' Then she turned to Honey. 'Come on – we'll find you a taxi.'

Vince heaved a sigh of relief as they walked off. He'd long abandoned all thoughts of cutting a percentage of the deal. He didn't want anything to do with it: never wanted to see any of these people again. So he walked off as well, heading in the direction of his own car.

'Not so fast,' snarled China Macfarlane, grabbing him by his ponytail. Jacques had just had a little word in China's ear, informing him of his plans for Vince. China wasn't at all keen on these plans. Jacques, however, had been adamant.

'Hey!' yelped Vince. 'What're you doing?'

'You're coming with me, beardie.'

Vince was horrified. Flower still at her flute lesson was bad enough. Missing the rest of the evening would be nothing short of catastrophic. 'But I can't! My old lady's expecting me.' He looked at China with his pleading, protruding eyes. 'We're having a Dungeons and Dragons night. It's the regional final!'

China's expression left Vince in no doubt as to what he thought of Dungeons and Dragons. He grabbed him by the lapel and headed towards the TransAm.

'But that's my car!' wailed Vince. 'You can't …'

'Oh yes I can.' China jabbed him in the ribs. Then he pointed towards the rear lights of the retreating Jaguar. 'We're going to follow them. In your car.'

'But …'

'You,' interrupted China, 'will hold the steering wheel. I'll be the one with the knife.'

They moved off, with Jacques Chevalier watching from the doorway of the warehouse. His face was devoid of expression: an inscrutable mask.

Ten minutes after leaving the industrial wasteland, the Jaguar, with Matthew driving, pulled to a halt in front of a row of taxis and Honey leaned forward to Grace. 'Are you sure?' she asked. 'Are you sure you don't want me to come with you?'

'Absolutely sure. It's all sorted. Everything's fine.' Grace turned to smile at Honey. But beside her in the driver's seat, Matthew was scowling.

'And thank you, Honey. Thanks for everything.'

'Not at all. It was …' Honey had been going to say it was a pleasure, but it hadn't been. Not at all. She had been terrified out of her wits and, once she had recovered them, had discovered that her Armani suit was stained with something unspeakable from the floor of the warehouse.

'Well,' she finished with a weak smile. 'If you ever need anything …'

'Yes,' said Grace, still smiling. 'I know where you live.'

A look of mutual understanding passed between the two women. It was all right. There was no animosity, no rancour. There was an understanding but not, in all probability, a friendship. They doubted they would ever see each other again.

'Take a headache pill,' cautioned Grace as Honey got out of the car. 'And go straight to bed.'

'Yes,' said Honey. 'And Grace?'

'Mmm?'

'Good luck.' Then, with a little wave at Matthew, she was gone.

'Who's she?' asked Matthew as they waited to see her safely into a taxi.

'Oh … just a friend.'

Matthew scowled again. 'That's what she said. "Just a friend." I thought you didn't have any friends.'

'Well I do.'

'Huh.' Matthew indicated and pulled out onto Marylebone Road. As the car picked up speed, so his anger at Grace escalated. She had trumped him, pulled rank, negotiated a deal, flirted with a criminal and thoroughly emasculated him. Worse, she looked as if she had enjoyed the whole experience.

'If that knife had slipped,' he said through gritted teeth, 'I'd be a dead man. There'd be a dead man driving this car back to Cornwall.'

Behind them, Martin began to snore. On no account, he had said when they left the warehouse, was he going to drive all the way back. It would have been irresponsible: he needed to stay alert and keep his hands free to treat the others for delayed shock. Grace patted the creases in her skirt. Honey's skirt, she realised with a start. She supposed she ought to get it dry-cleaned and send it back. To 44 Wilberforce Street.

'Don't be so stupid, Matthew,' she said. 'He was bluffing.'

Matthew snorted. He didn't want to admit it to Grace, but he had been really scared in the warehouse. Messing about with cannabis in a greenhouse in Cornwall was one thing: the reality of selling the stuff had been quite another. It had been sordid, unpleasant, dangerous and potentially lethal. And it was by no means over. Did Grace really think that she had shaken on a deal with the unctuous frog? The man had been toying with her; playing a game of cat and mouse. Matthew accelerated and moved into the fast lane. Then, realising his speed, he slowed down again. Breaking the speed limit was illegal. It was also irresponsible. Matthew didn't want to play that game any more. Grace thought she knew what was bugging him.

'Look,' she said after a long, uncomfortable silence. 'He doesn't know where it is, does he? As long as we have the merchandise, we have the power.'

Matthew looked, aghast, at the woman beside him. 'Excuse me? Do I know you? What are you talking about? "Merchandise and power"?' He snorted again. 'Look at you. Look at the way you're dressed. You're like Ma fucking Baker!'

'Language,' said Grace – a reproof that Ma Baker would never have voiced.

But that further incensed Matthew. 'Don't you "language" me! I nearly got my fucking throat cut because of you!'

'Well, you're not even supposed to be here.' But as soon as she'd said the words, Grace regretted them. Matthew and Martin had, after all, come up to London with the intention of saving her. 'Look, Matthew,' she said with a sigh. 'I'm really touched you came all this way; I'm really sorry about your throat; it was sweet of you to think I needed rescuing ...'

Matthew's face darkened.

'... but I wasn't in any trouble, was I?'

Matthew didn't reply.

'I'm convinced,' continued Grace, 'that once he sees how good the stuff is, we'll be able to use him as our dealer for as long as we want.'

'Or as long as he wants. Grace, he's a *gangster!*'

Grace bristled. 'I liked him. I think that ...'

'Fine! Fine!' Matthew's knuckles turned white on the steering wheel. 'You just go ahead and do it yourself with Jacques fucking Cousteau, then! I'm out! You hear? I'm out!'

'*What?*'

'I'm out, Grace. I don't want to be a gangster or a crook or go to jail. Nicky's right ... I'm out.' Matthew nodded to himself. 'I'm out. That's it.'

Grace looked at him in horror. 'But you can't be!'

'Watch me.'

Grace took a deep breath. All this shouting wasn't going to get them anywhere. 'Matthew,' she said evenly. 'You knew it was dangerous all along. Why the sudden change of heart?'

'I didn't think about it properly. London,' he finally admitted, 'really freaked me out.'

'But we can make so much money. And it's such fun.'

Matthew shook his head. 'It's not fun for me, and I don't care about the money. I don't want to end up sewing mailbags with a sore arse.'

Grace couldn't help grinning at that one. 'But Matthew, you'll need the money more than ever now that ...' Grace bit her lip. Matthew, she remembered, didn't know about the baby.

'Now that what?'

'Now that you … now that I can't afford to employ you.'

Matthew stole a glance at the passenger seat. His suspicions that Grace was trying a spot of emotional blackmail were allayed when he saw her expression. She looked thoroughly miserable; exhausted and bereft. He, Matthew, had Nicky to go back to. What did Grace have beyond a list of creditors and a repossession order for Liac House?

'Grace.'

'Yes?'

'I'm sorry I shouted at you.'

Grace sniffed. 'Apology accepted.'

'It's Nicky, y'see. She doesn't want to be in a relationship with somebody who's irresponsible and … and I don't want to be in a relationship with somebody who isn't Nicky.'

'I know.'

'So here's what I suggest: when we get back, we harvest the plants and we get the stuff up to London and we never do it again, okay?'

Grace didn't say anything for a moment. Then, looking dewy-eyed, she leaned over and pecked him on the cheek. 'Thank you Matthew. You've just saved my house.' The rest, she thought, could wait. She would sort something out. Liac House was secure.

The Jaguar sped on through the night, Martin snoring gently in the back seat, Matthew thinking about how pleased Nicky would be, and Grace trying desperately not to fall asleep. She didn't want to be haunted by dreams she couldn't control. She wanted to daydream about all the pleasant things that had happened.

No-one noticed the red TransAm with the painted eagle

on the bonnet and the furry dice hanging from the rear-view mirror. No-one had any reason to suppose that anything would go wrong. Or that the sleepy fishing village of St Liac was about to be plunged into chaos.

THIRTEEN

Quentin Rhodes from Rampton's was a patient man. He was also a polite and considerate one. He was well aware that Grace Trevethan was a grieving widow, utterly distraught at having lost her husband, too overcome with helplessness to be able to face up to the reality of losing her house as well. But patience had its limits, especially as it was delaying the repossession of a house worth several hundred thousand pounds – most of which was owed to Rampton's.

Exasperated by Mrs Trevethan's continued – and success-ful – attempts to avoid facing the issue, Quentin had decided to tackle it head-to-head. He took the early morning train to Cornwall, alighted at Bodmin and found a taxi to take him to the village of St Liac. The taxi driver didn't know exactly where Liac House was, but instead dropped Quentin at the village post office. 'It's run by two old dears. Very sweet they are too,' he said. 'They'll put you right. Nothing's too much trouble for them.'

This was normally the case. Diana and Margaret would usually go to enormous lengths to help people. Today, however, they were incapable. That morning, Diana had brewed their tea, not from the box of Darjeeling as was usual, but from the plant she had filched from Grace's greenhouse. By the time Quentin Rhodes walked into the post office, Diana and Margaret were stoned out of their minds. They were lying in a heap behind the counter of the post office, giggling and eating cornflakes from a box. When they heard the jangle of the bell as Quentin opened the door, they both put a finger to their lips to stifle their giggles. It didn't occur to either of them that the visitor might, just possibly, be a customer in need of help. Anyway, staying silent behind the counter was much funnier than serving someone.

'Hello,' said Quentin. 'Anyone at home?'

He looked around in bemusement. Then, noticing the golliwog and the mannequin with her vast pink bosom, he frowned. Very strange, he thought. 'Hello?' he called again. Nothing. Then, from behind the counter, Quentin thought he detected an odd, scratching sound. 'Hello?' he repeated.

Very slowly, what looked like a tea cosy began to rise from behind the counter. As it rose further, a woman's face appeared beneath it. Her grey hair was escaping in all directions from beneath the tea cosy, and her eyes were quite mad.

'May ... I ... help ... you?' asked the deranged apparition.

Quentin recoiled in horror. Then another head appeared. There were crumbs around the mouth of this one – and the eyes were even wider, even further distanced from any semblance of reality. Or so Quentin thought. Diana was under the impression that she was behaving perfectly normally. Here was a visitor. He must be in need of sustenance. With a great effort, she banged the opened cornflakes box on the counter beside her.

'Would you like some cornflakes?' she offered. Then she smiled. A stray cornflake popped out of her mouth. 'They're heavenly.'

Quentin's politeness, patience and consideration had never before encountered such a head-on challenge. 'Er ... no thank you,' he stammered. 'I've already eaten.' There was no way he could have known that his response was the funniest thing the two women had ever heard, and necessitated a bout of prolonged hysteria, followed by a re-acquaintance with the floor behind the counter. He frowned again, wondering if he was dreaming and had drifted into a very bad 1970s television series where holiday-makers came to a remote village, found it had been taken over by other life-forms, and never escaped back to normality.

Quentin blinked, coughed, and debated the wisdom of bolting. Then the women rose again from behind the counter. They were still overcome by paroxysms of helpless laughter, possibly due to the fact that both of them were wearing novelty glasses: the sort that included eyeballs on springs which bounced around with each movement of the head. In between convulsions, the creature on the right offered Quentin cornflakes again. Her companion tried to tempt him with a choc-ice – 'a choccy-icey' in her parlance – but to no avail.

'Look,' said Quentin to the giggling women, 'I'm looking for Liac House … I'm trying to contact Grace Trevethan. Do you know …'

'I love Grace,' said the woman with the madder eyes. She chomped on a few more cornflakes. 'I love her. I really, really, really love her.'

'Er …'

'She's an angel,' said the other woman. 'She has wonderful hair. Soft and silky.' The woman began to stroke her own coarse, greying bird's nest of hair which was making an increasingly successful bid for freedom from the tea cosy. 'Hair like a lovely, lovely, fluffy …Angora … rabbit.'

'Right.' Well, at least they had a passing acquaintance with normality. Very passing. Quentin tried again. 'So can you tell me how to get to Liac House?'

'Who?' said the cornflake woman.

'I love her,' said the other.

'Look,' Quentin all but shouted. 'Do you know where Mrs Trevethan lives?'

'Yes.'

'Where?'

The woman with the choc-ice looked at him in awe. 'She lives in a lovely, lovely, lovely house. I love her.'

Quentin sighed. 'So how do I get to the lovely, lovely, lovely house?'

He should have known the answer.

The woman waved the choc-ice. 'Up the lovely, lovely, lovely hill,' she sang.

'Right.' Quentin marched to the door. 'Thank you.'

'I love saying lovely,' said Margaret as the door slammed behind him. 'Lovely.' Then she collapsed behind the counter again, taking Diana's box of cornflakes with her. Diana screamed with laughter and then she, too, disappeared from view.

Quentin Rhodes trudged up the lovely, lovely hill towards Liac House: the first of the many unwanted visitors that day who would unwittingly cause complete mayhem, put St Liac firmly on the map and catapult Grace Trevethan to international fame.

———————

When Martin had dropped Grace and Matthew at Liac House in the early hours of the morning, they had found a semi-somnolent Harvey, still manfully minding the greenhouse. He had informed them of his successful (he thought) attempts at deflecting Diana and Margaret and, less happily, of Nicky's visit the previous evening.

'Nicky came here?' Matthew had been aghast.

'Yeah. Well, you didn't go home last night, did you?'

No, Matthew had thought. True. If he had been Nicky he would have come to enquire at Liac as well. 'So what did you tell her?'

'I told her that you had gone to London with Martin to help Grace sell the drugs.'

'Shit!'

'Well, it was true …'

'Yeah. Yeah. I know.' Matthew had turned to Grace and told her that he had to go to the boat and see Nicky; to placate her and tell her of his new resolution to be responsible.

'No problem,' Grace had said. 'Harvey will help me.'

So Harvey and Grace applied themselves to the task of harvesting the ripe crop and ridding the greenhouse of the hydroponic apparatus – which was what they were doing when Quentin Rhodes arrived at Liac.

The lack of response to his ring at the door didn't deter him. He knew that Grace Trevethan was an expert at the art of avoidance: she was probably cowering in an upstairs bedroom. He tried the door. Country houses, he knew, (from long experience of repossessing them) were never locked.

This one was.

Quentin sighed and decided to try the garden. She had probably seen him arrive and had bolted into a bush. 'Mrs Trevethan?' he called, heading towards the rhododendrons at the side of the house. 'It's Quentin Rhodes. From Rampton's.'

The words drifted over to Harvey and Grace as they dumped PVC tubing on the scrapheap at the back of the greenhouse. Grace went rigid with fear. 'Harvey! I cannot see that person. Not now. You've got to get rid of him.'

'How? What do I say?'

Grace shrugged. 'Oh I don't know. Tell him anything. Tell him … tell him I'm still in London. Tell him I've been kidnapped by aliens. Anything.' Then, terrified that Quentin Rhodes might appear at any moment, Grace bolted into a bush.

As she fled, she heard the faint ring of the telephone in the house. Quentin Rhodes again, she thought, calling from his mobile.

But it wasn't Quentin Rhodes: it was Charlie calling from The Anchor. He was as desperate as Quentin to get hold of Grace, but for entirely different reasons. He hadn't liked the look of the two men who had just come in asking for Grace. The one with the ponytail had been trying too hard to look like an ageing hippy. A disguise, obviously. The other one had tried too hard not to look like an ex-policeman – but that hadn't worked either. And it was quite obvious that they hadn't been friends: they hadn't even appeared to *like* each other. No, Charlie had thought as he sent them away saying he knew of a Grace who lived ten miles away in St Mayben, they had been colleagues. Colleagues from Customs and Excise. He supposed it was inevitable that the news of Grace's lights would spread beyond St Liac.

Charlie was just contemplating closing the pub and going to warn Grace in person when Nicky and Matthew rushed in.

'Hello. Bit early for you, isn't it?'

'We're celebrating,' said Matthew, grinning from ear to ear. 'We thought we'd have some whisky. Well,' he added, 'we thought *I'd* have some whisky.'

'No. *You* thought you'd have some whisky.'

Charlie looked at them. Nicky was grinning in the same slightly idiotic way as Matthew. Stoned, he thought. When

Matthew should be up at Liac House saving Grace from Customs and Excise Officers.

'Matthew …'

'We're celebrating,' beamed Matthew, leaning over the bar.

'Matthew, there were two men …'

'… I'm going to be responsible …'

'Yes, but …'

'… and Nicky's going to have a baby.'

'Oh!' Charlie looked up. 'That's great, Nicky. That's really good news.'

'Wonderful,' said Matthew, hugging Nicky close.

'And Matthew's never going to grow cannabis again and …'

'… and there are two men from Customs and Excise sniffing around asking for Grace at this very moment.'

'*What*?'

'Yes.' Charlie frowned. 'I've been trying to call the house but Grace isn't answering the bloody phone.'

'*Fuck*,' said Matthew. His elation of a moment ago had evaporated – and with it all thoughts of the rosy future he and Nicky had envisaged. They were so close. So near and yet … 'How did you know they were customs officers?' he asked suddenly.

Charlie shrugged. 'The way they looked. Trying too hard to behave like holidaymakers. Too casual in the way they asked for Grace. Said she was an old friend who they thought they'd look up.' Charlie shook his head. 'Didn't believe a word of it. I tried to send them off to St Mayben, but I don't think they believed me.'

Charlie was right about that. As he spoke, the two men were in the post office, discovering that Grace didn't live in St

Mayben at all but in a lovely, lovely house up the lovely, lovely hill.

'Shit,' said Vince as they left Diana and Margaret to their cornflakes and choc-ices. 'Those women were stoned.'

'So?' barked China Macfarlane. 'What the fuck's that got to do with you?' He pulled out his flick knife. 'Get in the car.'

'But …'

'But nothing. Get in!' China was heartily sick of Vince. A long drive through the night had been bad enough. The music that Vince had insisted on playing had been even worse. And then, to cap it all, Vince had lost the Jaguar somewhere ten miles outside Bodmin. China had been apoplectic with rage – even more angry when Jacques Chevalier had started to call on his mobile, asking if they'd found Grace and her hoard of cannabis.

There had been five calls, and five negative answers. China was beginning to run out of excuses. Now, thank God, they looked as if they'd hit the jackpot in this, the seventh village they'd tried.

'What the fuck are you *doing*?' snarled China as Vince, despite the flick knife, kept glancing back at the post office.

'That bucket and spade set,' wailed Vince. 'Can't I go back and get it? For Flower, y'see …'

'No!' China kicked him on the shins. 'No you fucking can't! Get in the car and get your fat arse up that hill!' Incandescent with rage, China propelled the hapless Vince into the TransAm and slammed the door behind him.

'That's them,' said Charlie, watching from the doorway of the pub further up the street. Then he frowned. Funny car for customs officers. Maybe it was all part of the disguise.

'Shit!' shouted Matthew as he saw China Macfarlane leap into the passenger seat. 'They're not customs officers!'

'No?'

231

'No. They're drug dealers!' He should have known; should have realised that Jacques Chevalier would have had them followed. He turned, wide-eyed, to Nicky. 'C'mon! We've gotta warn Grace! Where's your car, Charlie?'

Charlie pointed to the vehicle parked ten feet away. 'I'll come with you,' he said, fishing for his keys. 'Grace is going to need all the help she can get.'

Below them, China jabbed Vince in the ribs. 'Come on, beardie! Pull a fucking finger out, will you?'

'I can't.'

'Why the fuck not?'

'We've run out of petrol.'

Harvey had trouble with Quentin Rhodes. When Grace dived into a bush, he turned, ran back towards the greenhouse and, to his horror, saw Quentin peering through the open door. 'Stop!' he screamed. Quentin turned round.

'Who are you?' bellowed Harvey. 'What do you want?'

Good God, thought Quentin. Another one. 'I rang the doorbell,' he said, using his dwindling reserves of patience. 'But no-one answered.'

'That means there's nobody home.'

'You're here,' said Quentin.

'Yes, but it's not my home.'

'Then why are you here?'

Harvey blinked rapidly. What *was* he doing here? 'I'm … um … Security!' he said with a flash of inspiration. He pulled his membership of the Cornwall UFO society out of his back pocket and waved it briefly at Quentin. 'There's been an incident. We've got the whole place sealed off.'

'An incident?'

Harvey nodded. 'Can't say any more, I'm afraid. Please,' he added with polite authority, 'be on your way.'

Quentin didn't move. 'My name is Quentin Rhodes. I'm from Rampton's. I'm here,' he said with rather more authority than Harvey had mustered, 'to see Mrs Trevethan.'

'Never heard of her.' Harvey glared at Quentin and moved to stand between him and the greenhouse door.

Quentin's eyes narrowed. 'What's that in the greenhouse?'

'Greens,' snapped Harvey. 'For salad and such like.'

Quentin sighed in exasperation. He supposed they were all mad. That was probably why Grace Trevethan didn't want to leave. Clearly she felt at home here. 'Does Mrs Trevethan know you're here?' he asked.

''Course she does.'

'Ah! So you *do* know her?'

'I don't know anything.'

That, thought Quentin, was the sanest remark he'd heard all day. 'When is she coming back?'

'Never.'

'Right,' said Quentin, staring at Harvey with steely resolve. 'I'll wait.'

Harvey gave up. 'Would you like a cup of tea, then?'

From behind her bush, Grace heard their voices becoming fainter as Harvey led Quentin Rhodes round the house to the front door. Hoping that Harvey would have the good sense to take him into the drawing room and not the kitchen, she went back to the greenhouse. Half an hour, she told herself. That would be enough to get rid of the rest of the equipment and harvest the rest of the cannabis.

But Grace didn't get half an hour. She got precisely five minutes before Matthew, Nicky and Charlie came hurtling through the door.

'Grace! They're here?'

'Who? What? Matthew … what are you talking about?'

'Those stooges of your pal Jacques.'

'What? I don't understand?'

'They *followed* us, Grace.' Matthew's look held an element of 'I told you so'.

Grace's look was of pure horror – followed by one of bitter disappointment. She should have known; Jacques Chevalier was, after all, a gangster. Cutting people's fingers off was child's play to him: stealing cannabis was probably something he'd learned in infancy. She looked, distraught, at the mountain of the stuff now lying on the greenhouse floor.

'Jacques lied, Grace,' said Matthew.

'Oh. Then what … what are we going to do?'

'Hide it,' said Matthew. He looked at the mountain. It was almost waist-height.

'Where?'

'Er … in the shed.' Matthew picked up a handful of cannabis. 'If we can just …'

And then Martin came bursting into the greenhouse. 'Grace!' he said, gasping for breath. 'I've come to warn you. Parked outside the post office … the two men from last night …'

'I know.' Grace nodded. 'Yes, I know.'

Matthew whirled round to Martin. 'You mean they're *still* at the post office?'

'Er … yeah. Think so. They didn't look as if they were going anywhere.'

'Maybe,' frowned Matthew. 'Just maybe they haven't found out where we are yet. Maybe we've got more time ….'

'No,' interrupted Grace. 'We don't have much time. Harvey can't stall Quentin Rhodes for ever.'

Everyone else in the greenhouse looked puzzled. 'Who?' asked Nicky.

'Quentin Rhodes,' wailed Grace. 'He's come about repossessing the house.' Then she put her hands to her head. 'Oh God ... Quentin Rhodes ... you lot ... the man from last night. This would be like a French farce if it were even remotely funny.'

'What would be like a French farce?' asked Sergeant Alfred Mabely, striding into the greenhouse in his rubber soles. 'No farces around here, Grace. I've just come to warn you that there are two men who ...'

Then Alfred saw the cannabis.

Martin was the only one quick enough to react. 'It's lettuce,' he said.

Alfred shot him a withering look. Then he looked at the petrified Grace. 'It's marijuana, isn't it?'

Grace felt her life collapse around her. 'Yes,' she said with a miserable little nod.

Alfred sighed. 'I knew you and Matthew were growing it, but I had no idea ...

'... You knew?'

Alfred nodded and picked up a bunch. 'I live here, don't I?' Then he sighed. 'Seeing as how you had financial troubles, though, I thought I'd turn a blind eye to a bit of homegrown ... but this ... Grace, this is a *huge* amount.' Then smelling the bunch, he nodded in approval. 'Good stuff, too.' He looked at Matthew. 'Much better than that shit you had up at the vicarage.'

'*What?* You knew about that?'

'Oh yes.'

Grace took a deep breath. 'Sergeant Mabely?'

'Yes?'

'Another few minutes and we'll get rid of it. Can't you ...

can't you just turn your blind eye a little longer?'

Alfred looked pained. 'I'm sorry, Grace. If it were up to me, well …'

'But it *is* up to you. *Please?*'

'I'm sorry.' Alfred shook his head. 'Not any longer. That's what I came to warn you about. There's officers on their way from Coldock.'

'Christ!' bellowed Matthew.

'On account of the men down at the post office.'

'What?' asked Martin.

Alfred scratched his chin. 'Serious business. Old Jack Dawkins saw them. They stole a can of petrol.'

'That hardly counts as a serious crime,' scoffed Martin. 'Compared to …' Then he realised what he was looking at and bit his lip. 'Well …'

'Then one of them stole a bucket and spade.'

'Sergeant …'

'And the other pulled a knife on him.' Alfred looked grave. 'Not used to armed robbers around here. Don't like 'em at all. So, I called Coldock and … and if I were you I'd get rid of this stuff pretty bloody quick.' Then, somewhat embarrassed, he looked away. 'I'm … er … going to look for poachers.'

'Well,' said Grace, breaking the long silence that greeted his departure. 'There it is.'

She looked at the mountain and shrugged. 'We did it.'

'But what are we going to do now,' asked Matthew.

'Skin up?' suggested Martin.

'Not even you,' drawled Nicky, 'can smoke all that.'

Martin shrugged. 'I could try.'

'Maybe nobody should have it,' said Grace.

'What?'

'Maybe no-one should get it. Not the police; not Jacques'

236

men; not us.' She smiled sadly at Matthew. 'What if it just ... went up in smoke?'

'Oh.' Matthew looked at the fruits of their labours. It would be a shame. No, it would be a tragedy. But Grace was right: it had to be. Sighing, he pulled a box of matches out of his pocket and handed them to Grace.

Trying not to think about what she was doing, Grace extracted a match, struck it, and held it out above the beautiful foliage that she had hoped would be the key to her salvation. And then China Macfarlane stormed into their midst, holding a flick knife to Quentin Rhodes' throat.

'Put it out!' he screamed at Grace. 'Put it out!'

'I think,' squeaked Quentin, 'you'd better do as he says.' Or at least that's what Quentin thought he squeaked. Maybe he was just dreaming. Maybe the man who had offered him tea hadn't disappeared after all. Maybe the two thugs hadn't really come crashing into the drawing room waving a flick knife, a bucket and a spade.

And maybe Mrs Trevethan wasn't really standing in her greenhouse burning cannabis.

'Oh,' said Grace, dropping the match.

'Hello,' cried Vivienne Hopkins from the garden. 'I hope we're not too early?'

Looking back, Grace had difficulty placing subsequent events in the correct order. China Macfarlane, she thought, shoved Quentin Rhodes aside and chased after Vivienne Hopkins with his flick knife. Vivienne Hopkins let out a piercing yell and fled to the lawn where her thirty colleagues from the W.I. were admiring the garden. And they, in turn, chased China Macfarlane across the lawn and tried to beat him to a pulp with their handbags.

Then the posse of policeman arrived from Coldock and Grace, hearing the sirens, led everyone else out of the greenhouse. She wanted Matthew and Nicky well out of the way when the police found the cannabis. She stood in the garden for a full ten minutes, looking at the policeman, at the ladies from the W.I., the drug dealers and her friends from Liac. There was something faintly comical about the scene.

But there was nothing funny about the sudden explosion from behind her, about the shards of glass that went shooting in all directions and the smoke that billowed out from the shattered remains of the greenhouse. Grace had dropped the match, but she hadn't extinguished it. The several hundred cannabis plants had turned into the largest spliff known to mankind. Grace sighed. What a waste, she thought. What a terrible, terrible waste. And what a shame about the greenhouse. She hadn't realised the electrics had been so dodgy; that Matthew and herself had been in danger all the time. That a gentle smoulder was enough to blow the place up. Oh well, she thought, it doesn't matter now. I don't need a greenhouse any more. I don't even need the house. I'm going to prison. Grace walked across the drive to the front door and went into the house. She wasn't going to hide – there was no point. She just wanted a few moments on her own.

In a trance-like state, Grace trudged upstairs and into her bedroom. She was still, she noticed with amusement as she saw the mirror, wearing Honey's suit. Honey wouldn't want it now. Or maybe she would. She could come and get it in prison. Grace sat down on the end of her bed and wondered if she was going to cry. Then she realised she was too dispirited even to do that. It was a waste of energy, a waste of time.

'Grace?'

The police, thought Grace, not bothering to turn round. They weren't wasting any time. Then she frowned. Policemen didn't sound like that. Not British ones.

'Grace? Are you all right?'

Grace stood up and turned towards the door; to the imposing figure standing at the threshold.

Jacques Chevalier smiled and walked towards her. When he was still about a foot away Grace braced herself and, as hard as she could, slapped him across the face.

'Wow!' Jacques reeled – more in surprise than in pain. He rubbed his cheek and when he had finished Grace hit him again. Harder this time.

'Ouch!' Jacques had the good sense to stand back this time. 'Well,' he said, 'Yes. It's nice to see you too.'

'Bastard!' spat Grace. 'Can't even do your own dirty work.'

'Dirty work?'

'Yes. Why did you send your boys?'

'To keep an eye on you. To keep you from coming to any harm.'

Grace wanted to hit him again but her hand was too sore. 'Do you really expect me to believe that?'

'It's the truth,' he said softly.

Damn, thought Grace. That voice.

'I hope,' he said, sounding as if he meant it, 'that I haven't ruined everything?'

'No,' said Grace with a brittle laugh. 'Only the annual Cornish Women's Institute tea party. Everything will be fine tomorrow.'

But it wouldn't, and Jacques knew it. He knew Grace's life would never be the same again.

'Why did you do it?' he asked.

'Do what?'

Jacques gestured to the window. 'Grow the cannabis.'

'Does it matter?'

Jacques shrugged. 'It does to me.'

Oh what does it matter, thought Grace. 'Because I wanted to keep my house.'

'Ah.' Jacques nodded. 'You're broke. The ... the scummy husband?'

Grace didn't reply. 'Why,' she said after a moment, 'did you come?'

'To help you.'

'You can't help me, Jacques.' It was the first time she had used his name.

'Why not?'

'It might have escaped your attention, but my garden is swarming with policemen.' Grace walked towards the window. 'I'm going to be arrested.'

Jacques followed her to the window and stood by her side. Grace wished he wouldn't stand so close.

'Er ... Grace?'

'Mmm?' Grace was looking through the window, but she wasn't seeing anything expect the shattered remains of her life.

'Look.'

Grace looked. Where, only a few moments before, there had been a troupe of angry women beating up a drug dealer, and a swarm of police running across the lawn, there was now something else altogether: something Grace couldn't believe.

'Good God!'

'I think,' said Jacques with a lop-sided grin, 'you are right. There is a good God.'

Something very good was certainly happening to the policemen, to Vivienne Hopkins and her ladies, to Vince and

240

China Macfarlane and to several inhabitants of Liac. They were all, without exception, stoned out of their heads. And if Grace needed any proof of that, she had only to look at Vivienne Hopkins: she had dispensed with her hat, thrown caution to the wind, her inhibitions out of the window, and was dancing with China Macfarlane. Beside them, Vince was standing with his arm round Alfred Mabely. A little way off, Joyce Reid from the local library was disporting herself in a very un-bookish way with one of the officers from Coldock. Nearby, Matthew and Nicky were holding hands and dangling their feet in the lake, Martin Bamford was smoking a joint with Quentin Rhodes, and Harvey was discussing omens with Reverend Gerald Percy.

'The greenhouse,' whispered Grace. 'The cannabis.' Then she giggled.

Jacques, too, laughed at the scene in front of them. 'I don't think there is any need for you to run away after all. The police can't arrest you: they've smoked all the evidence.'

'I wasn't going to run away!' protested Grace. 'I was going to accept my fate with dignity.'

'Oh?' Jacques looked her in the eye. 'Fate is a funny thing, don't you think?'

'Er …'

'Some things are … how you say … fated to happen?'

'Are they?' Grace had a horrible feeling she was turning pink.

Jacques looked out of the window again. 'You said the fishing here was very good? You can fish in your lake?'

'No. It's full of bicycles and things.'

'What?'

'Oh … it's too shallow.'

'Shallow … yes. So you fish in the sea?'

'Yes.'

Grace waited for him to say something else, but Jacques seemed content to remain silent.

'I think you'd better go now,' she said, not meaning it.

'But I like it here.'

'Er ... thank you.'

Jacques looked out of the window again, then turned back to Grace. 'How will you keep your house now?'

'I won't.' Grace looked stricken. 'I'll have to sell.'

'Oh. A pity.'

'Yes.'

'There must be a way you can keep it.'

'No. There isn't.'

Jacques stroked the cheek that, minutes before, Grace had slapped. 'You could sell it to me.'

'That's not exactly keeping it, is it?'

'Oh.' Jacques shrugged in a Gallic sort of way and grinned at Grace. 'Isn't it?'

EPILOGUE

The old signpost to St Liac had been removed at the request of the Tourist Board. It had, they said, been too discreet and had anyway been partially hidden by tendrils of ivy. In its stead, a newer, more prominent and much larger sign had been erected; one that the documentary crew, crammed in a Renault Espace, couldn't fail to notice. At the wheel of the vehicle, Director Mike Reynolds nodded to himself, indicated right and turned into the narrow, high-banked road that wound down towards the sea. He sighed with satisfaction when the village came into view: it was picture-postcard perfect. On camera, he would make it look spectacular. The viewers would love it. But not as much as they would love the story behind the picture.

Mike was already cutting the film in his head. He had already decided to start with the grainy, black and white still of Grace Trevethan that some paparazzo had earned a fortune from. It was of Grace looking appropriately horrified and guilty, and trying to shield her face from the lens. Mike was going to accompany it with just one short, sharp line: 'Is this the face of a master-criminal?'

It had been just over two months since Grace Trevethan had burst onto an unsuspecting world with her novel *The Joint Venture*. Mike, like many others, hadn't been remotely interested in the first waves of publicity: it wasn't the first time some old dear from the west country had penned a raunchy little tale and shot to the top of the bestseller lists. But, a few weeks after publication, strange rumours had begun to spread and Mike, intrigued, read the book. It was then that he suspected he had a potentially explosive item on his hands. His initial research confirmed his suspicions: the truth behind the tale looked like being far stranger – and infinitely more incendiary – than what Grace Trevethan claimed was the fiction of *The Joint Venture*. Mike Reynolds' documentary was going to tell that truth – and it was going to tell a tale of corruption, collusion, international crime and Cornish chutzpah on a scale that beggared belief.

Reaching the village, Mike pulled up outside the post office and turned to the passenger seat. 'Who,' he said to camera operator Monica Hudson, 'have we got here?'

Monica looked at her notes. 'Margaret Sutton and Diana Skinner. Apparently they've been running this place since the world began.' She grinned up at Mike. 'And discretion *isn't* their middle name.'

Mike nodded. With any luck they'd get most of what they needed from these two old gossips and wouldn't need to contact everyone else on their list – they could go straight on up to Liac House. But Mike had a lot to learn about life in St Liac. And, more specifically, about Diana and Margaret. Neither of them was unwilling to talk: quite the contrary. When, the previous week, Mike had contacted them by phone, they had professed themselves delighted to be involved in his programme. Anything to help Grace, they had said. Anything to boost sales of her book. Not that it needed it. *The Joint Venture* had already sold over half a million copies. Another half million, Mike noted as he entered the shop, were on sale here. Along with a golliwog and a mannequin with an outsize bosom and a pink bra.

Margaret and Diana, dressed for the occasion in their best woolly hats, ushered Mike and his crew into a drawing room that was a shrine to chintz. Nervous at the prospect of appearing on camera, Diana twittered and offered them tea. The more assured Margaret told them how nice it was to have so many visitors this year; how wonderful it was to have St Liac firmly on the map. 'And it's all thanks,' she said, 'to lovely Grace.' Then she looked up at Mike. 'She really *is* lovely, you know. A wonderful woman.'

Mike nodded imperceptibly to Monica and sound recordist Jim Grant. They knew what he meant: get the camera rolling as soon as possible; ease into the interview without formality. A minute later, at the same time as Diana came in with the tea tray, they were up and running.

'You were saying how lovely Mrs Trevethan was,' said Mike.

Margaret nodded. Beside her on the sofa, Diana removed the tea cosy that matched her hat. 'Oh yes,' confirmed the latter. 'Grace is *really* lovely.'

'So success hasn't gone to her head?'

'Oh no.' Margaret was sure about that. 'Not a bit. Grace is the same as she always was.'

'Lovely,' said Diana, pouring the tea.

'So the money hasn't changed her?'

Margaret looked puzzled. 'What money?'

'The money from the book.'

'Oh no. Anyway, Grace has always had money. Well, apart from …'

Mike raised an eyebrow. 'Yes?'

Looking furtive, Margaret leaned forward on the sofa. 'Well … I don't think it's a secret any more. It's like the bit in the book, really. Grace wasn't very well off when her husband died.'

'No,' interjected Diana. 'She was going to lose her house, you see.'

'Yes,' said Mike. 'That's what I wanted to talk about: how the book mirrors Grace Trevethan's own life. It's very similar, isn't it? A widow … going to lose her house … makes a fortune from growing, well, you know …' He looked innocently at Margaret.

But Margaret just giggled. 'Oh no. Grace's heroine was growing drugs.' She leaned forward again. 'Grace herself was growing *tea*.'

'Ye-es,' drawled Mike. 'But she wasn't going to make money out of growing tea, was she? The money to save her house?'

'Oh no,' said Margaret. 'Jacques Chevalier saved her house for her.'

'He bought it, you see,' said Diana. 'He said Grace could keep it as long as he could come and stay for the fishing.'

'He's a lovely man,' said Margaret, sipping her tea.

'A bit like the Pedro character in the book?'

'Oh no.' Margaret shook her head. 'Pedro is Spanish. Jacques is French.'

'And Pedro,' added Diana, 'was a gangster. Grace would never get involved with a gangster.'

'Mmm.' Mike looked down at his notes. 'So when did Mrs Trevethan actually get involved with Jacques?'

Margaret looked at Diana and shrugged. 'It was around the time of the W.I. tea party, wasn't it, dear?'

Diana nodded. 'Yes, I think so.' Diana's memory of last year's W.I. tea party was a little hazy.

'What was Jacques Chevalier doing at a W.I. tea party?' asked Mike.

But neither woman was very sure about that. 'Fishing?' suggested Margaret.

Mike cast a covert look at Monica. He had anticipated the women might be evasive: he hadn't bargained on them being so open and honest – and so woefully ill-informed.

He sighed and tried again. 'The drug raid in the book. That was set against a tea party. Wasn't there some sort of similar incident up at Liac House?'

Margaret frowned. 'There *were* officers from Coldock at the house one day. I can't remember what that was about, can you Diana?'

Diana nodded. 'Salmon poaching, dear.'

'That's right.' Margaret beamed at Mike. 'Salmon poaching.'

Oh God, thought Mike. He looked down at his notes again. 'The *Aphrodite*; the trawler used in the book to smuggle the drugs. Where would Mrs Trevethan have got that from?'

Margaret smiled and leaned conspiratorially towards the camera. 'Now that *is* based on a boat here. Nicky's boat.'

'Except Nicky's boat is called the *Sharicmar*,' corrected Diana. 'And Nicky was a man in the book whereas she's really a woman ...'

'... with a lovely little baby girl ...'

'... born around the same time as Grace married Jacques, wasn't she, dear?'

Margaret turned to Diana for verification and Mike, sensing defeat, shook his head at Monica. They would wrap this up and try elsewhere. There must be *someone* in St Liac who was both willing and able to tell the truth about Grace.

But there wasn't. The man behind the bar at The Anchor waxed lyrical about the Joycean qualities of Grace's novel but said nothing about her life; the doctor rambled on about legalising marijuana; the vicar laughed out loud about the notion of cannabis plants in his garden ('that,' he said with a twinkle in his eye, 'would be *really* devilish'), and the young man with the wild eyes on the *Sharicmar* said he was writing his own book because Grace's had been such an inspiration and no, they couldn't interview Nicky because she and Matthew and the baby had gone for a picnic with Grace and Jacques.

'Where?' asked Mike.

But the young man shook his head. He wasn't going to let on to a film crew. Jacques would break his fingers.

Grace looked at Matthew. 'Do you remember the last time we were here?'

Matthew grinned. 'How could I forget?'

Grace giggled and sipped her wine. Then she gazed out at the sands of Pentyre, the white-capped waves beyond and, closer to them, the threesome at the edge of the water. Jacques was carrying Mary Jane on his shoulders and was roaring with laughter at something Nicky had just said. They looked the picture of contentment.

'Jacques,' she said, 'is over the moon at being made godfather.'

Matthew grinned again. 'Well ... it did kinda seem appropriate.'

Grace laughed. 'That's not fair. He's a reformed character now, Matthew.' She looked suddenly pensive. 'I never dreamed it could turn out like this. I got everything I wanted – and more.'

'Mmm. So did I. Grace?'

'Yes?'

'Why *did* you write the book?'

Grace thought about that for a moment. 'Fun, I suppose. I think I've developed a taste for the risqué ...'

'Aye, you could say that.'

'... and now that I've got a full-time gardener I have to keep myself occupied.'

Matthew grinned again. 'So what're you going to do next?'

Grace looked from the man she loved like a son down to the beach; to the man she adored with a passion. 'Well, you know how Jacques has that little wine business?'

'Yeah.' 'Little wine business' wasn't quite how Matthew would refer to it.

'Well, I thought it might make a good basis for another book ...'

The Bill:
The Inside Story

Rachel Silver

This is a comprehensive and highly illustrated behind-the-scenes look at what makes TV's *The Bill* so punchy and provocative. Full of facts, fun, gossip and revealing secrets about the making of the show, it also features extensive interviews with cast and crew and is essential reading for any fan.

Since its first transmission over fifteen years ago, more than one thousand episodes of *The Bill* have been broadcast, consistently pulling in some of TV's highest audience ratings. It has received critical acclaim for its hard-hitting, polished stories and memorable characters.

The Bill: The Inside Story is a unique look at the tough, fast-moving world of Sun Hill, both past and present, and what lies in store for the best police show on TV.

'A must-have for fans, providing a truly in-depth behind-the-scenes look at how the show is made.'

Belfast Telegraph

ISBN 0-00-257137-4

The Full Monty

Wendy Holden

Based on the screenplay by Simon Beaufoy

Original novelisation of the award-winning, smash-hit British film *The Full Monty*, the story of a group of redundant steelworkers in Sheffield and the reinvention of themselves as a most unlikely group of strippers.

When a visit by the Chippendales evokes a frenzied response from the local women, Gaz has a brainwave and manages to persuade Dave and four equally unlikely lads that stripping for cash is a good way to make money.

Their heart-warming journey between conception and performance is littered with tears and laughter. Will they turn their lives around and go the full monty?

ISBN 0-00-651192-9

Waking Ned

Wendy Holden

Based on the screenplay by Kirk Jones

Inspired by a true story, *Waking Ned* is an hilarious novelisation of the film about everyone's dream – to win the lottery.

Set in Southern Ireland in the tiny coastal village of Tullymore, *Waking Ned* follows the comic tale of Jackie O'Shea and Michael O'Sullivan and a lottery scam that changes the lives of the small community forever.

When Jackie and Michael discover that someone in the village has won the lottery, they decide it should not be too difficult to track down the mysterious winner and share in the jackpot. However, they are shocked to discover the winner's true identity and this marks the beginning of their problems, as they embark on a complicated scam that quickly threatens to spiral out of control.

The events that ultimately unfold are even more dramatic than winning the lottery itself...

ISBN 0-00-653151-2

Ally McBeal:
The Official Guide

Tim Appello

It's Ally's World…

Funny, charming and smart, award-winning *Ally McBeal* stole the hearts of critics and viewers alike from its premiere episode in 1997. The show continues to cultivate and entertain growing legions of fans.

Illustrated with more than 400 photos and in full colour throughout, this book is the who, what, where, why and how of this unique show which has become cult viewing. Chock-full of fascinating facts and tidbits, exclusive interviews with the cast and crew, and interesting trivia, this companion guide takes readers on an engaging trip through the hilarious, intelligent and quirky world of the endearingly odd Ally and her friends and colleagues.

'The hippest, hottest show on television'   *TV Guide*

ISBN 0-00-257119-6